THE ALPHA PARTICLE

TJ HAWKINS

This book is a work of fiction and, except for historical fact, any resemblance to actual persons, living or dead, is purely coincidental.

ISBN: 9798339324997

ACKNOWLEDGEMENTS

This book is dedicated to my father who sadly passed away in the year that this book was published at the age of 100, managing to even exceed the final age of his mother by 7 years.

The most decent person that I have ever known, he was not just a man of great integrity but was also blessed with a keen sense of humour and the most incredible memory even till the end. His amazing genetics are the inspiration for this series of books.

MICHAEL HAWKINS 1923 - 2024

INTRODUCTION

In 1898, Pierre and Marie Curie discovered a new element that they called Polonium. The rare silvery-grey radioactive semi-metal was named after Marie's homeland of Poland. The element is found in Uranium ore.

Polonium has a very short half-life of 138 days. As the element decays, deadly alpha radioactive particles are released. The emission of these alpha particles mean that a single gram of Polonium can reach 500 degrees Celsius (932 degrees Fahrenheit). The element is considered to be probably the most toxic element on the planet. As a comparison, a lethal dose has been calculated at one ten thousandth of that of the world's most potent nerve agent, VX.

Marie Curie died in 1934 from conditions relating to radiation exposure. Tragically, her daughter Irene, who followed in her mother's footsteps, was diagnosed with leukaemia and died in 1956. Exposure to X-rays and a laboratory accident involving Polonium have often been quoted as the causes.

Polonium is believed to be almost exclusively produced in Russia, with estimates of between 100g and 200g a year. Apart from being made in a nuclear reactor, the element can also be created artificially. It is sometimes called 'the perfect poison', because it is so difficult to detect and can easily be carried across borders in sealed containers. Airport scanners, for example, will generally not pick up on the radiation, as it emits alpha particles rather than gamma. On November 1 2006, former Russian KGB and FSB agent Alexander Litvinenko was fatally poisoned with Polonium in London.

Since the mid 1980's, Russia has been trying to develop a new type of weapon called a Hyper-Glide Vehicle. In March 2018, Russian President Vladimir Putin proudly announced that his country had successfully produced such a weapon. The Avangard HGV, he claimed, was unstoppable and could maintain speeds of Mach 20 or 15,345 miles an hour. London could be reached from Moscow in 6 minutes and New York in just over 18 minutes. The Avangard could carry a nuclear payload or something that was both deadly and silent …

PROLOGUE

Tom Rivers looked out of his hospital bedroom window and reflected on the recent events that had resulted in him now being sat in a wheelchair. A recommendation rather than a necessity according to his doctors and only on a temporary basis.

Up until recently he was just a normal guy. A middle-aged man with a good job as an architect, a comfortable home plus a beautiful loving wife and twin daughters. Then one day, he goes to a meeting with an important client and the next thing he knows, he is waking up in a bed at some secret section of Britain's MI5 intelligence service. There they tell him that he is a kind of *Sleeper* agent – a Counter-Terrorist Asset to give it the proper title. To call the whole experience surreal was somewhat of an understatement.

Many years earlier, he had been recruited and trained to an exceptional level in marksmanship, high speed pursuit driving and unarmed combat. His natural superior genetics, which were key to the programme, had also been enhanced by a Doctor called Prisha Patel, along with her special projects team. How that part worked exactly, they never properly explained. Too technical for a layman to understand, they said, and that he should just trust in their groundbreaking science. Until he was needed, they told him that they would temporarily wipe his memory and place him back into society. He would carry on a normal life, unknown to enemies of the state. He would be re-activated only in the case of the most severe threats to the country.

Tom was aware that he had been lucky genetically. His parents were both still fit and well, as was his grandparents who were both in their nineties. Just like them, he had gone through life with very few ailments. He was very similar to his father, physically. Taller than average at just over six foot and weighing in at around two hundred and twenty pounds, Tom was always proud of his triangular shape. Broad shouldered and large chested, with a comparatively small waist. The main downside with his shape, he found, was that he could never buy an off-the-peg suit. Now in his forties, the main difference from his youth seemed to be a few facial lines and the addition of some flecks of grey around the side of his otherwise thick, dark brown head of hair. Even he was surprised to see very little deterioration in his physical performance over the years and raised many an eyebrow at the gym, when the weights that he used were far in excess of guys half his age. He was very grateful to his parents.

Then one day, the severe threat arrived in the form of a terrorist called Mohammed Baqri. An eccentric psychopath who decided to launch an attack on London with an electromagnetic pulse device so massive that it could send Britain back to the Dark Ages. Tom was activated and then ended up racing around London and fighting the terrorists in an attempt to prevent its detonation. In the process he was shot and blown up and, while recovering in hospital, literally suffocated to death by one of the terrorists, Brigid Doyle, who was aggrieved at him killing her boyfriend. Fortunately, Captain Aaron Jax, an SAS officer who had been in his team and who happened to have decided to visit him at the hospital that day, had got to him in time and managed to resuscitate him.

If that wasn't enough, Tom also discovered that there is a secretive organisation called The Collective which was supporting Baqri and had members in powerful positions across government, industry, military and the intelligence service.

Even the director general of MI5 had been discovered to be one. To top it all, Tom then found out that his American wife, Luna, is also a *Sleeper*. Some well-planned and choreographed match-making by MI5 and the CIA years before, with the ultimate hope that they would get together and eventually have offspring. Their children, it was believed, would be something quite exceptional – having the benefit of both their parent's superior genetics.

***

Tom had just phoned Luna. She had been led to believe that he had died from his injuries, so it would be fair to say that she was more than just a little shocked to hear his voice. Incredibly, the same terrorist who had tried killing him had just arrived at their home and tried to kill her as well, causing her to prematurely reactivate from *Sleeper* mode. From what he gathered, it was Doyle who ended up running for her life. Tom shook his head. His story was something that even he found difficult to believe.

Soon, he would be on his way to MI5 headquarters and to see Luna again. It would have been fantastic to have then just gone home with her and had some quality time together. But thanks to Baqri, that was not going to happen. An urgent meeting had been called. The CIA had discovered that Baqri was moving straight on to the United States, without even a pause. It was difficult to believe that he once had such a normal, quiet life.

A knock on the door and two guys dressed in suits stepped into his room.

'It's time to go Mr Rivers.'

CHAPTER ONE

He could hardly feel his hands anymore. For almost nine months – nine whole months – he had been stuck in this depressingly bleak, desolate, artic hellhole. A featureless desert of snow, for as far as the eye could see. He thought only prisoners and those who worked on the pipelines got sent to Siberia. It never occurred to him, when he put himself forward for this programme, that the Russian army would choose that as a location for testing their latest weapon. All down to making sure that it could handle extremes of weather, apparently. Well, thankfully, this was to be his last day. Tomorrow, he got to go home to southern Russia – and some long overdue warmth. He couldn't wait.

Lieutenant Alexei Nevsky had not spoken to his wife or children since he started his training. Top secret, the army told him. Couldn't risk him accidentally mentioning something that he shouldn't. His phone had been taken off him, but today he was reunited with it and he wasted no time.

Disappointingly his wife had not picked up her phone when he rang. Nevsky had decided that while he waited for her to call back he would step outside the base for a cigarette. But he had finished that five minutes ago. Despite having resorted to jogging on the spot and repeatedly blowing in his hands, he had reached the point where he couldn't take the painfully bitter temperature anymore. As if he needed any more convincing, a huge snowflake had just hit his hand, indicating the start of yet another snowstorm. *Perhaps remembering to take your gloves outside with you would have been a good idea*, he considered. But in his defence, the excitement of speaking to his family had completely taken over his normally sensible thought process.

'God, if I never see snow again, it would be too soon,' he muttered to himself. 'Come on, Maria. Where the hell are you?'

Nevsky turned on his heels and started walking back to the entrance door to the base, when his cell phone rang. He looked at the screen. At last, the call he had been waiting so long for. He could feel a surge of excitement. He knew his wife would be feeling the same.

'Hi honey,' said Nevsky.

'Hi sweety,' a man's voice replied.

Nevsky stared out into the frozen landscape – initially unsure how to respond.

'Who is this?' he asked.

'I bet you got a lot of stick for marrying a westerner, didn't you Alexei? Well, a New Zealander to be exact. Does that still make her a westerner? More of a southerner really. But anyway, what a lovely story. There you were enjoying a relaxing holiday in Turkey and you literally bump into the girl of your dreams who has been back-packing across the world. Six weeks later and you're engaged to be married. It's just *sooo* romantic.'

'Is that you, Anatoly?' smirked Nevsky.

'Who? Anatoly … Anatoly. Give me a second. Don't tell me. Oh, yes, I remember now. Your best man at your wedding – right? No, sorry, not your friend Anatoly. Can I just say how pleased I am that your English is so good now. Another tick for you, Alexei. My Russian is terrible, so this will really help with our future communications.'

'What future communications? Who *is* this?' demanded Nevsky. 'And where's my wife?'

'I'm someone who has been closely following your progress, Alexei. And, may I say, someone who is very impressed with the results. Especially from the course that you have just been on. I have to say for a man who is as dull as dishwater, you have a real talent there. Top of your class! Bravo!'

Nevsky repeated again, 'Where's my wife?'

'Your wife is here with me. She's alive and well. For the moment anyway. Your children too. And they will not be harmed if you do exactly what I tell you to do.'

'I want to speak to them.'

A short silence was then broken by the sound of a familiar voice on the other end of the phone.

'Alexei?'

'Maria? Oh my God! Are you OK?'

'Who are these people, Alexei?'

The man's voice returned to the phone.

'She's lovely, your wife, isn't she? Very pretty. Punching a bit above your weight, don't you think? Well, a lot above your weight, actually. It must have been your sparkling personality that won her over.'

'What do you want?'

'I have a little job for you, Alexei. When you leave the army base tomorrow, a couple of my associates will meet you. We need those skills that you have perfected. If you do what I want, then you get to see your family again. If you don't … well, I have a reputation to preserve.'

'Who are you?'

'Who am I? I am the instrument that will deliver God's divine justice.'

CHAPTER TWO

Director General Sir Iain MacGregor gazed over the MI5 Operations Room table at the woman sat opposite him. There she was. Luna Rivers.

Magnificent … really, quite magnificent, thought Mac. *Who honestly would think that this wife and mother of two, with her girl next door looks, would be one of the deadliest women on the planet? That mix of slight tan with green eyes and highlighted blonde hair doesn't exactly scream genetically superior killing machine, does it? Honey Badger. That's what she would be if she was an animal. Looks harmless and even quite cute but actually is completely fearless and deadly,* he thought, remembering a nature documentary that he watched recently. And then there, sat beside her, was her husband, Tom. Living proof of the success of the 'Sleeper' project. Successfully thwarted the biggest terrorist attack on Britain ever seen. A middle-aged guy who even has a bit of grey around the temples and who, for the last twenty years, had been working as an architect – completely unaware of what he really was. On the face of it, just an ordinary man. But in reality, anything but. With incredible abilities plus the physical strength of a silverback gorilla and the constitution of an ox, he was someone never anticipated by the terrorists.

Mac's self-congratulatory thoughts ended abruptly as CIA Director Theresa Muller finished shuffling her papers and cleared her throat. Muller was a short woman of just five feet two inches, and of a petite frame. Her brunette hair swept back neatly and held by an ornate oriental design hair-grip, might lead the unsuspecting to assume a meek and mild personality. This couldn't be further from the truth.

'Good evening, everyone. Firstly, I would like to thank Sir Iain MacGregor for hosting this meeting. Can I start by introducing the Secretary for Homeland Security, Rachael Goldberg, and FBI Assistant Director, Hayden Marshall,' said Muller, indicating with her hand the two people sat on either side of her.

Mac nodded in reply. 'And this is Tom and Luna Rivers,' he said, mirroring the CIA Director's introductions.

'To get straight down to it,' Muller said, 'the reason we have asked for this meeting, and the assignment of Luna to us, is that we have received reliable intelligence that a terrorist attack on the United States is imminent. This threat is so significant that the president personally instructed us to come over here and meet with you.'

'Yes, she's spoken to the prime minister,' said Mac. I believe that Mohammed Baqri has decided to move on to you now.'

'It seems so,' Muller agreed. 'But as this is a direct domestic threat, then it means that Homeland Security and the FBI will be taking the lead, instead of the CIA. With that in mind, I'll now hand over to Rachael.'

'Morning, Mac,' said Rachael Goldberg with a friendly smile and a slightly prolonged amount of eye contact. 'Oh, and congratulations on your knighthood, by the way.'

'Thanks Rachael,' replied Mac, mirroring her facial expressions.

Goldberg's affirmation of Mac's successful career within MI5 actually meant a lot to him. Mac had known her since they were both section chiefs in their respective intelligence services and he had always greatly admired and respected her. Strong, competent, and highly intelligent. Her move to Homeland and subsequent promotion to the top position was well deserved.

On a personal note, she was also his sort of woman. Slightly younger at thirty-nine, slim, and with a dark bob hairstyle that wrapped around her face. Always in the most immaculately tailored suits. Her appearance seemed to have changed very little since he had known her.

Mac, however, had what could only be described as a 'well worn' face for as long as he could remember. The years and his career had now added a few extra facial lines, as well as the odd fleck of grey to his head of black hair. He always thought that they would have made a great power couple, had they ever got together. Shame she was now married. *Missed a good one there*, he mused.

'So, as Theresa mentioned, our intel suggests that Mohammed Baqri has, with hardly a pause, moved on to the US,' said Goldberg. 'This, to me, means that he has probably planned this some time ago – perhaps at the same time as the recent events here. It would be reasonable to assume then, that an attack on us is imminent. Mac, I think you have something to add?'

'Yes, I do. I've got a really good personal contact who is very well connected. Ears everywhere. This is the sort of thing that he might have heard whispers about. But he's not the sort that will just volunteer information easily. It will probably need someone who has their own style of persuasion. I think it would be a good idea for Luna to go and see him.'

'Sounds good to me. Right then. So, I'll now hand over to Hayden for the briefing,' said Goldberg. 'Hayden is head of the FBI's Counterterrorism Division or CTD, as it's known.'

Bit of a beanpole, Mac observed, noting the FBI assistant director's very tall and thin physique.

'Thank you, Sir Iain. And good to meet you both,' said Marshall, in a distinctive New York accent, nodding his acknowledgement to the other side of the table.

Tom looked down at his wheelchair. 'I'm sorry but I'm stuck in this for a little while longer apparently. The personal cost of Baqri's attack on London.'

'You definitely have no need to apologise, Tom. You are already a legend in my department … throughout the whole FBI, actually. What you managed to do was incredible. And the fact that you survived your injuries is … well … quite simply amazing.'

'I appreciate that. Thank you,' replied Tom.

'And as Baqri has now targeted the US, we've asked for you, Luna, to be assigned to us.'

'Sorry but can I just ask why you want *me*? You have other similar assets over in the States, don't you?' asked Luna.

Marshall said, 'Two reasons. Firstly, you have the advantage of being an American national who is familiar with Britain too. Baqri and some of his associates are British by birth, don't forget. Secondly, we have looked at your results from when you were reactivated from Sleeper status, and they are … well … off the charts. We need the best and I reckon that's you.'

'Perhaps it would be a good time to introduce Luna to the *Adalah* terrorist cell that she will be dealing with,' said Goldberg. 'I'm sure Tom will give you his own thoughts on them at some point as well. If you would, Sir Iain.'

Mac pressed a button on the remote control in front of him and three of the screens in the middle of a huge row of monitors that hanged over the end of the table changed from their MI5 logos to photos of individuals.

'So, Luna. Here they are. On the very left is Mohammed Baqri. He is British born from Yemeni parentage. Best described as a charismatic, eccentric psychopath,' said Marshall.

‘Or to put it another way, off his head,’ muttered Mac under his breath.

‘OK, that’s quite a change of look,’ said Tom. ‘In the last picture that I had seen of him, he looked like your average guy. Albeit, with a goatee. Now he’s shaved his head and … seems to have some marks under his eyes?’

‘Tattoos,’ Marshall said. ‘He’s had three tears tattooed under his right eye.’

‘Because?’ asked Tom.

‘We believe they represent the loss of the three most important people in his life. His friend Sal – killed in the attack on London; his brother Rahim – executed by the Egyptian authorities … and … his mother.’

‘And yes, this is the mother that *he* blew up with a letter bomb,’ said Mac.

‘So, he kills his mother and tattoos a tear on his face to remember her by. How lovely,’ said Luna.

‘Not that it makes it any better,’ Marshall said, ‘but the bomb was meant to kill his father.’

‘Oh, yes,’ said Luna. ‘That makes it so much better.’

Tom said, ‘Be careful with him, Luna. As Mac mentioned, Baqri may, on the face of it, appear nuttier than squirrel shit, but don’t let that fool you. He’s actually very intelligent and calculating.’

‘OK. So why does he hate America so much?’ asked Luna.

Muller leaned forward, ‘He was a lieutenant of Osama bin Laden. The British captured him and then handed him to us. It seems the CIA team interrogated him without too much restraint. Before my time, I might add.’

‘But to be clear he has always hated us,’ said Goldberg. ‘Although his time in our custody seems to have just taken it to a whole new level.’

'Moving on,' said Marshall. 'The next screen is the picture of someone who you've already met, Luna. A young woman from the United Kingdom by the name of Brigid Doyle. I understand she made the mistake of trying to kill you?'

'Yeah, psycho bitch! What the hell was that about?' said Luna, causing the American contingent to raise their eyebrows. Despite having lived in Britain for the last twenty or so years, the famous English reserved manner had not rubbed off on her as they had expected.

'She seemed to take exception to Tom killing her fiancé. So, she set about killing your husband in his hospital bed as revenge,' said Mac.

'And then after she thinks that she has killed him, she decides that I should die as well. Really?'

'She probably thought that you were an easy target – not knowing who or what you really were, of course,' said Marshall.

Mac said, 'Brigid's anger stems from witnessing the murder of her father by paramilitary loyalists, by the way, during The Troubles in Northern Ireland. Blasted him in the chest with a shotgun while he was sat drinking in the pub and then they put a bullet in his head. The killers got off at court thanks to a police procedural failure, and then the security services killed all her brothers when they tried to take justice into their own hands.'

'Baqri stepped in and put a bomb under their car and then let Brigid press the button. Now she is completely loyal to him,' added Mac.

Luna looked at the face of her would-be assassin once again. She was certainly pretty. Bright blue eyes, fair skin and shoulder length red hair – rather than the dark hair that she had when she had turned up on Luna's doorstep with the intention of killing her. *Sort of get why she's such an angry person.*

'And the third and final one is Doctor Alim Farooqi,' said Marshall pointing at the last screen. 'The technical brains who build the electromagnetic pulse device that nearly sent Britain back to the dark ages.'

Mac said, 'He's in hospital after Brigid stuck a knife in his back in an effort to prevent him telling Tom how to stop the EMP.'

'Wow. She's such a lovely person too. I can see why she gets on with Baqri,' said Luna.

'The point is, Luna, that Farooqi will know that she was acting on Baqri's orders. So, our thinking is that he may be reconsidering which side of the fence he should be on. We want you to go and pay him a visit at St. Thomas's hospital and try to persuade him to help us find out what Baqri is planning against the US.'

'Where's Baqri now?' Tom asked.

'He's been spotted in North Korea. Casually sitting outside a café in Pyongyang, having a coffee and dressed like a tourist,' replied Goldberg.

Tom smiled and nodded. *Of course, he would be.*

'He then met up with a North Korean general by the name of Kim Sun-woo,' continued Goldberg, as Mac switched the next monitor over to a photo of the general in full military uniform. 'It's fair to say that North Korea isn't our greatest fan, but this guy has made it clear that he would love nothing more than to level the US. Worryingly, he's in charge of their nuclear weapons development.'

'God. That really is worrying,' Mac added.

'So, Mac, you can see why the President wanted us to see you personally. Our on-going relationship is critical – particularly on intelligence sharing. She'll be attending the Coronation of King Edward at Westminster Abbey tomorrow, as you know. I would then like us to be able to provide her with a positive update when we fly back on Airforce One,' said Muller.

'Yes, of course. Whatever we can do.'

'So, with that in mind, we have one more request,' said Goldberg. 'We would very much like Tom to be seconded to the FBI for the duration. His knowledge of Baqri and his terrorist cell will be vital. I know you're not up to field work yet Tom, but you could really help us. If Mac is agreeable, you would be working out of the J. Edgar Hoover building in Washington DC. Then after Luna has finished her assignment here in the UK, she will be able to come over and join you. I believe both your girls are now at University and under the charge of Mac and MI5, so hopefully you won't think that's an issue. We're happy to fly them out to see you between terms, of course.'

Mac spun his chair round ninety degrees to face Tom, who just nodded.

Tom muttered, 'And just when I thought I would never have to deal with Baqri again.'

CHAPTER THREE

Sir Iain MacGregor, Director MI5, read the shiny stainless-steel plaque on the door. Just as Luna was about to knock, the door opened. Mac's assistant stood on the other side.

'Please take a seat,' she said pointing to the other end of the very long and modern office with a distant figure in a pin-stripe suit sat at the end.

'Ah, Luna,' said the familiar voice.

Luna smiled. All it needed was to substitute her name with 'Miss Moneypenny' and he would have sounded just like Sean Connery.

'Nice to see you smiling. Please have a seat,' said Mac gesturing towards one of the much smaller chairs on the other side of his desk.

'Good morning, Mac. And good morning, Doctor Patel,' said Luna, nodding an acknowledgement to the person occupying the other chair beside hers. 'Nice office, by the way, Mac. Very minimalist. Love the river views. Very you.'

Mac smiled. 'Right then. So, the reason you're here is just a de-brief before you start your new career with the FBI. We haven't had as much time as usual to transition you from Sleeper status to active agent.'

Patel added, 'We've also had the major issue that you've been snapped out of your Sleeper state in an uncontrolled manner – thanks to Brigid Doyle trying to kill you. We've never had that before.'

'Oh right. So, you want to be sure that before you hand me over to the Americans, my brain is wired together properly? Before I go and kill a load of people?'

Mac raised his eyebrows and glanced over at Dr Patel.

'Kidding, Mac. Don't look so worried,' said Luna.

'You do have a famously short fuse though, and so Dr Patel just wants to have a chat and make sure the old you and the new, or should I say the recently remembered you, are successfully fused together.'

'OK, Luna,' said Patel repositioning her small square glasses and picking up her notepad. 'Tell me about some of your favourite childhood memories.'

Luna paused for a moment. 'Well, I guess some of the best times that I had was with my dad and all the different countries we lived in as I was growing up. He was in the US Diplomatic Corps, as you know, but he had this passion for really getting into the culture of a country. So, for example, when we lived in Japan it wasn't just things like eating Japanese food for him. He would learn their customs … like when you should bow a little lower to some people as a sign of respect. One of my favourite memories was Cherry Blossom Day – which is in March. The whole family used to take a picnic and sit under the cherry trees. It's a popular Japanese tradition. Mom loved it too. My little brother not so much.'

Patel smiled. 'Sounds lovely.'

'It was. Then, when we moved to the UK, Dad got into British culture. He felt that should include the pub – every Saturday without fail. Lunchtime drink with his friends. He even got into soccer – or football as you call it. Became a big Chelsea supporter. He loved going to the matches and used to drag me along with him.'

'Well, there doesn't seem to be any issues with your childhood memories. So, let's look at the next stage – when you were recruited.'

'OK. I can remember that clearly too. Dad had been offered a promotion, but it meant a return to DC. It looked like we were on the move again.'

'Was that when you decided that you wanted to join the FBI?'

'Actually, I had wanted to be an FBI agent since I was a little girl. With us all moving back to the US, I decided that it was the right time to apply. I flew back to the States and went through a three-day assessment.'

'But then when you came back to London, you met a tall, dark, handsome man, right? Tom?'

'Yeah, at an Embassy party. Do you know, the funny thing is, I didn't even fancy him when I first saw him. But then we were introduced, and he made me laugh. He also had this sort of strength about him – like nothing would phase him. We had a few dates after that and then we had *the night*. Do you know what I mean by that? We stayed up all night and just talked. We really connected and I thought *this could be the one*.'

'Must have caused you some problems with your plans to join the FBI though?'

'It did. Initially, I had no idea what the hell I was going to do. The trouble is, I had already fallen in love with Tom. I think they could see my dilemma. Then they approached me and said that they had a special position available where I could stay in Britain and still work for them. I was told that their tests on me in the States had identified superior genetics. They said there was a joint US/UK project where I would be trained to my maximum potential and far beyond what a normal person could take. For me, that was a win/win.'

'Ok, great. That was the first part of your memories that we had suppressed, when you were put into a Sleeper state. If

I had asked you a month ago, you would have said that you decided not to proceed with your application to the FBI and that you got a marketing job in Britain instead. So, let's move on to your memories of being trained.'

'I went to some sort of secret MI5 centre. Lots of weapons instruction. Even more unarmed combat training. There were some FBI and CIA guys there too, who seem to be setting the agenda. And you were there too.'

'Indeed, I was. I remember watching you in action. Extremely impressive. Never forgot it. I recall that, on one of your sessions, you disabled three armed attackers in about thirty seconds flat.'

Luna smiled and nodded.

'So, last part,' said Patel. 'Your life as a Sleeper.'

'I remember it, but it also feels slightly strange. Bit like I have been living a lie. I was a highly trained agent pretending to be a normal wife and mom. At the same time, I also realise that I wasn't pretending, as I consciously didn't know what I was. I'm still finding it a bit confusing and just trying to square it off in my mind.'

'What about major events like your wedding. How do feel about those – now you have these new memories.'

'Well, it was an amazing day. But now it sort of feels like it was someone else there. I was a Sleeper asset and bizarrely, I was marrying another Sleeper. And neither of us realised what we were. It's a bit mind blowing, to be honest.'

The phone rang on Mac's desk. He picked it up with an irritated sigh.

'I did say that I didn't want to be disturbed,' he said curtly, and then fell silent. 'What? How the hell has that happened? Great. That's just bloody brilliant.'

'Problem?' asked Luna.

'You could say that. You won't be able to speak to Dr Farooqi as he's escaped custody.' Mac scribbled on some paper in front of him.

'How?'

'Someone decided that he was well enough to be transported from St Thomas's hospital to Belmarsh prison. The prison van got ambushed on the way.'

'And they just happened to know his route and timetable?'

'I smell *Collective.*'

'Excuse me?' What's *Collective*?' asked Luna.

'Who, actually. I guess I had better tell you about them, as they've surfaced again. I know you haven't had a proper catch-up with Tom yet but get him to tell you about his experiences with them as well.'

'Sure.'

'Alright then. During Tom's mission to stop Baqri's attack on London, it transpired that the terrorists were getting help. They were not only being given top secret information but the satellites that we had tracking them got repositioned, and then police units were dispatched to block Tom's progress.'

'How the hell did they manage to do that?'

'We discovered that my predecessor, Sir Nicholas Meads, was behind it. He wasn't alone though. He told me that he was a member of a secretive organisation called The Collective. They are a group of wealthy, powerful, and influential people from around the world who manipulate events to make money. They were betting on Baqri succeeding in his attack on London and taking down the financial system. Then when it looked like he was going to fail, they intervened in his favour.'

'OK. And wow. The Director General of MI5. But that whole incident nearly ended up in a war between Britain, America and Russia. It could have gone nuclear. Are they nuts?'

'Well, he also told me that The Collective had manipulated all the countries involved. He was trying to convince me that there was never a real risk of nuclear war. It was all part of their money-making agenda. I don't see how anyone could be sure of that. What that did tell us, however, is that they must have people with a high degree of influence in those governments.'

'I assume that intelligence agencies around the world are trying to track them down?'

'We're trying but getting nowhere. Sir Nicholas told me that they operate an anonymous messaging system to talk to each other and each member has a codename. They never meet in person and so even those in The Collective don't know who the other members are.'

'Why don't you just get into their messaging system? Draw them out.'

'Because their messaging system keeps changing. They hijack an app and insert a secret messaging system within it. So, my advice to you is not to trust anyone.'

Luna nodded as Mac handed the piece of paper over which he had written on.

'First job for you. This is the guy that I mentioned in our meeting with the American contingent. I suggest that you go and pay him a visit. He may be able to give you some info about Dr Farooqi and he might also have heard something about Baqri's plans.'

Luna looked at the paper. 'Razor Rutter. Interesting name. Did he just have cruel parents or something?'

'His real name is Harry Rutter. He was a small time East End gangster in his younger days. Called Razor as he had a reputation for using a razor blade to peel the top layers of skin off those who crossed him. Got banged up in prison, of course, and when he got out, he decided to change his career to become *a conduit of information*, as he puts it.'

'He sounds nice. I assume his new job came with a little help from you?'

'Indeed. He already had some great contacts, so it made sense. We have a mutually beneficial relationship. See if you can get him to tell you anything about The Collective too. The address on the paper is the private member's club that he spends most of his time in.'

'How do I recognise him?'

'Oh, I think you'll work it out. If you have any doubt, he's the one with a bowling ball for a head. Big lump. I'll tell him to expect you.'

***

As Luna exited the office, Mac looked at Dr Patel.

'Well? What do you think?'

'Difficult to say. You did cut my assessment short, Mac. Hopefully, she'll be ok.'

'Hopefully? That's not a word that fills me with confidence – especially as we have just handed her over to our closest ally.'

'The issue is that we have never had a Sleeper prematurely activated before. Brigid's attempt to murder Luna meant an uncontrolled wake-up. This is new territory. Hell of a gamble, Mac, sending her out so early. I could have done with more time with her. We've just despatched a killing machine and I'm not convinced that we have an off button.'

CHAPTER FOUR

'Good afternoon, Madam. May I help you?' said the doorman standing outside *The Raglan* private members' club.

'I'm here to see Harry Rutter.'

'Ah yes. Ms Rivers, I assume? Mr Rutter is expecting you. Third floor and right down to the end.'

Luna stepped through the black doors, framed by marble columns on either side, and into the lobby of the impressive early 19th century Regency era building. As she made her way up the ornate, sweeping oak stairs – complete with crimson red carpet-runner down the middle – she couldn't help smirking at the numerous photographs of the past and present members of the club that adorned the walls. Among them, she recognised several former prime ministers, a few members of the royal family and some major business leaders who had been knighted for their services to their country. But it was the fact that, with all its grandeur and air of superiority, she was now going to see a common, convicted, east-end gangster in this so-called gentlemen's club, that made her smile.

One more flight of stairs, a short walk down to a quiet cordoned off area and there he was. The man with the bowling ball for a head. Bursting out of his pin-stripe suit, matched with a white shirt and spotted blue tie, there was little chance that he could be confused with anyone else. Luna was about to meet one of the most feared villains in England.

Having put his knife and fork very slowly and deliberately down on his plate, Harry 'Razor' Rutter picked up his napkin and wiped both sides of his mouth before placing it back down on the table in front of him. He looked up and gazed intimidatingly at Luna.

'Hello, treacle. 'Ow are ya?' said the bowling ball, in a deep, gruff East London accent.

'Is that your best hard man look? It's not going to work on me, honey. May I?' said Luna rhetorically, immediately sitting down in the chair opposite.

'Well, you're a cocky one, aren't you?'

'Cocky? No. But I am used to getting my own way.'

'I'm a bit baffled. Why has Mac sent you? I checked you out and I can't work out what's going on. As far as I'm aware, you were 'till recently, living a normal life. A marketing executive with a husband and kids. But then your husband – who was supposed to be an architect – ends up fighting terrorists and saving the country from disaster. Now, I can't say that I'm intimate with the workings of an architect, but I'm pretty sure that they're not normally highly proficient in high-speed pursuit driving and the use of semi-automatic weapons.'

'I don't work for Mac. I'm American, as you probably guessed. He did, however, suggest that you may be able to help with an FBI operation that I'm involved in.'

'Yeah, it hadn't escaped me that you were a septic.'

'A septic?'

'Septic tank.'

'Oh, OK. Yank, yeah? I've got to understand a bit of cockney rhyming slang since I've lived in this country. So, can you help, Mr Rutter?'

'So, in reality, you're really just a glorified housewife. Your husband's a hero, and the snowflakes thought, let's be all politically correct and give his missus a job? Is that right or am I missing something? No offence, by the way.'

'Offence taken, by the way. Actually, I have a special skill set of my own,' Luna replied, glaring at the big lump opposite her.

'Alright, sweet cheeks. Calm yourself down. You'll start giving that pretty little face of yours some stress lines.'

'Mmmmm … Not so keen on the *sweet cheeks* either. You see, phrases like that could confuse people into thinking that you're just a misogynistic pig.'

Rutter sat bolt upright. 'Who the f—'

'Tell me about Dr Farooqi, Mr Rutter,' interrupted Luna.

Rutter leaned back in his chair again. 'You've got some *orchestra stalls* on you, girl. Alright then. As a favour to Mac, I'll tell you what I know. Dr Farooqi is now out of the country. Baqri needs him to build some weapon and he's gone to join him.'

'Must be another electromagnetic pulse device. What about Baqri? What's he planning? And what's with this group? The Collective?'

'That's all I know. Never heard of any Collective. All I have heard is that Baqri's in Russia, planning some attack on America.'

'And that's it? I got the impression from Mac that you were the font of all knowledge, when it came to this stuff. Sorry, I'm struggling to accept that's all you know.'

'Oh really?' said Rutter, gazing out through the open window across the river Thames. After what felt like a very long thirty second pause, Rutter broke the silence. 'Let me tell you a little about my life. I grew up on a really poor council estate in the east end, you know. My dad was locked up in prison when I was six and so my mother brought me and my brothers up on her own. She worked three jobs just to pay the rent and put food on the table. And I learnt from a very young age that I had to fight to get what I wanted in life. I wasn't born with a silver spoon up my arse, like you. Then one day, I remember looking across the river at this building and wondering what sort of people would be in here. My mother told me that powerful people went to this place, and it wasn't for the likes of us. I made a vow to myself that I was going to prove her wrong. And look at me now. Here I am. I have powerful countries around the world wanting to do business with me.'

Rutter leaned forward again in his chair and scowled at Luna. 'So, what I'm getting at is that I don't actually give a shit what some little American girlie thinks – with your blonde hair and cheap suit. I spoke to you as a favour to Mac. And now feel free to just piss off.'

'Just because you're in a gentlemen's club and wearing a suit and tie, doesn't make you a gentleman, Mr Rutter. Or, as my husband would say, you can't polish a turd.'

'You little bitch,' said Rutter springing to his feet.

Luna's strike to Rutter's neck was so fast that he had no time to react. He staggered back a step, holding his throat and gasping for breath. A kick to his chest followed, sending Rutter crashing over his seat. By the time he had managed to stand up again, Luna was already stood in front of him. He lurched at her but was immediately met with a barrage of punches to his face. Another kick sent him staggering back again – but now towards the open window. Frantically grabbing at anything within reach, Rutter just managed to stop himself falling out by gripping the side of the window frame with one hand.

'Speak ... properly ... to ... women,' said Luna, punctuating each word with a punch to Rutter's face.

Rutter fell backwards through the open window. Luna lunged forwards and grabbed him by the tie.

'Pull me in … pull me in.'

'Tell me what you know, and I will.'

'I'm Razor Rutter, you psycho. Do you know how I got that name? I'm going to peel your skin off for this.'

'Wrong answer,' said Luna, briefly letting go of his tie before grabbing it again.

Rutter glanced down at the busy road below. 'Alright, alright. I know Baqri is backed by The Collective. They've got people everywhere.'

'What people?'

'I don't know who exactly. But they're powerful people – you know generals and top politicians. I swear to God that's all I know. Nobody knows who they are. Pull me in.'

'My arm's going to tire soon. Pretty sure even from three storeys, a dive into the middle of that road isn't going to do you much good.'

'OK, OK. I also know Baqri's got hold of some special Russian missiles. They're called HGVs.'

'And he wants to fire them at America?'

'Yeah. And the Yanks won't be able to stop them.'

CHAPTER FIVE

WEDNESDAY JULY 5th

'Doctor!' said Baqri excitedly. 'How absolutely wonderful to see you again.'

Alim Farooqi blinked repeatedly and tried to focus his eyes as the hood covering his head was removed. He was in a large dark room with just one small window. He had already felt the cold. In fact, he had felt a distinct drop in temperature as soon as he had walked off the aircraft that he had been bundled into.

'How are you, Alim? Welcome to Russia!'

Dr Alim Farooqi just scowled in reply.

'Oh dear. As the barman said to the horse, what's with the long face?'

'It's not like I had much of a choice, did I?' said Farooqi, looking around at the two men behind him.

'Zane and Idris are both loyal members of *Adalah*, just like you doctor. You were off to prison, Alim, but we rescued you. You're welcome, by the way.'

'You rescued me? I assume you didn't want me helping the British Secret Service? That's why you *rescued* me. And you probably want me to build a new device of some sort, so that you can try to kill more people?'

'Oh, Alim. A little bit of time with those infidels and you seem to have completely lost your way. Remember, what *Adalah* means in Arabic? Justice. Remember how they were responsible for the death of your wife and daughter? Remember how you swore revenge? We didn't manage to achieve that revenge on

London but now we have a much bigger target. And we now have the support of The Collective. We will not fail this time.'

'I regret my part in the attack on London. I see that it was wrong now. People died. Innocent people. They had nothing to do with the death of my wife and daughter. My wife would never have wanted me to do that.'

Baqri bowed his head. 'I see that they have truly corrupted you, my friend. We must try hard to put you back on the right path.'

'What, by getting her to stick a knife in my back again?' said Farooqi, as Brigid Doyle walked into the room.

Baqri looked at Brigid. 'No. Really? Did I ask you to do that?'

Brigid simply nodded in reply.

'Oh, yes. OK, I remember now. But if we hadn't done that then you would have been forced by the British to tell them how to stop the bomb. Obviously, we couldn't let that happen. As Confucius said, 'silence is a true friend who never betrays us.'

Brigid rolled her eyes and shook her head.

'And anyway, where she stabbed you was designed to incapacitate rather than kill. You're fine now, aren't you? Really not sure what you're whingeing about.'

'I'm not doing it, by the way.'

'Not doing what? I haven't even told you what it is.'

'It doesn't matter. Whatever hare-brained scheme that you've come up with. I'm not helping you.'

'Bet I can change your mind.'

'I don't care what you say or what you do, I'm … not … helping … you,' Farooqi slowly and deliberately repeated.

Baqri picked up a small cake box from the table beside him and handed it to Farooqi, who looked bewildered by the gift. A neat red cotton bow adorned the box and hanging down the side was a tag.

To my friend, Alim. Hope this gives you the motivation that you need.

'Oh my God,' shouted Farooqi, dropping the now opened box. As it hit the ground, a finger bounced out the top and landed beside his foot. 'What is wrong with you? And why the hell do you think cutting a person's finger off and giving it to me is going to be motivation? Is this supposed to scare me? If you cut off my fingers then I can't help you, can I?'

'Look more carefully at the finger, Doctor. Then you'll understand. That's a really beautiful ring on it, I have to say. Recognise it?'

Farooqi lent down and squinted through his square spectacles. He recognised the ring but for a minute couldn't place it. Then he staggered backwards with his hand over his mouth.

'Oh my God. What have you done? That's my mother's ring. What have you done with her, you bastard?'

'I thought I better leave the ring on. I mean, an old wrinkly finger on its own just could have been anyone's, couldn't it? But don't worry, Alim. Apart from that missing digit, she's alive and well. For the moment, anyway. She may find playing the piano slightly more difficult now. But I bet she likes a challenge.'

'You're sick. You're not right in the head. You do know this, don't you?'

'What I know is that America must be punished for its crimes. And you need to help me do it. My promise to you is this. If you help me, then your mother will be set free. If you don't then you better buy a shovel to scoop up the rest of her.'

A ping drew Baqri's attention to a new message on his phone.

'Mmmmm … interesting,' said Baqri, looking up at Brigid. 'Our new associates tell me that a couple of friends of yours are now in the United States and helping the Americans.'

'Who?' asked Brigid.

'Tom Rivers and his equally dangerous wife, Luna. You remember her, don't you,' Baqri said with a smirk. 'Stay away from her, Brigid, unless you want another beating.'

Baqri tapped away on his phone with a slight look of irritation on his face.

'What is it?' asked Brigid.

'The Collective are suggesting that Tom poses a threat to our objective and we should look at eliminating him. They seem to feel that his knowledge and understanding of my modus operandi, means that he could provide the Americans with a critical insight. He's still wheelchair bound from his London injuries, so should be an easier target at the moment, they say.'

'So, what did you say?'

'I told them that going after him was an unnecessary distraction and I wasn't interested.'

'Or is it because you lost the first battle of wits with him and want a re-match? For a much bigger prize. You seem to treat this as a game between you. It's not a game, Mo. You should let me finish what I started. You do remember that this shit killed my fiancé, don't you?' Brigid's building anger was now beginning to heighten her Northern Irish accent.

'Stay away from them, Brigid. You were lucky last time. Be patient now. I will help you when the time is right.'

Brigid was alerted to her own phone and a new message.

'My mother. Just checking that I'm ok. She's such a worrier,' she said, aware that Baqri was looking at her.

She turned around and looked at the message again. Not a message from her mother but one from The Collective. A broad smile spread across her face.

CHAPTER SIX

FRIDAY 26 JULY

It was 8 a.m. and the president's chief of staff, James McInnis, had already been awake for three hours – a firm believer that a productive day's work comes from an early start. Joining him for his morning meeting with the US president in the Oval Office was the director of the United States Secret Service, John Barratt.

'Right then John. Let's have your update on King Edward's state visit,' said President Jane Monroe, looking over her glasses.

'Are you OK, Madam President?' said Barratt, noticing that the President's eyes were starting to stream.

'I'm fine, John. Thank you for asking, though. Need to pop some more tablets. Picked up a stinking cold when I was at the Coronation. The French president was coughing away behind us and now both me and the First Gentleman have caught it,' said Monroe reaching into her desk drawer for the necessary medicine.

'Do you know what? I think that you're the first president to ever attend a British King's Coronation,' said McInnis.

'Really? Monroe said, 'That's interesting. Don't forget that he's a good personal friend as well. I wouldn't have missed it for the world. Sorry, John. Please, continue.'

'As you know, Madam President, the King's aircraft, RAF *Voyager*, is due to land at Andrews Air Force Base around 4 p.m. this Sunday afternoon. After you greet the King, we will be transporting you both from the airport directly to the White

House via Marine One. I have assigned a Secret Service detail for the King's protection during his visit, of course, and they will work with his own royal protection officers,' replied Barratt.

'I understand that the King and Queen are spending Monday at the White House meeting the British ambassador and other dignitaries during the day and then later there is the state dinner, of course.'

'Not forgetting that you are having a private dinner with them Sunday evening as well,' interjected McInnis.

'I haven't forgotten that one, Jim. This state visit is actually something that I'm really looking forward to. Can't say that about many of them. John, please carry on.'

'On Tuesday, we have the main event – his royal address to Congress. The King's motorcade will leave the White House at 11 a.m. and proceed slowly down Pennsylvania Avenue to allow him to wave at the crowds. Barrier control will be in force, of course, along with a high level of uniformed police officers. I have, with the assistance of his royal protection team, managed to reach a compromise with the King, in that he has agreed not to leave the protection of his vehicle and not fully lower his window on route. This is the time when he will be most vulnerable, since he will have lost the benefit that blacked out bulletproof glass provides. I have, of course, coordinated with the FBI and other agencies as well.'

If Barratt had a family moto, it would be 'organized and thorough.' His meteoric rise through the FBI and then Secret Service was mainly down to these two qualities, rather than any sort of charisma. Dependably efficient with a look that matched. Crew cut dark hair, sharply pressed black suit and shoes that you could see your reflection in. The King would be safe on his watch.

'Has the King been given a code word for this visit?' asked Monroe, taking off her glasses and then raising her imposing six-foot three-inch frame out of her chair. She continued to walk around her desk before sitting down on the front of it.

'He has, Madam President. *Sceptre.* It's the staff that the monarch holds in their hand.'

'Oh, yes. I remember it from his Coronation. It has a huge diamond on the top called the Star of Africa. I remember Prime Minister Hatcher telling me about it. Five hundred and thirty carats. Now, that's a big diamond. Largest clear diamond in the world, in fact. Sorry John, please carry on.'

'I was only going to add that we will employ a full range of security precautions including snipers and a significant number of plain clothed agents mixed into the crowd. I would have preferred it if we could have cleared his route from any spectators, but the King was adamant that he wanted to appear normal and approachable. I am trying my best to try and persuade his people that the less time the King spends outside the protection of his vehicle meeting people, the better.'

'I thought that he had agreed not to get out at all?' queried Monroe.

'He's keen on getting out near to Congress and talking to some of the crowd.'

'That's dangerous.'

'I know, Madam President. But no one has been able to persuade him not to do it.'

'Trouble is the guy is very charismatic and his high profile before he was King with all his charity work around the world, has given him rock star status with the American people. And we're his first visit as the new British monarch. I've also been told that huge numbers of tourists are already descending on Washington,' said the thirty-five-year-old fresh face, James McInnis.

Monroe said, 'He is amazing, isn't he? I'm not sure we have ever seen the likes of him in our lifetime. Probably won't see anyone like him again. Did you see that series on tv? When he was travelling around Africa? And then all that aid and finance that he subsequently managed to secure from other countries.'

'Including us, Madam President,' said McInnis.

'True. But who could refuse? Tell me you didn't cry when he held that little girl in his arms, all thin and weak? And she just quietly passed away. He cried, I cried and I think the world cried at that moment. I'll never forget it.'

'A rock star to us but a living saint to Africa.'

'Indeed. *The Saint of Africa*, the President of Nigeria called him.'

A brief knock on the Oval Office door and Homeland Secretary Goldberg walked briskly into the room.

'Madam President, my apologies for the interruption but I'm sure you will want to hear this immediately.'

'Of course, Rachael. Please take a seat,' said Monroe gesturing to a couple of chairs next to Barratt.

'We have just received some troubling news. We have reliable information that, three days ago, Mohammed Baqri and his terrorist group *Adalah*, managed to acquire three Russian Avangard HGVs,' said Goldberg.

'HGVs?'

'Hypersonic Glide Vehicles, Madam President. These are like small, unmanned aircrafts without any propulsion system of their own. Bit like a glider.'

'And we're only just hearing about it now?'

'The Russian's have been keeping it quiet – hoping they would regain them before anyone else found out.'

'I sort of remember something about these in a briefing from a couple of years ago. The Russians were still trying to perfect the technology at that time.'

'Our understanding is that any development issues have now been resolved and they are fully operational. Three mobile launch vehicles carrying RS-26 Rubezh intercontinental ballistic missiles with Avangard HGVs as a payload, were hijacked on their way to a base in southern Russia. Madam President, these ballistic missiles have a range of about 3600 miles. And we believe that Mohammed Baqri is the hijacker,' said Goldberg.

Monroe stared incredulously at Rachael Goldberg. Her mouth literally dropping open with the news. 'And what is the range of these HGV things on top of that?'

'Well, the Russians have proved a range of 2300 miles during testing.'

'So, what does that mean?'

'What it means is that Baqri could potentially hit any city within the United States from deep inside Russia.'

McInnis just muttered, 'Dear God.'

'How the hell did he manage to steal some ballistic missiles off them?' said Monroe.

'Somehow, this convoy only had one army vehicle and a total of six soldiers as protection.'

'Somehow! And Baqri also somehow just managed to find out about it? Please tell me that these things don't come fitted with nuclear warheads.'

'The Russians tell us that they weren't.'

'And we believe them?'

'Our intelligence reports seem to indicate that that is correct. They also state that the Russians are frantically trying to track them down. Our sources tell us that President Petrov is furious. The Russians are concerned that they have no idea who Baqri may target with those weapons. But of even greater concern is that their technology might fall into the wrong hands.'

'Our hands you mean.'

'Yes, Ma'am. But I also have to remind you that Baqri was recently spotted in North Korea having a coffee with the general responsible for their nuclear weapons programme.'

'This is sounding worse and worse, Rachael. So, do we think he may have been successful in getting some nuclear material from North Korea then? And he's constructing some sort of nuclear weapon? Or could they have just given him a bomb?'

'It's possible, yes. But I can't imagine the North Koreans just handing over a nuclear weapon – that would be a declaration of war against the United States. What is more likely is that Baqri is trying to put together some sort of dirty bomb. If you remember, Madam President, the scientist that built the EMP bomb that nearly crippled the UK, Dr Alim Farooqi, was recently sprung from a prison van which was transporting him. We believe he has now joined Baqri in Russia.'

'So, do you think he's got Dr Farooqi to build it for him then? Is that why Baqri broke him out?'

'His speciality is EMPs but I guess he has the knowledge to turn his hand to building other devices.'

'Tell me we have the defences to take these things out.'

'Actually, we might have a problem there. The Avangard was designed by the Russians to be unstoppable. It detaches from the missile carrying it at sub-orbital levels – about sixty-two miles up – and then it is believed to be able to reach speeds of between Mach 20 and 27 towards its target. That's around 15,000 to 21,000 miles an hour. We don't have anything that can catch that, so we will be relying on our defence missiles trying to intercept it.'

'And the probability of us successfully being able to do that?'

'The thing is, the Avangard isn't technically a missile. Missiles follow a predictable trajectory, which is how we can intercept them. HGVs like the Avangard are remote controlled – like a drone. This makes them highly manoeuvrable and able to quickly change course. In short, we're not sure that we *will* actually be able to stop them.'

President Monroe stood up once again and then put her face in her hands, brushing back her dark brown bob-cut hair with her fingers. After what felt like a very long minute's silence, she looked up and spoke again.

'But surely these things can't be piloted by just anyone?'

'You're right Madam President. But we've just received intel that a Russian officer by the name of Alexei Nevsky has gone missing. And Nevsky is one of just a small number of people who have received training in piloting the Avangard. He is generally regarded as being the best of them.'

'And you think Baqri has him as well?'

'I do.'

'We need to find Baqri … and quickly. Put every resource available on it. I gather that you have managed to borrow Tom Rivers from the British? Put him on point for this – his knowledge of Baqri will be invaluable. I'm going to tell Admiral Womack to get a Black Ops team together. I'm not waiting for the Russians to find him. Perhaps we should also get Tom's wife, Luna, on standby. She seems to be effective at extracting information, I believe.'

'Luna's currently suspended from duty, Madam President. She was the one who got us the information on the HGVs but she went a little too far in her questioning of a contact.'

'Really? She got the result, didn't she?'

'Yes, but she punched a British national several times in the face before dangling him out of a third-floor window over a busy road. The man was well connected politically and we received a formal complaint.'

'Bet my political connections are better than his. I'll call Prime Minister Hatcher. I want her ready to go when we need her. Make no mistake people, Baqri is coming for us.'

CHAPTER SEVEN

MONDAY 29 JULY – 9 a.m.

As usual for that time of the week, the president had started her foreign affairs meeting in the Oval Office with the secretary of state and her chief of staff.

'Good morning. Well, I think the King and Queen's visit is going well, so far. Always look forward to the stories he comes out with over dinner,' said Monroe with a smile. 'By the way, I don't think we should worry him with the Baqri threat. OK? Anyway, let's get down to business. So, Walt, what's the latest on the Democratic Republic of Congo?' said President Monroe, putting on her reading glasses and then picking her pen up from the desk.

Secretary of State Walter Houston, sitting opposite the president, peered down at his notes through the square glasses perched on the end of his nose.

'It appears that, despite being in self-imposed exile, Colonel Joseph Banza has started making significant progress in his efforts to gather support from within the Congolese military. His narrative is that the DRC is merely an American puppet state, so long as President Mwamba is in charge. He's getting ground roots support from the people as well, Madam President.'

'Puppet state! It's not a puppet state!' exclaimed Monroe. 'But it is a country that is doing very well from all the billions of dollars that the US government has invested in their cobalt mining industry … and is still investing. A country where American corporations have also invested billions in developing the plant and processes to extract the minerals. They asked for our support and we gave it.'

'I know Madam President, but Colonel Banza is propagating the idea that America is taking Congo's valuable resources and the people are getting nothing in return. American imperialism, he calls it. He proposes to nationalise all the businesses, quarries and infrastructure that are involved in cobalt mining in the DRC. His friends in the media there are really pushing it out to the public.'

'Nationalise them first and then, no doubt, sell them off on the cheap to newly established companies that he is the majority shareholder of. He will end up as one of the richest men on earth,' interjected Chief of Staff James McInnis.

President Monroe said, 'Walt, I'm sure I don't need to remind you of the importance of securing a reliable source of cobalt. Like most other countries, the shift away from fossil fuels to that of electrification is at the heart of our environment strategy. Batteries need cobalt and the DRC has more of it than all the other countries in the world combined. If Banza seizes power in the Congo then every country will be held hostage by him and he will control the market.'

'I agree, Madam President, but it's not clear what more we can do to support President Mwamba. As you know, the only thing currently holding back Colonel Banza from seizing power is the threat from the surrounding African countries that they will send forces to assist the President.'

'Encouraged by the financial support packages that we have offered them all, of course,' interjected Chief of Staff McInnis. 'Can we not just send in American troops as well?'

'Really bad idea, Jim,' Houston said. 'That would play straight into Banza's hands. Wouldn't go down well with all the other countries in Africa either. It would be regarded as an unwarranted invasion.'

'Well, let's hope that our African allies stand firm then,' said Monroe.

'There is another issue, of course,' said Secretary Houston. 'The Russians. They are very aware that their natural resources are dwindling and that electrification is the future. So, they've been cosying up to Banza for a while now. And if he does nationalise our companies out there, as Jim suggested, then it will be the Russians at the heart of the new private companies when they emerge again. It won't just be Banza who will be incredibly rich but the shareholders of those Russian companies too.'

A triple knock on the Oval Office door announced the arrival of FBI Assistant Director Marshall.

'Come in Hayden. Have a seat,' said President Monroe, pointing to an empty chair by Secretary Houston. 'I've asked Assistant Director Marshall here to give us an update on the Baqri menace. Where are we up to, Hayden?'

Before Marshall could respond, a buzzing noise from his suit jacket pocket alerted him to an incoming call on his phone. He looked at the screen. It was his office. *Must be urgent*, he mused, having left specific instructions that he was not to be disturbed during his meeting with the President.

'Do you mind if I take this Madam President? It may be relevant to our discussions.'

Monroe nodded and for the next few minutes Marshall just listened to a report being delivered by his assistant. As he ended the call, he continued to stare at his phone – but now with a furrowed brow.

'Everything OK, Hayden?' asked Monroe.

'I'm not sure. We have just received reports of an explosion centred on London. That's London, Ohio, by the way.'

'Any casualties?'

'Not really. That's the strange thing. A few people with minor injuries from some flying shrapnel.'

'Obviously I'm sorry for those people, Hayden, but am I missing something?'

'Well, it seems that the explosion came from the air. Eyewitness reports are that the object looked like a small glider. Travelling at incredible speeds and with no engine noise.'

President Monroe shuffled uncomfortably in her seat. 'Are you thinking that Baqri's behind it?'

'Maybe. London is a very small town of around 11,000 people. No strategic significance, so why would he waste detonating one of his HGVs there?'

'So, no fatalities then? No EMP?' asked Monroe.

'No fatalities. No EMP. No nuclear explosion.'

'I agree that doesn't make sense. Maybe we're just getting too paranoid about him? Best make sure that CDC still test for radioactive material; in case it was a dirty bomb,' said Monroe.

'I will, Madam President. But I'm struggling to join the dots if that turns out to be the case. It just doesn't make any sense. If this was a dirty bomb, he could have picked on a much larger city for his attack. This restraint doesn't seem to fit his personality,' said Marshall.

'Perhaps it was just to get our attention. Or perhaps it's nothing to do with Baqri.'

Marshall said, 'One thing that I have learnt from Tom Rivers and the attack on the UK, is that Baqri always has a reason for what he does. If this is him, we need to find him and his remaining missiles before whatever plan he has comes to fruition.'

The silence in the room was broken by the ringing of Hayden Marshall's phone once again, which he promptly answered.

'Thanks, Tom. That's good news,' said Marshall as he ended the short call.

'Did I hear the words *good news*, Hayden?' Monroe said. 'We could do with some of that right now.'

'Yes, indeed, Madam President. As per your previous instructions, Tom Rivers was tasked with trying to locate Baqri. And he has, over the weekend, made some progress. He told me that he is getting near to discovering the area that he may be hiding but is waiting for a few enquiries to come back. From that, and his personal knowledge of how Baqri works, he thinks he should be able to piece the puzzle together over the next day or so,' said the FBI's Deputy Director.

'That's incredible. I can't tell you what a relief that is, Hayden. Getting Tom on board really was a good move,' said Monroe.

'Can't you share what you have with us now?' asked McInnis.

'Nothing really to share yet. It's all in his head. Shouldn't be long though.'

***

Later that morning, and on the other side of town, Brigid Doyle was relaxing in her small hotel room when a ping alerted her to a message on her phone. Another message from The Collective. But this one included a time … and an address. She put her phone back down on the bed. That excited feeling had returned. And she smiled.

CHAPTER EIGHT

'Good morning,' said Tom as he approached the reception desk in his wheelchair.

'Good morning, Mr Rivers. How are you today?' replied the bubbly young female standing behind the counter, in her smart black uniform.

'Do you know what? I think we're making good progress. Thankyou. Is it Jenny again today?'

'Indeed, it is, Mr Rivers,' said the receptionist, pointing down the corridor towards an approaching petite figure.

Tom had now visited *The Sanctuary* sixteen times since his arrival in the United States. Conveniently located just twenty minutes' drive from his new apartment in Washington DC, the medical centre was an impressive sprawling modern single storey building of chrome and glass, which supposedly housed some of the best physiotherapy facilities anywhere in the country. Tom was just glad that he wasn't the one footing the bill.

'Hey, Tom,' said Jenny Chan, with a cheery smile. 'How are you today?'

Tom said, 'All the better for seeing you, Jenny … OK, OK, that sounds like a cheesy line, I know, but it's the truth. I can't thank you enough for all that you are doing.'

Ever since he first started his treatment at *The Sanctuary*, Miss Jenny Chan had been his rock. Tom was aware that his superior genetics played a part in the dramatic improvement of his physical health, but he was also sure that a great deal was down to the exceptional skills of his physiotherapist. Her unusual technique had its roots in the oriental – knowledge that had been passed down from her Chinese grandmother who practiced the technique of Tui Na in her hometown of Wu-Han. All Tom knew was that he was making a rapid recovery from the massive injuries that he had sustained during the London terrorist attack.

'Come in, Tom' said Jenny, opening the door to her treatment room.

Tom smiled as he walked in and looked at the black therapy table. It still remained a mystery to him as to how a tiny person like Jenny could exert such powerful massage techniques on someone twice her size.

'Now on your last visit, you did promise to tell me the story of what happened to you,' said Jenny, with her arms folded over her black tunic. 'All that you've revealed so far is that you work for the FBI.'

'You're not going to let this go, are you? OK, but it's really boring. Just a nasty accident at work. Before I worked for the Bureau.'

'Well, that wasn't what I had imagined. I had thought that since the federal government were paying the costs for your treatment, and with those scars all over your body, then you were some amazing, unstoppable, FBI agent or something. Like a Jack Bauer.'

'Ha! Nothing as interesting as that, Jenny. A nice quiet life for me. I just do some advisory work for them. Not very exciting, I'm afraid.'

'Oh, Tom – you've completely destroyed that image I had of you!' said Jenny laughing. 'We better get on with your treatment, Mr FBI adviser. Make yourself comfortable on the table, under the towels, and I will pop back in a little while.'

***

As Jenny Chan left the room, she could see the receptionist frantically beckoning her over.

'Jen, isn't that your car over there?' she said pointing at a small red Honda in the car park.

'What the hell? What's with all the fire trucks?'

'Looked like there was a little blaze going on at the back end. They've just put it out.'

Jenny threw her hands up in the air and shook her head. 'I'll be back in a minute,' she sighed.

Jenny Chan strode out through the front door towards her car, briefly pausing to hold the door open for a slim, blond-haired woman who was entering the centre.

***

'Hi there,' said the woman, holding up her FBI identification. 'I believe you have one of our agents here, receiving treatment? Tom Rivers? I need to have an urgent chat with him.'

'Yes, of course,' replied the receptionist. 'He's in room 14c – right down the very end of the corridor.'

'Sorry, but I don't want to catch him in … shall we say … a state of undress.'

'Oh, right,' said the receptionist with a grin. 'Got it. Don't worry, his therapist has just left the room, so he should be settled onto the massage table by now. Probably best if you give the door a knock first, just in case.'

'I will. Thank you,' said the woman walking down the corridor.

The FBI agent approached the door and appeared to knock on it. But the knock was silent. The woman looked back at the receptionist, smiled, and held her hand up as a thank you.

She quietly and gently turned the door handle and walked in.

Ahhhh … there you are, said Brigid Doyle to herself, looking across at Tom lying face down on the table. *How you survived first time round is a complete mystery. But as they say, if you don't succeed at first then try, try again.*

Brigid crept her way towards the table, making the most of her soft-soled sneakers – a detail completely missed by the receptionist. She scrutinised Tom for any movement and then reached to the back of her blue suit trousers and under her jacket for her weapon of choice – a FNX-45 tactical pistol with silencer. Slowly and quietly, she withdrew the gun. Brigid looked down at the pistol and put her thumb on the safety catch. She could feel a huge surge of adrenaline fuelled excitement. *This has been a long time coming. Even you can't survive a bullet in the head.*

But as she did so, she felt a cold, hard, metallic object press up against the back of her head. The distinct sound of a gun's hammer being pulled back then followed.

'Hello, Brigid,' said Tom, still looking down at the floor from his table. 'I believe you have already met my wife.'

CHAPTER NINE

MONDAY 29 JULY – 1 p.m.

For a man who was famous within the Bureau for his lack of visible emotion, Hayden Marshall looked decidedly upbeat – in an awkward, 'trying to keep it restrained' type of manner. He stretched his tall skinny frame towards the remote control and stood up from the long table of the White House Situation Room. It was now just 22 hours before the King was due to leave The White House and present his speech to Congress.

'Madam President, I am pleased to report that we have taken one of Baqri's closest associates into custody. Brigid Doyle,' said Marshall putting a photo up on one of the monitors at the far end.

'That's good Hayden, but I'm slightly confused. The last I heard from you was that Tom Rivers was close to pinning down Baqri. Is this still the case?' asked Monroe.

'Well, Madam President, capturing Ms Dole was the method by which Tom believed he would get this information. We can now interrogate her and hopefully get some detail on that objective,' replied Marshall, looking slightly sheepish.

'That's not quite what you sold to me, was it? Did you know about this Rachael?'

Homeland Secretary Goldberg shook her head.

Marshall said, 'I apologise, Madam President, but Tom was convinced, after his experience in Britain, that there would be elements within our government and security services that would be working against us. Members of the group called

The Collective. So, we conducted a sting operation to ensnare Brigid Doyle by letting it be known that Tom would be alone and vulnerable at a physio appointment.'

'I understand your reasons, Mr Marshall, but you're skating on thin ice by not telling me.'

Monroe stood up and placed her hands on top of the table, leaning down towards her advisers. 'Nevertheless, I think this has proved Tom's point with regard to The Collective. It is clear that we also have a powerful group working against us and we have absolutely no idea who they are.'

The silence in the room was broken by a short buzz. This time from the phone of James McInnis. He opened the app and replaced his phone back on to the table.

'Apologies, Madam President. That was just a news alert telling me something that I already knew. I've put it on silent. Apologies again,' said McInnis.

'Excuse me, Madam President,' said the assistant chief of staff, entering the room. 'I thought you might want to take this. Baqri's on the line for you.'

Jane Monroe sat and stared at the phone in front of her, trying to predict what Baqri would say and then what her response would be. Perhaps, the confusing situation that they were facing would become a little clearer. She pressed the speaker button.

'This is President Monroe.'

'Madam President. Thank you so much for taking my call. And could I just say *Good Morning* to some of the more interesting members of your National Security team? Now let me see. I guess the Chairman of the Joint Chiefs, Admiral Womack, is going to be present. How are you, you silver fox?'

Admiral Womack responded with just a frown.

'And then there would be that old fossil – Secretary of State Walter Houston, of course. Lovely to see your granddaughter graduate, by the way, Walt. You looked so proud at the ceremony.'

'How the hell …' said Walt Houston under his breath.

'You know what, Walt? If it all goes horribly wrong in politics for you, I reckon you could double for Morgan Freeman – the similarity is just uncanny. Go on Walt, give me your best line from The Shawshank Redemption. I just love that film. *I remember thinking it would take a man six hundred years to tunnel through the wall with it. Andy did it in less than twenty.*'

Secretary of State Houston just stared blankly at the President. *Difficult to know what to say when a complete mad man is trying to engage you in conversation*, he thought.

'Then, there's that little firecracker, CIA Director Theresa Muller. And next we must have Vice President Jed Stone. Now you, Jed, just remind me of Major Chip Hazard out of *Small Soldiers*. Rugged and serious. I reckon if they could bottle and sell the scent of Jed Stone they would call it "Alpha Male" or maybe just "Alpha." If you make millions from that idea; I want a cut. Just saying.'

Vice President Stone, who had a habit of talking to himself, just muttered 'completely nuts' under his breath.

'Oh, OK. Maybe another time, Jed. And finally, there must be your loyal Chief of Staff James McInnis. Don't take any notice of those idiots, Jim, who keep suggesting that you're so young you haven't started shaving yet. They're just jealous,' said Baqri, laughing at his own joke.

The looks around the table were of bewilderment. How Baqri was in possession of such detailed information was very unsettling.

'Have I missed anyone? Oh yes, Secretary for Homeland Security Rachael Goldberg,' said Baqri. 'I believe that you were responsible for the arrest and subsequent execution of my brother, when you were the CIA section chief in Afghanistan. I hope to pay you back for that, one day.'

President Monroe said, 'What do you want, Mr Baqri.'

'Can I call you Calamity or Calam for short?'

'No, you may certainly not … Calamity?'

'You know. Calamity Jane. *Oh! The deadwood stage is a-rollin on over the plains,'* sang Baqri. 'You're a Texan cowgirl, aren't you?'

President Monroe looked around the Situation Room at the baffled faces, who were all wondering how their boss, who had been an oil magnet for much of her life, was in any way similar to a cowgirl.

'You can call me Mo. Or how about you call me Mojo?' said Baqri with a chuckle.

'What do you want, Baqri?' Monroe repeated curtly.

'You see that's the trouble with the world today. No one has time for a bit of small talk. No chit-chat. No little chinwag, as the Brits would call it. It's all business. I try to be nice and it just gets thrown back into my face. Well, I'm not going to be deterred from being the lovely, caring sort of person that I am. I just wanted to say that I hope the nasty cold that you caught in London is getting better. Very rude, I felt, for the French President to pass that on to you.'

President Monroe again looked around the table before just staring at her chief of staff, who simply shook his head in reply.

'So, then Calam. I just thought I would give you a quick call. Two reasons really. Firstly, just wanted to see what you thought of my calling card?'

'Your calling card?'

'Oh, you know. The calling card that I liberated from the Russians. I was asking myself, what would be the best way to introduce myself to the American people. Then I thought, *it would be nice to send them a gift.* I was, after all, brought up to show good manners, Madam President. Anyway, then I thought *where the best place would be to send my present.* And, in a lightbulb moment, I thought, *let's carry on where we left off and send it to London.* That's London, Ohio, of course. Did you see what I did there? Genius, eh?'

'You're a deranged lunatic, Mr Baqri.'

'Well, that's not very nice, Calam. And I thought we were getting on so well. Anyway, back to me. I thought I would sprinkle some love over that little town. A special type of love from me to your people. A gift that will keep giving.'

'What was in that missile, Baqri?'

'You'll find out shortly. Those lab results from CDC will be with you very soon. Then I'm sure you will take me seriously.'

'I'll ask you again, Baqri. What was in that missile?'

'Something to get your attention, Madam President. I'm pretty sure if I just made my request to you nicely, you would have ignored it.'

'What request?'

'Oh, I'll get on to that in a minute. There's still a second thing. Something that I have to insist you do.'

'Go on.'

'Stand down your Black Ops team that you're sending to try and kill me.'

'I don't know what you mean, Mr Baqri.'

'Oh, come on now, Calam. Your memory isn't that bad, is it? Or perhaps it is? Perhaps it's your age. Do you remember when you told the Silver Fox to send a team to Russia to kill me?

Two reasons why this is a bad idea. Firstly, the Russians may not be so keen on having your troops on their soil. Especially as they are trying so hard to find me themselves. And secondly, because if you do send them, then I will be forced to launch the second Avangard HGV, towards an American city. A much larger one than little old London in Ohio.'

'I've told you; I don't know anything about sending a Black Ops team.'

'Now you're not lying to me are you, Calam?'

'We are entitled to defend ourselves, Baqri. If you attack us then we will always retaliate. And, Mr Baqri, you will refer to me as Madam President.'

'As you wish, Madam President. Well now. I do have a deal for you. If you agree to three conditions, then I can assure you that no more weapons will be launched at America. It was originally just going be two conditions, but as you've engaged the services of Britain's favourite bloodhound, Tom Rivers, then I've had to add a further one.'

'Go on.'

'Part A of the deal is that you immediately release my impetuous young apprentice, Brigid Doyle, whom I gather has been arrested and is on her way to FBI headquarters for interrogation. I'll give you just fifteen minutes to do that. If she doesn't call to tell me that she's free within that time or if you try to interrogate her, then I will send the next missile.'

'And your second condition?'

'I want you to guarantee my safety. That means no special ops and no sending assassins after me – especially that psycho, Luna Rivers. Dangling one of the hardest gangsters in London out of a third storey window by his tie! I mean, she should be called Looney not Luna. Can't believe that she's Tom's wife. What a family.'

'Continue, Baqri.'

'The condition for my safety, and that of my group, extends to the British by the way. I want protection from them too.'

'Well, I can understand why you would be on their hit list. You did try to blow up their capital.'

'Yes, but they might be even more upset shortly. So, I want you to tell them that *Adalah*, including myself, is not to be touched. Which brings me onto the last part of the deal.'

'You want more?'

'If you want to avoid the biggest loss of lives in American history, then, yes, I do, Madam President. It concerns the current state visit by the new King. We want you to help us do something.'

'What?'

'Kill him.'

CHAPTER TEN

'Do wut? Someone please tell me that I heard that wrong,' said Jane Monroe, in her usual Texan drawl, ending the call. 'Do you know, I could have sworn he said that he wanted us to help him kill King Edward? And then protect him after he's done it?'

'He's nuts,' repeated Vice President Stone – out loud this time. 'Completely nuts.'

'Yep. That boy's got a big ol' hole in his screen door.'

Stone said, 'I don't get it. If these weapons are armed and ready, as he seems to suggest, then why doesn't he just launch them at the United States? Why would he hold back? Just to kill Britain's King?'

'Well, he does hate the British,' said Walt Houston.

'Sure. But he hates us more. And what's to stop him launching the missiles anyway?' said Admiral Womack.

'Well, if you think about it, keeping this threat aimed at us is the best way that he can secure protection from the British. I mean, how long do you think he will last out there after he's assassinated their King?' said James McInnis.

Jane Monroe slumped back into her chair and stared at the ceiling. Everyone else in the room knew the President well enough to know that this was her thinking posture and silence was required. Several long minutes went by before she sat upright again.

'OK. So, this is where I'm at. This Baqri guy is making my nose twitch. And that's 'cause I can smell horseshit. My first question is why, in the name of all that's holy, would he not just kill the King himself with one of those HGV things? Secondly, why kill the King at all? As you correctly pointed out

Admiral, he hates us even more than the British. So, why not fly one of them straight into The White House?'

'Maybe because he knows that if he assassinates you, no country in the world would offer him protection,' postulated Secretary Houston.

'And you honestly think that we can provide him with protection from the British after he has murdered their King? Trust me, there will be nothing that I could say to Prime Minister Hatcher which would prevent him from issuing a kill order on Baqri.'

'I'm sure Baqri knows that,' added Homeland Secretary Rachael Goldberg.

'So then, what's the real reason why he wants the King dead? That's the key question here. Jim, I want you to get Tom Rivers in for me. And I mean *now*. I want him present at all future meetings regarding this threat – along with FBI Deputy Director Marshall. Tom understands this madman and it's clear that, without him, London and Britain would have faced disaster. It would be wise to make use of him. In the meantime, let's discuss the options. What do you think?' said Monroe, turning to her chief of staff.

McInnis said, 'Well, the first option is that we agree.'

'You're kidding, right?' snapped Jed Stone.

'Well, before we just dismiss this, let's just remember that the primary role of the US President and the government is to protect its people. We know Baqri has these weapons. We also know that they are capable of reaching anywhere within the United States.'

'But so far, his threats have been empty. Specifically, the HGV that detonated over Ohio. No one's died, so he's clearly got nothing. It's a bluff.'

'Not nothing, Jed. There's something you need to see,' said Goldberg, ending a phone call with her office and grabbing the television remote control.

Everyone in the room looked on as a tv reporter explained that the hospitals in Columbus, Ohio, were being overwhelmed by a flood of new patients.

'And these patients have one thing in common,' said the reporter in an inappropriately excited manner. 'They were all residents of the nearby small city of London. Reports from the hospitals say that these patients are all exhibiting signs of poisoning. But, so far, tests have failed to identify the particular toxin involved.'

'Madam President, I need to show you something. You should be prepared. It's quite upsetting,' warned Goldberg, opening up her tablet. 'This video has been taken by an FBI agent inside one of the hospitals.'

It was clear from the outset that Rachael Goldberg had not exaggerated. Monroe and her team sat and watched aghast, as the footage travelled through hospital corridors crammed with patients on trolleys – some unconscious, and some vomiting or coughing up blood. Monroe held her hand to her mouth as the video continued into the children's wing and focussed on a young boy who had just flat lined. Clumps of hair were missing from his head and his pillows were soaked in fresh blood.

'Turn it off,' said the President, taking a deep breath. 'And they're all from that one small town in Ohio? London?'

'Well, not necessarily all from London but it appears that they were all in that town when the explosion occurred,' replied Goldberg.

'That does seem like some form of radioactive poisoning,' added Walter Houston.

'CDC used radiation detectors at the blast site – as the president had instructed. And the doctors at that hospital did the same because that was their first theory too. Everyone tested negative.'

President Monroe looked down at her desk and said a single word. 'Polonium.'

'Madam President?' asked Goldberg.

'I pray to God that I'm wrong, Rachael. I really do. But get them to test for Polonium.'

'Did you say Plutonium?' asked Secretary Houston.

'No, Walt. Polonium. I'm not an expert on this stuff but I do know that the Russians assassinated one of their former agents with it. He had defected to Britain and they dropped a tiny quantity of it into his tea. His name was Alexander Litvinenko and all I can tell you was that he suffered similar symptoms. The British doctors didn't pick up on it at first either. It's difficult to detect. They will need a specialist lab to test for it.'

'So, where do we go from here?' asked Secretary of State Walter Houston.

'Firstly, we need to know exactly what we're dealing with, Walt. But let's be clear, everyone,' said Monroe staring intensely down the table, 'whatever comes back, America has a long-standing policy of not negotiating with terrorists. And surprise, surprise I have no intention of helping Baqri kill the Monarch of our closest ally. It's just not happening. Let's find out what this Brigid Doyle can tell us and then we're going to deal with this threat head-on.'

Everyone around the table nodded their acknowledgement as the president, once more, stood up, straightened her back and rebuttoned her suit jacket.

'Admiral, ready your team. We're going to take out that lunatic.'

CHAPTER ELEVEN

So, there he was, in the rear of a black FBI SUV, on his way to the White House with FBI Deputy Director Hayden Marshall. Tom's brief: to provide his insight on what will certainly be the biggest threat to America in its modern history. He knew Baqri. And he knew what he was capable of. A man with an egocentric personality and no conscience, who had never showed any sign of remorse for his previous actions. A psychopath, in the true sense of the word.

The news that he was going to be advising Jane Monroe personally on the crisis was, truth be known, not entirely welcomed by Tom. He had put up with MI5 Director MacGregor's rantings during the London attack but dealing with the President of the United States was going to be a whole new ballgame. He would much have preferred to be working in the field, pursuing Baqri. But he was, for a little while longer, wheelchair bound. It would be some time yet before he would be able to hit the gym and start building back up to his usual muscular sixteen stone frame. It made sense, therefore, that in the meantime, he used his brain rather than his brawn to deal with the new threat. And instead, it would be his wife, Luna, that would be doing the pursuing.

Since the attack on Britain's capital, he had tried hard to come to terms with the fact that his wife was a *Sleeper* – just like him. Both of them had to try and accept each other's new lives, as strange as they seemed – they just had no choice. At home, everything seemed just like it always did. The previous evening, they were in their new apartment in DC, sat on the couch, and watching a horror movie together after Tom had just cooked one of Luna's favourite meals – chicken linguine. They both loved horror movies, which they had discovered on their first date together. Luna had enjoyed a crisp, cold glass of Sauvignon Blanc with her meal and for Tom it was a bottle of Peroni. This was their Saturday night routine and nothing seemed to have changed. And everything felt normal. She had even teased him about some new flecks of grey hairs that she believed she had spotted to the sides of his otherwise short but thick dark hair. Just a normal Saturday night.

Except that earlier in the day, someone had tried to assassinate him. A terrorist whom his wife had almost beaten to a pulp during their previous encounter and then this time had been taken into custody for interrogation, after a sting operation that they had jointly set up. This was to be the new 'norm' for their lives. Their domestic lives, which were just as they always had been, and their professional lives which was now something entirely different.

Tom knew that Luna was able to take care of herself. He was well aware of her capabilities. But it didn't stop him worrying – even though he tried hard not to. His wife would be out there, pursuing one of the most dangerous terrorists in the world.

'What was it like?' blurted out Marshall, interrupting Tom's thoughts.

'Sorry?'

'My apologies, Tom. That just came out of nowhere, didn't it?' said Marshall with a sheepish grin. 'It's just that I've been wondering about this for a while and been trying to find the right moment to ask you.'

'No problem. What's on your mind?'

'You were an architect, right?'

'I was, yes.'

'Just living a normal family life. And then one day, you went to a meeting with some clients. But these clients turned out to be MI5. They then tranquilized you, and the next thing you knew, was when they woke you up and told you that you were actually some sort of super spy? And that you'd been in a Sleeper state for the last couple of decades. Is that about right?'

'Sounds mad, doesn't it?'

'Highly trained with exceptional abilities and a genius level IQ, our report says.'

'Yeah, apparently so.'

'Must have been absolutely mind-blowing for you.'

'Yup. I think that's a fair assessment. I need to correct you on one thing though. I'm not a spy. Nor am I an assassin. Or anything like that. I'm technically classed by MI5 as a Counter-Terrorist Asset. I got a peep at my file. At the top it says *to be deployed in the event of a major national terrorist threat.*'

'Sort of like a *break glass in case of emergency.*'

'Something like that.'

'But how does it feel. Do you feel ... well ... like you. Or do feel like a completely new person?'

'Do you know what, Hayden? I'm not sure I've really figured that out myself yet. Sometimes it feels like an out-of-body experience. It's so difficult to explain.'

Tom's attention was snapped back to the present, as he realised that they had arrived at the White House. Hayden Marshall showed his credentials to the guards at the entrance.

'Good morning, Mr Marshall,' said the guard. He looked through the open window into the rear of the car. 'And good morning to you, Mr Rivers.'

The guard nodded, and Tom definitely got the feeling that his recent exploits in London had become famous "across the pond." The SUV moved forward as the barriers raised. They were on their way to see the president.

CHAPTER TWELVE

Tom had little time for introductions and pleasantries with Jane Monroe before the phone rang in the Situation Room. Everyone knew who would be on the other end. Twenty minutes had gone by since Baqri demanded the release of Brigid Doyle. Chief of Staff McInnis answered the call and immediately started scribbling on a piece of paper in front of him.

McInnis said, 'It's Baqri, Madam President. He wants to speak to you.'

Monroe, after a little hesitation, nodded and McInnis pressed the speakerphone button.

'Mr Baqri. This is President Monroe.'

'Madam President. I'm disappointed that you haven't taken me seriously.'

'I *am t*aking you seriously, Mr Baqri, and I can assure you that your associate has been processed and will be released imminently.'

'Really?' said Baqri menacingly. 'I was under the impression that you decided to continue taking her to FBI headquarters for interrogation and that you still intend to assemble a black ops team to try and find me.'

'I'm not sure where …'

'Oh, spare me your deceitful rhetoric, Madam President. You Americans. Your false, insincere words just ooze so naturally from your mouths, don't they? You had the opportunity to prevent the deaths of civilians. American civilians. But you decided not to. Watch now the consequences of your actions.

I have given your chief of staff an IP address. Use this now, Mr McInnis.'

Jane Monroe nodded again and shortly the picture on the main monitor in the Situation Room changed from the image of the Presidential Seal.

'What the hell am I looking at?' said President Monroe.

'What you are looking at, Madam President, is the live image from the second Avangard HGV that I launched a little while ago. I did that as soon as I became aware of your treachery. It was clear that I needed to demonstrate my resolve.'

Monroe stood up and walked past the rest of her National Security Team to the end of the table, nearest the monitor – her blue eyes transfixed to the image on the screen.

'Do you not want to know where it's heading?' Baqri asked.

'Where?'

'Surprise!'

'What?'

'Surprise!'

'Just tell me, Baqri,' said Monroe curtly.

'I just did. That's the city of Surprise in Arizona. I've been *so* looking forward to you asking me that, I can't tell you.'

No one in the room muttered a sound as they watched the Avangard racing towards its target – covering the last two hundred miles in just over thirty seconds. A boom followed by a blank screen indicated that the device had detonated over its target.

'What the hell have you just done?' said Monroe.

'That's something called retribution, Madam President. I know you are waiting for the CDC lab report but let me save you some time. The HGVs are all loaded with Polonium 210 – which I believe you had already guessed. I'm sure you will be briefed shortly about how devastating that material is.'

Monroe slammed her hand down on the table. With wide eyes and gritted teeth, she rose to her feet.

'Temper, temper,' said Baqri calmly. 'You need to realise, Madam President, that so far, I've been remarkably restrained.'

'You're kidding me, right?' replied Monroe, almost frothing at the mouth.

'For the calling card that I sent to Ohio, I had deliberately chosen a small city of only around eleven thousand people and used just a tiny amount of the Polonium that I have in my possession. The state capital of Columbus is only twenty-five miles away, to assist. You're welcome.'

'You're welcome? Did you just say, *you're welcome?'*

'Yes, I did. You should have thanked me for the gracious mercy that I had shown you and then simply did what I had asked.'

'And so, your next play was to potentially kill well over a hundred thousand people with another strike?'

'You caused this, Madam President. You alone are responsible for all those civilian deaths that will result. If you had taken notice of my original warning, then you could have avoided any further loss of life. I gave you a chance, Madam President.'

'You're insane!'

'Well, you might be right but, as Aristotle said, *no great mind has ever existed without a touch of madness.* Or to quote Einstein, *the only difference between genius and insanity is that genius has its limits.* So, I'm sort of hoping for the insanity option.'

'You're going to murder innocent civilians with a deadly radioactive material? Just to prove a point?'

'Madam President, you are to release Brigid Doyle immediately. If you fail to comply again with *any* of my demands, then the next target will be much larger – as will be the amount of polonium used. It might be New York. Or perhaps Los Angeles or to really cripple the American machine, then Washington DC could be a good choice. The result will be so utterly devastating, that it will scar your country forever.'

'It seems that I don't have much choice,' replied President Monroe, slowly lowering herself back into her chair.

'Just to be clear, Brigid should not be followed or tracked in any way. You know the consequences if she is. Release her now, Madam President.'

Monroe looked across at Hayden Marshall and nodded.

'The FBI's Assistant Director has been instructed to do that immediately, Baqri.'

'Good. And now on to the main event. The King. His Majesty is due to travel from the White House to Congress tomorrow morning. You are to provide me with a copy of his motorcade route and escort details. You have until 6 p.m. to do this. That should give CDC enough time to confirm the presence of polonium. Then I want you to supply us with a piece of military hardware. The armour piercing kind. More detail on that later.'

'You want us to assist you in the assassination of the British King? Do you know how mad that sounds?'

'Insane. Mad. I shall rise above your insults, Madam President. Genius is the word that you are looking for.'

'Genius? You've murdered thousands of innocent people just to make me help you kill the King!'

'I am giving you a chance to save your people. It's just one person's life for that of millions. Surely not a difficult decision. If you comply, then I see no reason for more civilian casualties. But you know, Madam President, what will happen if you don't. And one more thing.'

'What?'

'The King should suspect nothing. So, you need to keep a lid on the Ohio and Arizona attacks with the media. And no disappearing to that bunker of yours. Everything must appear completely normal. If the King doesn't die … then millions of Americans will. There's enough polonium on that last HGV to completely wipe out the entire population of any of your cities.'

Monroe looked around the table. Her face now grave and solemn. The same facial expression was mirrored by the rest of her advisers.

'I understand,' said President Monroe.

'I want to hear your agreement to my terms, Madam President.'

'What?'

'I want to hear you confirm that America will help us kill King Edward and that you will supply the weapon system that we need to do it.'

'If the polonium is confirmed, then I agree to your demands,' mumbled Monroe.

'No. I want to hear you clearly say the words. Just as I said them.'

'Don't be ridiculous!' snapped Monroe.

'Millions of American lives are at stake, Madam President. You don't want to give me an excuse to launch that attack, do you?'

President Monroe looked across at Jed Stone and then Tom Rivers, who both slowly nodded.

'Very well, Baqri. I agree to America helping you kill the British monarch, King Edward, and we will also supply you with the weapons system that will allow you to do it.'

CHAPTER THIRTEEN

'I see … I see. What sort of quantities are we talking, do you think? Have a guess. Right. And how much is needed for it to be fatal? Really? That's incredible. I'll advise the president,' said Goldberg, scribbling away frantically on the pad in front of her, before ending the call.

After what felt like a very long period of silence to everyone else, she looked up at the President with a grim face.

'That was CDC. They've done their first set of tests on those civilians from London, Ohio who have been hospitalised. And the results have confirmed the presence of Polonium 210.'

Monroe said, 'Dear God. I was so wishing that I was wrong. Are you able to explain to everyone what this means?'

'As I believe you know, Madam President, Polonium poisoning is incredibly serious. Actually, it doesn't really get much more serious. CDC have given me some facts and figures. I'm not a scientist but I've got them to give me some headline facts and figures,' continued Goldberg, picking up her pad.

Everyone in the room, without exception, felt the same terrible, sinking sense of disaster and braced themselves for what Secretary Goldberg was to say next.

'So, here we go,' continued Goldberg after taking a deep breath. 'Polonium is a highly unstable radioactive material. It's not toxic in itself but when it decays, it emits lethal amounts of something called *alpha particles.* These alpha particles carry incredibly high amounts of energy which results in the destruction of genetic material within the human body. As it travels around the body, it takes electrons from every molecule in its path. The alpha particle radiation damages a person's

DNA to the extent that cell suicide occurs. It is, by mass, probably the deadliest material on the planet.'

'Sorry Rachael. How deadly are we talking?' asked Tom.

'Well, it's about two hundred and fifty billion times more toxic than cyanide. In theory, one microgram of Polonium 210 is enough to kill a person. In the type of attacks that we have just seen, the CDC toxicologists believe that one gram could kill fifty million people and make another fifty million seriously ill.'

The silence in the room was deafening. It took just over a minute before anyone spoke.

'Dear God. But, in theory, one microgram could kill someone?' Monroe repeated back incredulously.

'That's correct, Madam President,' replied Goldberg.

'Sorry Rachael. I've no idea what a microgram is,' said Secretary Houston. 'Never got to grips with that metric nonsense.'

'It's one millionth of a gram, Walt. So, a single raisin weighs about a gram. Imagine, if it's possible, that raisin chopped into a million pieces. One of those pieces could potentially kill you.'

Walter Houston and several others in the room simultaneously slumped back into their seats.

'And how much do we think was on those Avangard devices? And how much do we think Baqri has left?' asked Tom.

'There's no way of telling, Tom. But the Russians, for example, are believed to generate about two hundred grams a year of it.'

'So, if Baqri got this from North Korea and they had dedicated significant resources to the creation of Polonium – then we may be talking about much more?' asked James McInnis.

'Potentially, yes.'

'And do we have an estimated casualty figure from the two attacks?' asked Vice President Stone.

'That's a difficult one, Jed,' replied Goldberg. 'Those who were outside and in the immediate vicinity of the detonations are unlikely to survive. Those that were indoors will have a better chance.'

'Why's that?' asked Houston.

'It's because the alpha particles, which are emitted, pose little danger outside of the body. They can only travel an inch or so in the open air and can't penetrate skin. So, the polonium has to be ingested – by swallowing or breathing it in. Some people may have avoided that. But I still think we could be talking about potentially tens of thousands of deaths. And if a major city is hit next, then probably hundreds of thousands – if not millions.'

'What's the diagnosis for those that are poisoned by it?' asked President Monroe.

Goldberg said, 'Initially, the symptoms are as we witnessed from the Ohio attack. Extreme nausea, hair loss, vomiting and diarrhoea. In high doses there could be convulsions and potentially comas within minutes of poisoning. The alpha particles are likely to go on and damage bone marrow, and also the cardiovascular, gastrointestinal, and central nervous systems. Some may survive but most will die.'

'And what does that depend on?' asked Vice President Stone.

'That really depends on how much polonium they ingested, Jed. Some might die in days or weeks and others may take much longer. For those that do initially survive, then they will carry a very high risk of developing cancer – which ultimately is likely to kill them in the end anyway.'

The room fell silent once again. Each person around the table trying to process the information that they had just been given and its implications. President Monroe looked up and again briefly glanced at everyone in turn.

'OK. So, this is what we're gonna do,' said Monroe, picking up her pen to use as a pointer. 'Jim – first job – I want you to make sure that CDC and the hospitals that are dealing with the casualties from both attacks get everything that they need. I then want you to talk to the Communications Office and prepare a press statement. This will hit the media very soon. We have to make sure that it's played down – so tell them that initial reports have been received of two unfortunate and tragic accidents. Keep away from specifics. And tell them that a full investigation is underway.'

'Do you think they'll swallow that?' asked Tom.

'We just need it to buy us a little time,' replied Monroe, who then turned towards the Secretary of State. 'Walt – I want to talk with the North Korean President. Are they responsible for supplying Baqri with polonium? If so, he needs to know that we consider that to be an act of war and that there will be consequences.'

'I will get straight on it, Madam President.'

'And Rachael – I need answers. Where is Baqri? What's his next target? And … this is something I really don't get … why the hell is he so obsessed with killing the King? We'll reconvene at 5 o'clock, at which point we will need to decide what the hell we're gonna do. Let's go people.'

As the National Security team filed out through the door, President Monroe said, 'Tom, please stay behind. I want to have a chat about this Baqri guy.'

Jane Monroe sauntered back down to the other end of the Situation Room table and sat down beside Tom's wheelchair – the unprecedented threat to her country still not encouraging any change of speed to her trademark walking style.

'I know that you're not happy with my decision,' said Monroe glancing down at Tom's fist, which was resting but clenched on the arm of his wheelchair.

Tom exhaled heavily and shook his head. 'We've just given up our best chance of getting to Baqri, Madam President.'

'I really didn't see how I had any choice. We've already lost hundreds of American lives and it looks like that will be followed by thousands more. And then if Baqri launches an even bigger attack on somewhere like New York ...'

'I wish that I could just get out of this wheelchair and set about hunting him down. But don't get me wrong. I do understand, Madam President. And you did make the right decision, by the way. At the moment you *do* need to dance to his tune.'

'But I'm the President of the United States! I shouldn't have to dance to anyone's tune!'

'I get it. But the problem we have is that he is one step ahead of us. The help that Baqri's getting from The Collective is just going to keep undermining every move that we make.'

'I know. And today's events have confirmed my worst fears, Tom. It is clear that The Collective have infiltrated my government. The information that Baqri knew was far too detailed and current to have come from anywhere else except from inside my administration.'

'I think you're absolutely correct, Madam President,' replied Tom. 'And the leak has really cost us. Interrogating Brigid Doyle was our best chance of finding out where Baqri and his missiles are. Or were. He will have moved them and himself by now.'

'I need someone that I can trust, Tom. I've obviously got people nearby, who are working against me. And I've no idea who they are.'

'You can trust *me*, Madam President. But if I was a member of The Collective then I would say that, wouldn't I?'

'I spoke to Sir Iain MacGregor at MI5 about you. He suggested that since you had pursued Baqri and his group all over London; been shot and blown up in the process, as well as being suffocated to death – literally – in your hospital bed by one of the terrorists, then, actually, I probably could trust you.'

'I think that's a fair argument.'

'Tom, I want you to work directly for me. I'm going to appoint you to be my Special Adviser on the basis of your knowledge of Baqri. This means you will have a direct line to me. I'll get Secret Service to give you an encrypted phone so that our discussions can remain just between us.'

'Madam President, may I suggest that you should assume any communications we have in the open with your National Security team will get straight back to Baqri.'

'That's good advice.'

'In fact,' said Tom with a wry smile, 'we could make this work to our advantage.'

CHAPTER FOURTEEN

Brigid Doyle strode out of FBI headquarters into the warm afternoon summer sunshine. She had only been in the building for ten minutes before the instruction came through for her release. She would never forget the look on the face of Luna Rivers. Or the tantrum that followed. Like a toddler who had been denied the opportunity to play with her new toy. Brigid was more than a little relieved that Luna wouldn't be allowed to interrogate her. It wouldn't have been pleasant; she was sure of that. And she couldn't help smiling at Luna as she walked past her. Nothing quite like adding a bit of fuel to the fire. Something had happened though in the meantime. The way that FBI agents were frantically moving around the building could only mean one thing. Baqri had hit America.

Brigid dialled his number on her sat phone.

'I'm out,' she said. 'Now what?'

'Now we make sure that the Americans haven't bugged you and aren't tracking you,' replied Baqri. 'I have explained the consequences to Calamity Jane if she does. But we need to be sure. Take the Metro subway from Federal Triangle on the silver line. Just in case they're using satellite. Stand right at the front of the platform, as if you're going to get on a train. My guys will meet you and give further instructions.'

As instructed, Brigid made her way down the escalator and walked on to the crowded platform. Spotting a gap, she made her way down to the end and stood near the edge. It wasn't long until even that area started filling up with passengers and she found a woman with blonde hair, dressed in a pink jacket and sparkly pink trilby hat, standing immediately to her left. Brigid became aware that other people were now all around her. She looked to her right at the heavily built man in a grey suit. Here was a guy who looked positively awkward wearing a suit. Brigid could feel her heart racing. Her obsession to kill Tom Rivers had backfired once again and she had gone against Baqri's specific orders not to go after him. Baqri wasn't the forgiving kind. She could hear the train coming down the tracks. She turned around but was blocked by an even larger man. Someone grabbed her right arm. She looked to her side. It was the woman in the pink trilby.

'Brigid, squat down on the floor,' the woman said. 'Hurry up.'

Baffled by the request, Brigid complied and dropped to the ground. The two suited men closed ranks, standing right up to the two women. The woman took off her hat and a blonde wig, which was underneath. She gave them to Brigid and then took off her jacket to reveal exactly the same clothes that Brigid was wearing.

'We knew what you were wearing when you were arrested,' explained the woman. 'Now hurry up and put everything on. Keep your face down and get on the train with me. Then get off at the next stop. I'll stay on and it should buy you enough time before they realise what's happened. You'll be picked up outside that station and taken to Baqri. Oh, and don't worry about any trackers or bugs. My large friend here, who was stood behind you, already scanned for those.'

Brigid stared at the woman. There was a remarkable similarity to herself in looks. Shoulder length red hair, blue eyes, and a similar facial bone structure. *Slightly shorter in height but would anyone really notice?* Brigid wondered. So long as her body double didn't look at a camera directly, she could see how the security services would be fooled.

And they were. Brigid's double had been on the subway train for almost forty-five minutes before the FBI realised something was wrong. By that time, Brigid had been delivered to Baqri's apartment and was stood in front of him.

'I thought at one point that you were going to have me killed,' Brigid said.

'Can't say it hadn't crossed my mind. If you disobey me again and put my plans in jeopardy, then … well, you know,' Baqri replied.

'I won't. I'm sorry. Really, I am. It will never happen again.'

'The thing is, Brigid, Tom knew you were my weakness. Give him his dues, he's a great judge of character. He knew how to reel you in – hook, line, and sinker. He knew that you wouldn't be able to help yourself and that you had to have another go at killing him. Reminds me of Aesop's fable about the scorpion and the frog. Do you know it?'

'Errrr … no.'

'Well, to paraphrase it, a scorpion wants to cross a river and asks a frog to carry him over on its back. The frog points out that the scorpion could sting him. The scorpion argues that, since he can't swim, if he did sting the frog, then they would both die. The frog sees the logic in that and agrees. Halfway across the river, the scorpion stings the frog and dooms them both to death. The dying frog asks the scorpion why he did it and the scorpion replies that he couldn't help himself. It was in his nature. You need to control your nature, Brigid, before it is the death of all of us.'

Baqri's phone buzzed and he looked down at the screen.

'Well, they're on their way back.'

'Who?'

'Idris and Zane.'

'Who the hell are Idris and Zane?'

'You met them at the station. They're my muscle.'

'What about my body double – whoever she is.'

'An out of work actress. Told her that an ex-boyfriend of yours was having you followed. Gave her a wad of cash and she didn't ask any questions.'

Brigid nodded. 'So, I assume that you sent the first HGV?'

'I did. And then another one. I'm sure that I now have their attention and co-operation.'

'Do you think that the president will now comply with your demands?'

'She doesn't really have a choice.'

'One thing I have to ask. Why did you risk so much to get me back? I couldn't have told them where you were or even where the missiles are. So, you could have just left me in FBI custody.'

'I didn't want to lose my investment. I spent a lot of time on your training since London and it has paid off. You have become one of the most competent people in our organisation with military weapons. We've got a King to kill. And you're going to be the one doing it.'

CHAPTER FIFTEEN

MONDAY 29 JULY – 5 p.m.

'Jim, can we have your update please?' asked President Monroe.

'Well, we've sent out a press statement. And the general reaction to the two *incidents,* as we've called them, is currently just confusion within the media. They've not really got enough evidence at the moment to come up with any proper hypothesis.'

'Good. And what about the casualties?'

'Getting the best treatment that can be offered, Madam President. But the number of fatalities has started to rise rapidly, as the alpha radiation works its way through the bodies of the victims. By this time tomorrow, CDC estimate that we will be looking at the number of deaths to be in excess of ten thousand. And that figure will keep rising.'

President Monroe sat back in her chair with her hands firmly clasped behind her head. She stared at a blank space in front as the room fell silent.

'Walt, have we spoken to the North Koreans?' Monroe continued.

'They're denying any responsibility, Madam President. A representative is on his way here to see you,' replied Houston.

'That will be interesting.'

'Should we put our military on readiness, Madam President?' asked Admiral Womack.

'The American people will expect a full and uncompromising response against any country that has aided the terrorists,' added Vice President Stone.

'But this will mean war against another nuclear power – not some minor middle eastern regime,' argued Houston.

'Agreed,' said Monroe. 'Start compiling strategies, Admiral, but go no further at this time.'

Admiral Womack simply nodded his acknowledgement.

'We have an hour to supply Baqri with the King's motorcade route to Congress or our nightmare will go to a whole new level. What do we do people? Tom, what do you think? Why does he want us to help him kill the King?'

'Well, he could have killed the King himself if he had wanted to. One of those HGVs straight into Buckingham Palace with a bomb or perhaps a big dose of polonium. But the point is, he wants our help. More importantly, he wants the world to see that we helped him.'

'But why?' asked Secretary of State Walt Houston.

'I believe the main purpose of this attack is to destroy the relationship that you have with your allies,' replied Tom, looking over at the president.

'I get that the Brits won't want to stay best of friends when this gets out,' said Womack.

Tom said, 'Not just the Brits, Admiral. Don't forget countries such as Canada and Australia. We will be aiding and abetting in the assassination of their Head of State as well. Plus, the King is head of the Commonwealth. That's another fifty-six countries who aren't going to be overly thrilled.'

'OK, I know we won't be popular. But we will be saving American lives by giving him up,' said McInnis.

'It's more than just not being popular, Jim,' said Rachael Goldberg. 'The reason why we prevent so many terrorist attacks on this country is because of our intelligence network. But it's only as effective as it is because information is shared between us and our partners.'

'What's the likely impact on our intelligence, Rachael?' asked President Monroe.

'We will lose Britain, of course. Even your close relationship with Prime Minister Hatcher can't stop that. So, immediately there's a big hole in our net. Then there's a very high probability that other countries will follow. We will lose all credibility and trust. There will be complete outrage across the globe at what we have done.'

'Surely, we can mitigate that by explaining to the British and the rest of the world that Baqri had murdered thousands of our civilians and would have killed maybe millions more if we hadn't complied with his demands. What country wouldn't have done the same?' asked McInnis.

'But Baqri, along with his Collective partners, will be using the media to spread a different message – one that I'm sure will show the US in the worst light,' said Tom.

'That we wanted the King dead, no doubt,' added Goldberg. 'Many countries will take his assassination particularly badly.'

Secretary Houston said, 'Particularly in Africa, of course, where many countries already regard him as a living saint.'

'I have heard murmurings from the Vatican, by the way, that the Pope is trying to find a way around the usual Catholic protocol to canonise the King – not that the Holy Father would be expecting him to die so soon,' added Monroe.

'Can he do that?' asked VP Stone. 'The King is the head of the Anglican church. He's not Catholic.'

'Technically he could, I think,' replied McInnis. 'Pretty sure it's never happened before but I don't think there's anything that specifically says he has to be a Catholic. There appears to be a huge amount of popular support for his canonisation in that community.'

'So, you can just imagine how this will go down. We will forever be known as the country that helped murder a future saint. America gets to alienate not only numerous countries around the world but one of its major religions too.'

Houston said, 'About twenty percent of our own population, in fact.'

'Plus, any Anglicans, of course. Let's not forget them,' said Monroe, raising her eyes towards the ceiling'

'We could take Russia's place as the world's pariah,' added Goldberg.

Womack said, 'You're right about Russia. They will revel in this, of course. And they will take advantage of the situation in Congo, if our African allies turn their backs on us.'

Tom said, 'Sorry. Congo? I know there's some unrest going on there but am I missing something?'

'A man called Colonel Joseph Banza is trying to un-stabilize the government there. We've been relying on the Congo's neighbouring countries to offer military support. That's what's been keeping Banza in check and preventing a coup,' said Monroe.

'And we've been giving those countries financial packages on ... shall we say ... very advantageous terms,' added Walt Houston.

'OK. But why is Congo so important?' asked Tom.

'Because they have the largest deposits of cobalt in the world – by a long way. And cobalt is needed to make batteries. Along with most countries, we're committed to battery power as a major part of our sustainable energy plans for the future.'

'Interesting,' said Tom. 'So, if those African countries decide that the current American backed regime doesn't deserve their support anymore?'

'Then we have a problem,' said Walt Houston.

Down the other end of the table, Chief of Staff James McInnis, was tapping his pen on the pad in front on him.

'What's up, Jim?' said President Monroe.

'Madam President, I get that we are in a no-win scenario. I really do.'

'But?'

'But what I've heard so far is pure conjecture. We don't know just how bad the fallout will be from the King's assassination. What we *do* know for certain, however, is that Baqri has another one of those Avangard HGVs and is prepared to use it. So, unless Admiral Womack is close to locating whereabout it is in Russia, or Deputy Director Marshall has identified the whereabouts of Baqri, then I can't see that we have any option but to comply with the demands.'

Marshall shook his head.

'We've got a radius where the last launcher is likely to be, after calculating the distance that it could have travelled from where Baqri seized them all. We're hoping that we may even be able to use satellite to track it down,' said Womack.

'Well, that's good news, isn't it?'

'Not entirely. Even if we do track it down, the Russians have made it clear that the Avangard is their property and they will be the ones to retrieve it. They stated that any black ops by the US into Russia will be regarded as an invasion and an act of war.'

'I assume you explained the urgency to them?'

'I did, Madam President. They said that it would be dealt with promptly and it was just a matter of time.'

Jane Monroe fidgeted around in her chair. Leaving the fate of America in Russian hands was not an appealing notion. The dilemma that she faced seemed an impossible one. The crisis could be ended if Russia acted swiftly.

'Time is a luxury we don't have, Admiral,' said Jane Monroe. 'And I assume from your body language that the FBI hasn't made much progress on identifying Baqri's location, Hayden?'

'I'm afraid not, Madam President. We lost our best chance of that when we were forced to release Brigid Doyle,' replied Deputy Director Marshall.

'I would be surprised if he wasn't already in the US,' said Tom. 'He's a bit of a voyeur. He loves to personally be there to see the results of his handywork. Not the sort that would be happy just watching it on an iPad.'

'Jim, America has a long-standing policy of not negotiating with terrorists for a reason,' said Monroe. 'Because we know that if we do, then we open Pandora's box. The message that we will be sending out is that if you threaten America then we will just buckle. Every terrorist organisation out there will think it's open season on the United States.'

McInnis said, 'I understand that, Madam President. But there is one cold, hard fact that simply can't be ignored. In less than an hour, unless we capitulate, another HGV will detonate over a much larger American city than the previous ones. It could be New York, Los Angeles, Chicago or maybe even Washington itself. Hundreds of thousands – maybe even millions – of Americans will die as a result. And, as you just heard, we are not in a position to stop it. Our top priority must surely be to save American lives. If the King has to die, then that is the price that must be paid.'

'I can't believe this is our only option,' said Monroe. 'Tom, what do you think?'

Tom paused for thought. 'I think that I would have to agree with your chief of staff. I don't see that you have any choice, Madam President.'

'Really?' said Monroe.

'Really. The King must die.'

CHAPTER SIXTEEN

Baqri looked out from his apartment window across the Potomac. The afternoon was nearly at an end and the sun's strength was starting to fade. His moment had come. All that America had done to him – his incarceration and torture; the death of his brother – all this he had sought retribution for, and at long last, justice had prevailed. Thousands of Americans had already paid the price for the sins of their leaders – and many more would follow.

He had put the President of the United States in an impossible, no-win position. Capitulate to someone that America regards as a terrorist, lose your closest ally along with many others, and open the gates of hell to every single America-hating group out there. The alternative was just to sit by and watch hundreds of thousands, if not millions, of fellow countrymen die horrible deaths. He was sure that he had left the president with just one move. It was like a game of chess. But instead of placing the King in check, the game would be won by his death.

All of the evidence that he had amassed of America's complicity in his assassination would be made public. He would make them look like the villain on the world stage.

The six o'clock deadline had arrived. Time to call the president.

'It's showtime, Madam President!' Baqri trumpeted down his sat phone, like a gameshow presenter.

For the next couple of minutes, Baqri stared at the ground and, unusually, just listened. Finally, he looked up at Brigid.

'Very good, Madam President. I will contact you again shortly with a list of buildings along the route that I want cleared. No one – I mean no one – is allowed in any of those buildings. Make sure the FBI or Secret Service clear them and then ensure that they are themselves removed. I will be watching.'

'I'm sure you will,' replied Monroe.

'I will also want to know where the television cameras will be based. I mean to ensure that the world gets the best view possible of this momentous occasion. They say that revenge is best served cold, Madam President. The temperature for America's dish will be positively sub-zero,' Baqri laughed.

'So, I assume that the president is playing ball,' said Brigid, as Baqri ended the call.

'As expected, she is. Not that I don't trust Calamity Jane – well I don't, of course – but I will still ask The Collective to confirm everything.'

'Aren't you worried that the feds will track us from your phone signal?'

'Not at all,' explained Baqri, waving around his phone. 'The very latest in scrambled sat phone technology – courtesy of Benny Erickson. You remember him, don't you?'

'Yeah. Wasn't he the arms dealer who got you the EMP detonators for the UK attack?'

'Indeed, he was. Without a doubt, my most favourite of criminals. If it's out there, Benny can get it.'

'I assume that he also provided you with your weapon of choice?'

'The *Spike SR*? Oh no. That's being supplied courtesy of the US government.'

'Sorry? The Americans are giving you the missile launcher that will blow up the King?'

'Yep!' exclaimed Baqri. 'Part of my demands to Calamity. So, to the rest of the world, the Americans are all but pulling the trigger. And that's the line that will be pushed to the media and other governments through The Collective's connections.'

'This really isn't going to make the US look good, is it?'

'Oh, and there's more. I also believe that the Russians are preparing to put a couple of US servicemen in front of the cameras to confess that *they* were the ones who took their Avangard HGV launchers and not us. All part of America's plans to assassinate the King, they'll say.'

'That's ridiculous.'

'Yes, it is, but if you throw enough mud, some of it will stick. They're going to be peddling a theory that the King was interfering in American business overseas and that's why they wanted him dead.'

'Where the hell did they get those servicemen?'

'Who knows. Probably already had them detained in some Siberian gulag for years.'

Brigid stared at Baqri's face. His new look was certainly a surprise when she first saw it. The crew haircut and facial tattoos provided him with a much more menacing look. A physical image that matched his personality perfectly.

'What?' asked Baqri.

'I was just wondering if I died, whether you would add another tattooed tear to your face?'

'I'm surprised you haven't done something like that to remember that boyfriend of yours who was killed by Tom Rivers. What was his name?'

'Connor. His name was Connor. I can't believe you have already forgotten his name. He died for you.'

'Pretty sure he died for you, Brigid.'

Brigid turned around. She was not going to let Baqri get the satisfaction of seeing her cry. She swallowed and told herself to get a grip.

'So, what happens now?' asked Brigid.

'Now, I will select a suitable building for you to get set up. The President will be told to clear it and all others to both sides. The crowds will also not be allowed directly in front, so you shouldn't get spotted. I will also mention to her that if the King doesn't die, for some reason, then American civilians will. Idris and Zane will go with you and help you assemble the missile launcher on to its stand and ensure that the guidance system is functioning properly.'

'Then I guess, I just wait.'

'This will be your moment, Brigid. You will take your place in history.'

CHAPTER SEVENTEEN

TUESDAY 30 JULY

The day had finally arrived. It was 10.55 a.m. and the King was in the lobby of the White House surrounded by royal protection officers. Secret Service Director John Barratt was surveying the scene across the North Lawn. Agents were positioned exactly in line with his directive and the King's motorcade was ready to depart.

'Thank you so much for your hospitality, Jane,' said King Edward, leaning forward to kiss the president on the cheek. 'I'm so lucky to have a friend as good as you.'

'As always, Edward, it's been an absolute pleasure,' replied President Monroe, smiling at the dark-haired man holding both her hands. A nice change, she always felt, to be able to have someone of her own height to speak to – rather than having to look down or feeling the need, out of politeness, to slouch in order to be at the same height.

'You look tired. Are you alright?'

'Yeah, I'm fine. Bad night's sleep,' replied the president.

'Something on your mind? I'm always there for you, if you just want a chat.'

President Monroe felt her stomach turn. The King was not just the reigning monarch of America's greatest ally but he was also a good personal friend – and had been for many years. He was generous and down to earth, and his sense of humour was legendary. One of the few people who could actually make the First Gentleman roar with laughter. It seemed as if every time they got together, the King and her husband would be sitting up drinking brandy together until the early hours, exchanging stories. Yet underneath his seemingly normal exterior was an exceptional human being. His tireless work for charities and deprived communities around the world was utterly inspiring, and sometimes she had to remind herself that *she* was friends with this man who was adored by so many. But now she would have to betray him.

'Thanks Edward. I appreciate that. Sorry to hear that the Queen won't be joining you today, by the way.'

'Yes, I'm afraid she's feeling a little queasy this morning.'

'I really hope that wasn't down to the food at last night's state dinner.'

'Oh, I'm sure it wasn't. The food last night was exceptional, Jane. And all the staff did a fantastic job. I tried thanking as many of them last night as I could but would you be so kind as to pass on my gratitude to them all?'

'Of course, Edward. With regards to today, I will be following on a little later to the Capitol Building for your address to Congress. Gives you a little more time to wave to the crowds. Not too much though or you'll be making my secret service chief very nervous,' said Monroe with a forced smile. 'At the end of the day, the crowds are there to see you – not me. Think they probably don't need to see any more of me.'

'Oh, I'm sure that's not true. You're a great president, Jane … And thank you, Mr McInnis,' said King Edward, turning to his side. 'As always, your professionalism is peerless.' He extended his hand to the chief of staff. 'And your assistance with my speech to Congress has been invaluable.'

'You're very welcome, Your Majesty,' replied James McInnis, with a courtesy nod.

'How do I look?' Kind Edward asked, turning back towards the president and straightening his mauve tie.

Monroe didn't need to look. 'Immaculate, of course. You always are – well when you're not dressed like a Bedouin on your African trips.'

'Ha! Well, in my defence, a pin-stripe suit like this might look a bit odd out in the desert, don't you think? I have to admit that big public events always make me slightly nervous, Jane. Always think there's going to be a disaster and I'll make a spectacle of myself. Perhaps today will go better than I have feared.'

With that, the King turned towards the White House doors, glanced over at Secret Service Director Barratt and nodded.

'*Sceptre* is exiting. I repeat, *Sceptre* is exiting. Everyone on your toes,' said Barratt into his covert microphone.

With that, King Edward walked out of the White House and into the morning sun. Cheers erupted from the large crowd standing outside the perimeter fence and the King stood and waved warmly in reply. A little too long for his security personnel, who gently ushered him into the rear of his black armoured Rolls-Royce. A royal protection officer dressed in a black suit with red tie joined him in the rear, as two others climbed into the front. The motorcade pulled away but stopped again a short distance down the drive.

'What's going on?' asked James McInnis, noting that the King's vehicle had still not moved after several minutes.

'Apparently, it's due to the protection officer being in the rear. When it became clear that the Queen wasn't able to go, then I suggested that it would be a good idea if an officer sat by the King,' said Barratt, with his finger pressing against his earpiece. 'It seems the King is not in agreement.'

'Because the King doesn't think that anyone else should be that close to him?'

'No, he just thought it might make it more difficult to see the crowds and for them to see him. That particular protection officer is now going to join one of the escort vehicles instead.'

'Well, as far as the King is concerned, it's all about connecting with the people. Most of us have to put on a front, half the time. Not him,' added President Monroe.

With the reshuffling complete, the motorcade once again moved off. Almost immediately the blacked-out rear window of the royal limousine lowered slightly and the King started waving enthusiastically at the crowds. Once it was level with the outer perimeter, a small group of teenage girls tried pushing past the police lines but, finding themselves held back, decided to exclaim their adoration instead.

President Monroe looked at James McInnis. 'What have I done?' she asked.

'The only thing you could do, Madam President.'

CHAPTER EIGHTEEN

It seemed slightly strange. Brigid had to remind herself that it was a Tuesday. A normal working day. But there she was on the third floor of an office block, located just down from the Capitol Building. An office which would normally be a hive of activity with workers busily typing away on their keyboards, running paperwork from one side to another or perhaps sneaking off to grab a cup of coffee. Instead, the computers were off and empty chairs were sat under tidy desks. Well, mostly tidy. There were always some exceptions. But today, thanks to Baqri's arrangement with the president, a whole block of offices was empty. Cleared by federal officers and guaranteed to stay like that for the duration. Just Baqri's henchmen, Idris and Zane, to keep her company.

Brigid looked through her binoculars for signs of movement from the top of Pennsylvania Avenue. It was a beautiful clear, sunny day. In fact, the conditions for her couldn't have been any better. She looked at her watch. It was 10.55 a.m. No movement yet.

She looked down at the crowds that had amassed a little further up from her on both sides of the street. An incredible amount of people, many of whom were armed with a Union Jack flag in one hand and a Stars and Stripes in the other. It was clear that the nearby street sellers were having a very lucrative day. Many people had been waiting hours just to get a fleeting view of King Edward waving at them. On the other side of the barriers, an evenly spaced police line stood facing the crowd, and then behind them were men and women in dark suits. What none of them could ever have imagined was what was about to happen instead. They were about to witness something that they would never forget and something that they would retell to others for the rest of their lives. They were there, on that fateful day.

Brigid turned her head in the other direction, towards the Capitol Building. There, located halfway up, was the massive media podium crammed with journalists and reporters from around the world, still jostling to improve their positions. All those tv cameras that would soon be transmitting the most shocking pictures of a high-profile assassination since JFK. Millions of people would be tuned in, not just on their televisions, but listening to their radios or streaming live on tablets. Brigid could hardly comprehend the repercussions of that one action which she would perform – pressing a trigger. And just past the media platform, were even more crowds, crammed in on both sides.

Any minute now she was bound to get a call from Baqri confirming that the King's motorcade was leaving the White House for his speech to Congress. Her phone rang. Bang on time.

'It's me. He's in the lobby area of the White House, according to our friends. Just checking that you're all set up and ready for this?'

'Yes, as I was two hours ago – when you first called and asked me the same thing. Strangely enough, nothing's changed,' bristled Brigid.

'OK, OK. Calm down. You'll end up with lots of stress lines all over your face if you carry on.'

'You're the one that gives me the stress.'

'It's just because today is so important. The Collective have an expectation for the King to die today. I don't intend to disappoint them.'

'I *do* get that.'

'Any sign of American interference?'

'No. None.'

'I'm surprised and disappointed in equal measures. Just so unlike them to take it lying down. One little punch to their nose and they've held their hands up.'

'I imagine that the idea of having millions of civilians die in a scaled-up version of your previous attacks probably had something to do with it. Guess you're gonna have to hold off launching your other HGV then.'

'Patience is the best remedy for every trouble. Plautus said that, you know.'

'Who?'

'A famous Roman writer … oh, never mind,' replied Baqri with a sigh. 'Looks like the King might be about to step outside. Do you know the last time I saw him on tv was his Coronation. Funny to think that we will be witnessing the end of his very short reign this morning.'

'Yes, hysterical,' replied Brigid sarcastically.

'Just to recap, once you have fired the missile then make your way down the rear fire exit, where a car will be waiting. The president has guaranteed a clear road out of the city for you.'

Brigid had mixed feelings about the assassination of the King. On the one hand, she came from a Republican family who had been fighting the British establishment in Northern Ireland for two generations. The Royal Family was certainly not something that her father would have encouraged anyone to preserve. In fact, they epitomised everything that her own family hated about being under British rule.

On the other hand, she wasn't her father. Things had moved on in her country with a peace between Loyalists and Republicans. The Good Friday Agreement had set up power sharing for the two sides and a new devolved parliament was established, so that the people of Northern Ireland could make their own decisions. So, it was difficult to see how the new King was relevant to her family's past. Apart from that, he actually seemed like a genuinely good man who was making a difference in the world.

The big sway for her, however, was Baqri's promise of revenge. Her nemesis, Tom Rivers, had calmly and coldly gunned down her fiancé, Connor, on the streets of London. Twice she had sought retribution. On the first occasion, she had literally suffocated him in his hospital bed – only to find out later that he had been resuscitated. On the second occasion, she had been lured into a trap with his terminator type wife, Luna. Brigid knew that, even though Tom seemed immortal, anyone could be killed under the right circumstances. With Baqri's help, she believed that her day would come. For that to happen, the King had to die.

CHAPTER NINETEEN

'He's walking out of the White House. Now he's waving at the crowds. Get ready Brigid, they're about to leave!' gushed Baqri excitedly. 'To be clear, he's in the third car. Not difficult to identify. A black Rolls-Royce Phantom with a Union Jack on one wing and a Stars and Stripes on the other. The Royal Standard Flag is on the front of the roof.'

'Again, you already told me that. But I have to say, they couldn't have made that any easier for me, could they?'

'Do you know that more than sixty-five percent of all Rolls-Royces ever made are believed to still be on the road? They've been building cars for 117 years and the large majority are still out there. That's a quality car, isn't it?'

'Great. Thanks for that. And now I'm about to blow one up,' Brigid said, ending the call.

Brigid looked again through her binoculars up Pennsylvania Avenue towards The White House. The Royal motorcade gently loomed into view, travelling at a suitably sedate speed in her direction. The Rolls-Royce certainly stood out – strikingly different to the SUVs in front and behind it, and with a certain presence about it. She could make out a hand waving through a partially opened blacked out window. *Time to get ready.*

Brigid placed her binoculars down on the desk behind her, looked at Zane and nodded. With the opening of the window came a wave of noise from the crowds on either side – cheers had started from the left and the sounds of excited anticipation from the right. The motorcade was still almost a quarter of a mile away – crawling its way down Pennsylvania Avenue. Brigid thought to herself that if it continued at its current speed, she could probably throw the missile at the Rolls-Royce and hit it. It almost seemed ridiculous to use one of the most technically advanced infantry missile systems in the world to shoot at a large, slow target at such close range.

She stood behind the *Spike SR*, turned it around on its stand, and looked through the unit's thermal camera at the approaching motorcade. She locked on to the Rolls-Royce, which was now just over a hundred and fifty yards away. Brigid could feel her heart pounding. But she had trained for this. Two deep breaths. She squeezed the trigger. The *Spike* did not fail her, as the missile burst out of the end of the armature tube and in just seconds exploded through the roof of the Rolls-Royce. A blinding light with a deafening bang, accompanied a force so powerful that not only the bulletproof windows, but the armoured doors themselves were blown out into the road.

Some in the crowds started screaming and some just stood transfixed. Some were doing both. They were the lucky ones. Strewn across the side of the road were others lying on the ground. Many motionless, having been killed instantly by the blast, and many more critically injured, crying out for help. Those still standing, were just staring at the King's car – now completely consumed by fire. A huge plume of smoke towering high up into the sky. Even the noise from all the emergency vehicles arriving on the scene couldn't drown out the screaming.

Many in the crowd then instinctively decided to just run away - fleeing in every direction but without really knowing where they were going to. The inevitable and futile cordoning off of the area by the police and Secret Service followed, while the royal protection officers simply looked on dumbstruck and in the knowledge that they had failed in their duty to protect the Monarch.

***

In the Oval Office, the President stood staring at the television – her hand clasped over her mouth. The shocking images of the blazing Rolls-Royce were being transmitted live across the world with the caption *King Edward assassinated* underneath and a stunned Fox News presenter who kept repeating the words *we have just witnessed the assassination of King Edward on American soil.*

The phone rang. James McInnis picked up the handset and held it out.

'It's Baqri.'

'President Monroe,' she almost whispered.

'Wooooo-eeeeee! Oh yeah! Not that's what I call a barbeque! I could almost feel the heat from that. Did anyone order one British King well-done? Did you see that, Calam?' Baqri crowed.

'You're disgusting, Baqri. What is wrong with you?'

'Well, I thought that as you're a Texan girl, you would appreciate a good barbeque.'

'Your attempts at some sort of sick humour are not welcome. What is wrong with you?' Monroe repeated.

'Nothing wrong with me, Calam. The King, however … well he's just in bits about it.'

Baqri laughed like he had just told the world's funniest joke.

'You're sick. Unlike you, the King was a great man. And what about those other people that died? How did any of those civilians harm you in any way? What did they do to you that was so bad they deserved to die so horribly?'

'He died because it was necessary. They died because … well …because all wars have their casualties. I imagine you're just about to have every major world leader call you, Madam President – starting with the British. Wait until the world sees the depth of your involvement in the assassination.'

'I've complied with your wishes, Baqri. Now, hand over the other weapon.'

'Oh, I never said I would hand it over. All I said was that if you did what I told you to do, then I wouldn't launch it. But I'm not going to just give it up, am I? Not when I have America in the palms of my hands.'

President Monroe replaced the phone handset and looked up at her chief of staff. Before she could say anything, the phone rang again.

'Madam President, I have the British Prime Minister on hold for you,' said the White House communications officer. 'The Canadian, Australian and New Zealand Prime Ministers are also insisting on speaking to you and are on hold. I'm sorry, Madam President, but so many other world leaders are leaving messages for you to call them, we're barely keeping up.'

President Monroe sighed heavily and walked back to the other side of her desk before lowering herself into her chair. 'I think I would like to deal with these calls privately, Jim. Could you check where we're up to with the FBI and police operation? Better arrange for a press conference later, as well.'

As McInnis left the Oval Office, President Monroe reached for her mobile phone.

'Tom. Do you have him?'

'I certainly do, Ma'am. I'm looking at him right now,' replied Tom, refocussing his binoculars.

'How did you know where he would be?'

‘I didn’t. Well, not exactly. Baqri may be as mad as a hatter but he’s also very predictable with certain things. In particular his voyeuristic tendencies. He just had to have a front row seat for the assassination. Couldn’t help himself. I wasn’t sure which building he would choose, of course. But I knew he would turn up.’

‘I wish there had been another way to have got him out into the open. The cost has been huge.’

‘I know Madam President. There really wasn’t.’

Monroe paused briefly to take a deep breath. ‘OK, Tom. Let’s proceed with your plan. I’m sure I don’t need to remind you that everything’s riding on this succeeding. And now, I have the unenviable task of talking to the British Prime Minister.’

CHAPTER TWENTY

Perhaps surprisingly, the FBI tactical unit tasked with capturing or killing Baqri, had no objection to Luna's appointment as team leader – even though almost all of them had more on the ground law enforcement experience than her. But they knew her capabilities and had seen her in refresher training. Faster reaction speed, marksman-like precision with a gun and unmatched unarmed combat abilities. They knew that she would lead from the front and that was just fine with them.

'Luna. You've got a green light from the president,' said Tom over his radio, but still keeping a watchful eye on the beautiful 19th century old post office across the other side of Pennsylvania Avenue. 'He's in the Waldorf Astoria. According to my plan of the building, he's in the Capitol Suite. That's on the fifth floor.'

'Tom, I have to tell you that it's insane down here. Complete panic and chaos. I've got cops, medics, Secret Service and even the fire service getting involved. Mixed in with that, we have civilians who are all running around like headless chickens. It's difficult to see the wood from the trees.'

'Yeah, I can see that,' said Tom focussing his binoculars in on Luna's six-man team, which was trying to force its way through the masses. 'It also looks like a fire has broken out on the first floor of the Waldorf. Maybe as a result of the explosion. A large number of the firefighters have been re-directed to deal with it.'

'Ok copy that. Are the fire exits covered in case Baqri's using this to escape?'

'Affirmative. Every escape is covered. Anyone who leaves via an emergency exit will be detained.'

'How many hostiles are we looking at?'

'Can't be completely sure. So far, it looks like just Baqri and one other male, as far as I can see. But there may be more that are out of my view.'

'Has the hotel been cleared?'

'Supposedly. The FBI had already cleared The Waldorf and all the other buildings on the King's route to Congress. On security grounds, which is a bit ironic. But it looks like some civilians have run into the reception of the Waldorf out of sheer panic when the bomb went off. The firefighters are trying to escort them back out.'

Tom looked back up again at the fifth floor.

'Luna. I've lost sight of Baqri.'

'OK. Copy that. We've just arrived at the Waldorf's reception. The whole place is full of smoke and the fire's still raging. The fire service is struggling to contain it. Looks like it's moving up through the floors.'

'The hotel should have an automatic sprinkler system. Has that not activated?'

'Doesn't look like it.'

Luna grabbed a nearby fire officer by the arm, who seemed to be in command.

'I need to get to the fifth floor,' she said, lifting her goggles on to the top of her helmet.

'You're kidding, right? That's not happening. My priority is to get this fire under control. No one should be trying to go higher into the building – not even you guys.'

'Look. You know the British King has just been blown up – right? Well, we believe the terrorists responsible are in the Capitol Suite, on the fifth floor. I can't tell you what's at stake here but it's not over. Trust me, it's no exaggeration to say that hundreds of thousands – if not millions – of lives are still at risk. And just to be clear, I wasn't asking for your permission. We're going up there whether you like it or not.'

'OK, OK,' said the fire chief, slightly taken aback. 'It's your risk. I can't afford to send any of my guys with you, so you're on your own.'

'Have you got anyone upstairs?'

'No, the building was declared empty by federal officers – so we're using all available resources into getting this fire under control.'

Luna nodded and reached again for her radio. 'Tom, the smoke is getting really bad. We're going to have to put on breathing apparatus. We're moving now.'

'Copy that. Be careful, Luna.'

Luna and her team vigilantly and methodically advanced through the thick smoke and up the stairs from each floor until they reached the door leading to the fifth floor. Progress had been painfully slow due to the density of the smoke and then she realised why. The fire door to the fifth floor had been removed. It then dawned on her that this had been the case on every floor. Someone had deliberately taken off every fire door.

She made her way slowly and carefully down the corridor, with her FBI team behind her in tactical formation, until they arrived at the door of the Capitol Suite. In a seamless, well-choreographed action, one of the team moved up, placed a small charge by the lock as the rest of the squad stood to one side. The explosion was quickly followed by two stun grenades, which were rolled along the short inner hall and into the main living room.

'FBI. Get on the ground,' shouted Luna, which was then echoed by every member in her team.

Smoke rushed through the open doorway and into the suite. Luna raised her MP5 and stepped inside, advancing cautiously along the hallway. Her team mirrored her actions, staying close behind. Luna stopped and squinted. She held up her hand to her team behind her. She edged forwards. Something had caught her attention. And there it was. A thin piece of wire going across the threshold between the hall and the living room. She had almost missed it thanks to the smoke. She peered around the corner to see the other end of the wire. Tied to it, a grenade. Luna looked behind and beckoned with her hand to one of her squad. She pointed to her eyes and then down at the wire below, before stepping back. The agent knelt down, peered at the wire and followed it along to the grenade. She removed her wire cutters and, after gently but firmly holding the wire with one hand, she carefully snipped the wire. Luna moved back to the front and continued slowly advancing into the living room with her gun raised. She then indicated in two directions with her hand to the rest of her team, who then rushed in behind her and fanned out.

One by one, the rooms were searched. A feeling of dread swept over Luna. It wasn't long before her worst fears were confirmed. The only thing left behind was sat on the coffee table in the middle of the room. A copy of Sun Tzu's book, *The Art of War.* Luna picked up the book. Inserted into it was a bookmark. She opened up the book to that page. Part of one line had been highlighted with a yellow marker. *If your enemy is secure at all points, be prepared for him. If he is superior in strength, avoid him.*

'Are you kidding me?' shouted Luna, throwing the book across the living room and narrowly missing one of her colleagues who had just exited a bedroom. She grabbed her radio, paused briefly as she took a deep breath and then held down the button.

'Tom. Baqri's escaped. I repeat. Baqri has escaped.'

CHAPTER TWENTY-ONE

'How the hell did he escape, Tom?' barked President Monroe.

Tom knew that this was going to be a difficult phone call. In his heart, he believed that capturing Baqri at the Waldorf Astoria was going to be a long shot. He was always going to have had an escape plan of some sort.

'I've reviewed the recordings and it looks like Baqri and his sidekick were disguised as fire fighters.'

'And nobody spotted it was them? I mean the guy is pretty distinctive these days with those tears tattooed on his face.'

'I'm afraid not. Don't forget that the whole hotel was full up with smoke and so Baqri would have been wearing full face breathing apparatus – like all the genuine fire fighters. They only took that off as they got into a fire service vehicle, which was parked outside, and made their escape.'

'But it sounds like they must have used the same stairs that your wife Luna, and her FBI team went up … yet somehow managed to get past them?'

'That seems to be the case, Madam President.'

'How?'

'Baqri knew they were coming and their position in the building. I had the whole team checked when they returned to the FBI field office and we found that one of the team had a tracker on him. Baqri probably hid in another room until they went past.'

'Is this agent in custody?'

'He is, yes. Awaiting questioning. But I doubt very much that he was aware he had a tracker on him. I mean, who plants a tracker on themselves?'

'So, someone else in the Bureau then?'

'That would seem most likely.'

'I don't mind telling you, Tom, that the longer this goes on, the more difficult it becomes for me. The British want answers and I've got a big ol' line of other countries stacked up behind them, wanting the same thing. At the moment, none of them are aware of our involvement and believe it to be just a terrorist attack. But I'm sure Baqri is preparing all his evidence to send out to the media and across the Web. That's when the solids hit the air-conditioning – if you know what I mean.'

'I do understand that Madam President. That's why we have to immediately move on to *Plan B*. As we discussed previously, the only ways we can stop this is by either capturing Baqri or his missiles. We are now forced to turn our attention to the latter. The last Avangard that has the potential to cost millions of American lives.'

'You're right, of course, Tom.'

'Have you managed to look at that file that I sent over to you?'

'I have … but I can hardly believe it. That was a hell of a shock.'

'I know, Madam President. But the evidence is irrefutable.'

'I would agree. Do you think there are others in my administration?'

'I'd be amazed if there wasn't. I would imagine that there are members of The Collective in every major government around the world as well. From what I have seen, they will probably be in high political, intelligence, military and law enforcement positions and also major names in big business.'

'Even world leaders?'

'I would expect so.'

'How do you fight that?'

'One step at a time, Madam President. That's all we can do.'

Monroe sighed and shook her head. 'You better get going then, Tom. I'll call in my chief of staff now and let's pray that your *Plan B* works. Good luck,' she said ending the call.

***

Jane Monroe sat back in her black leather chair and stared at the ceiling. A high stakes battle of wits was being played out between Tom Rivers and a genius level lunatic armed with a weapon of mass destruction. The outcome could determine the fate of hundreds of thousands – maybe even millions – of Americans. To make matters worse, there was a secret organisation which was so powerful, it was able to manipulate current events on a global scale. And they were helping the terrorists. For the first time in her Presidency, she felt powerless and helpless. There was little she could do except pray that Tom would defeat Baqri. She knew that he was the only one who could.

'Madam President,' said McInnis entering the Oval Office.

'Sit down, Jim. What's the latest on the Ohio and Arizona attacks?'

'The latest report now has twenty-two thousand people already dead.'

'Dear God.'

'But the even larger number will be what's called the *walking dead*.'

'The *what*?'

'It refers to the people that took a minute amount of polonium into their bodies. As you know, even a millionth of a gram is likely to be fatal. But the smaller the quantity, the longer it will take to kill them. There are probably many thousands of people in both towns who have been given a death sentence but just don't know it yet. CDC are still testing the population.'

'And the media?'

'There's rumours flying round about it being a dirty bomb but they're still lacking evidence to give that theory any momentum.'

'We're definitely running out of time on that one. It won't be long until our allies and the whole world finds out the truth.'

'Talking of which, how did your call with the British Prime Minister go?'

'Tense. I've known Bob Hatcher for many years. He's not stupid. He knows there's something that I'm not telling him.'

'So, our line is still that it was a tragic assassination by terrorists that we're actively pursuing. As you say, it's just a matter of time before he finds out the whole truth.'

'That's why I need to send you on an assignment, Jim.'

'Me?'

'I need someone that I can trust. Someone who understands the dire situation that we're in. You're the only person who has been through this all the way with me.'

'What do you want me to do, Madam President?'

'I've made an appointment for you to see the Russian ambassador. I want you to deliver an official letter from me and explain the contents. Specifically, that their lack of progress in retrieving the Avangards and their launchers, could be interpreted as deliberate. Furthermore, should the last HGV hit one of our major cities, then they need to know that we will be holding them responsible. The letter will serve as formal notice of that.'

'Of course, Madam President. Do you think that will work?'

'Not sure. Probably not. But so long as they think that there are no repercussions for them, then I think they will do nothing to stop it and just let things play out. There's a big upside for the Russians if Baqri is successful. This threat from us might just make them think again.'

'I agree. I think that it's worth a go. Do I take it that talks with President Petrov have not been fruitful then?'

'Well, he says the right things. Promises that they're doing everything that they can. But then comes a load of excuses. *Russia's a huge country. The mobile launcher is easy to hide from view. Etcetera, etcetera.*'

'To be fair, there is some merit to that argument. The last intel report that I read was that even our own satellites have failed to find it. Probably hidden in some cave somewhere.'

'What I can guarantee, Jim, is that if Baqri was threatening Moscow instead of us, the Russians would have found it by now. Anyway, you better get on your way.'

'OK, will do. By the way, there is a representative from North Korea waiting outside to see you.'

'Send him in.'

'Madam President,' said the representative striding towards Monroe with an outstretched hand, as McInnis exited the Oval Office.

Monroe rose briefly from her seat to shake hands. 'Mr Lee. Please,' she replied, indicating a chair opposite.

'How can I help?'

'You may be aware of a potential threat to this country that involves a polonium-based weapon.'

'Potential threat? We were under the impression that two had already detonated over American soil?'

'I'm not sure where you are receiving your intel from, Mr Lee.'

'Yes, of course. My apologies, Madam President. My information must be wrong. Otherwise, you would have told the American people about it by now, wouldn't you?'

'Mr Lee, we have received intelligence reports that the polonium acquired by the terrorists has been supplied by your country.'

'That accusation is outrageous, Madam President.'

'Mohammed Baqri was seen sitting outside a café in Pyongyang with General Kim Sun-woo. I believe that he is in charge of your nuclear weapons programme?'

'You are correct. And it's true that they did meet – at the request of Mr Baqri. The general was offered the opportunity to be given the schematics for a Russian weapon called an Avangard. The price for this was that we had to provide Mr Baqri with a large quantity of polonium.'

'Go on,' said Monroe.

'The General asked what the polonium would be used for and Mr Baqri explained that he was planning an attack on the United States. The General said he would consider it but then reported it immediately to his superiors.'

'But you decided not to tell us?'

'I hope that you will forgive me, if I am very candid with you. We do not consider America to be our friend, Madam President. But I'm sure you also realise that my country does not involve itself in the business of the West. Having said that, we are not your enemy either – despite what you may think.'

'Oh really?' said Monroe mockingly.

'We are not the ones that supplied him with that polonium, Madam President. If we were the ones to supply the polonium, do you think we would have had a meeting with Mr Baqri at an outdoor café? In plain sight of everyone?'

'I would love to believe you, Mr Lee. But I need to advise you, that if a weapon detonates over an American city, and people die, then the United States will have to respond.'

'I don't appreciate your threats, Madam President. We are also a nuclear power. Any attacks on us will be responded to in kind. May I give you one piece of advice?'

'Go on.'

'Don't make the catastrophic mistake of starting a nuclear war because of false information. North Korea is not the enemy. You need to look elsewhere for your villain, Madam President.'

CHAPTER TWENTY-TWO

Nothing brought greater joy to his heart than watching America suffer. And today, he was in a state of complete euphoria. Russian Premier, Sergei Petrov, was sat in his office in the Kremlin as the news reports started coming in. He leaned back in his chair, clasped his hands behind his head and smiled. The latest headlines on national media, heralded not only the death of the British monarch but now added rumours of America's complicity. Petrov picked up the phone.

'General. What is the update on the remaining missing Avangard?' asked Petrov, while still smiling at the images on the television.

'I regret to report that we have still not been able to find it, sir,' replied General Volkov.

'Why?'

'Because every time we receive intelligence as to its whereabouts, the information turns out to be incorrect.'

'So, you're blaming the FSB then? The fact that you have not found it is completely unacceptable,' Petrov barked.

'All I'm saying, sir, is that I can't be expected to track it down if I am given faulty information. We are having to search a huge area with no help. It could be anywhere in southern Russia.'

'That just sounds like a lot of excuses to me, General. We have promised the Americans that we will find it – but we're now running out of time. Very soon they will feel that they have no choice but to send a special forces team after it. You need to find it before they do. Don't disappoint me again, General. I will hold you personally responsible,' said Petrov, ending the call.

Petrov turned his seat to the man sat on the other side of his desk. Major Viktor Gorsky was a large man. At six feet and six inches, he was a whole foot taller than his boss. He was also blessed with a full head of black hair – unlike President Petrov. It had always been a bit of a national joke with the Russian people that, for the past two hundred years, their leaders alternated between bald and not. Petrov was definitely in the bald camp. His physical appearance, however, did not detract from his surprisingly intimidating demeanour.

'I'm not sure how long I can keep the army running around, sir,' said Gorsky.

'Hopefully, you won't need to for much longer. But, right now, we need American intelligence to believe that we are trying our best to find the remaining Avangard.'

'There is a risk that the FSB is going to look incompetent soon. In particular, I'm going to look incompetent.'

'It's true that the reputation of the FSB may take a knock. But it will only be temporary and soon forgotten. At any rate, it will be worth it.'

'I'm not sure I understand, Mr President.'

'As you know, we have been spending huge resources in gaining closer ties with numerous countries around the world. Many of those countries, which have been traditional allies of America, are teetering on the brink of allying with us instead.'

'Like some of the African countries?'

'Correct. What we have been waiting for was something that would push them over the edge.'

'The King's assassination.'

'Exactly. Those countries, and many others around the world, will be outraged when they hear evidence of American complicity with the terrorists. And those governments will get the excuse that they need to turn to us.'

'It sounds like you knew that the King would be assassinated?'

'I'm sure it will be no surprise for you to learn that I have ears everywhere. And my ears heard whispers.'

'Do I assume that a number of leaders will also personally benefit from their country's new friendship with Russia.'

'Of course,' replied President Petrov.

'But at the moment, I've only heard rumours about the American involvement in the assassination.'

'Which means it's time to stoke the fire, Colonel.'

'Colonel?'

'I told you at our first meeting, that I would reward you for your service. So now, Colonel, we have to do our bit for the conspiracy theory and start putting meat on the bones.'

'Of course. Thank you, sir,' said Gorsky, slightly flustered by his unexpected promotion. 'What would you like me to do next?'

'I want you to proceed with the televised confessions of the two American servicemen that are in our custody.'

'Can I ask what they will be confessing to?'

Petrov stood up, strolled over to the window, and looked across at the other Kremlin buildings – while observing the bright sunshine glistening off the top of Moscow's famous onion domes. The weather had been particularly good for the past few days with temperatures well above the seasonal average and this certainly added to Petrov's feeling of optimism.

'They will admit that they have been undertaking covert missions into Russian territory.'

'But the Americans will say that those servicemen had left the military years earlier and were operating as private individuals in our recent conflicts, when they were captured by us.'

'They will, yes. But we will refute that. After the assassination of the King, I think that the world will have very little confidence in anything that America says.'

'Sorry, Mr President. I'm still not clear as to what they should be confessing to?' repeated Gorsky.

'They will state that they were actually part of a CIA Black Ops team which was sent by their government to attack one of our convoys in southern Russia. The objective was to acquire the HGV Avangard systems.'

'Well, their country believes that they were killed abroad. We left enough evidence behind for that. So, for them to be CIA would seem plausible to the intelligence services of most other countries. I'm confident that we will be able to come up with some military records as proof.'

'Excellent.'

'What about the remaining Avangard that we can't find?'

'The American prisoners will say that Russian forces caught up with them after they launched the first two missiles. There was then a fire fight, during which they were captured. But the rest of their team managed to escape with the remaining Avangard HGV.'

'And can I ask why America would launch missiles at its own cities?'

'So that they can accuse us of supplying the terrorists. Monroe and her government wanted the King dead because he was interfering with their colonial plans in Africa. To kill him, they needed to blame someone else. Blame us. That's the narrative that the prisoners need to give in their confession.'

'Colonial plans in Africa?' asked Gorsky.

'Colonisation by stealth. In the same way that Britain had managed to create its empire. They didn't do it through some massive standing army, Viktor. At the height of the British Empire, it ruled a quarter of the globe. Ruled it by consent. Well, consent of the leaders, of course. Not necessarily the people.'

'And these leaders were incentivised, no doubt.'

'That's generally how it works, yes. And as I said before, just as we will do.'

'Do you think that this will work?'

Petrov turned from the window. 'Those whispers weren't the only ones that I have heard. Other whispers say that proof will be coming which shows the Americans not only provided the terrorists with the King's motorcade details but also supplied them with the anti-tank missile system that killed him.'

'That will be a disaster for them diplomatically.'

'Indeed, it will. And the first domino to fall will be the Democratic Republic of Congo. Colonel Banza is ready to seize power.'

'With the help of our weapons and mercenaries to support him.'

'Absolutely. And the rewards for us will be enormous. The world is obsessed with electrification, as if it is some sort of saviour from fossil fuels. Cell phones, laptops, mobile devices and soon every motorised vehicle on the planet will need battery power.'

'And batteries need cobalt with the Democratic Republic of Congo having more of it than all the other countries put together.'

'Very good, Viktor. It won't stop at cars, believe me. And there isn't enough cobalt in the world to satisfy the demand. It will soon become more and more valuable as the world realises there isn't enough to go around. In return for our assistance, Russian companies will be given major interests in Congo's cobalt mines and the future of global sustainable electric power. Every nation – including the Americans – will have to come knocking on our door. And that will just be the start.'

'We could end up as the world's economic superpower!'

Petrov smiled. A menacing smile worthy of The Cheshire Cat.

'We will, my friend. It is time for Russia to take its rightful place at the centre of the world stage.'

CHAPTER TWENTY-THREE

James McInnis gazed out of the blacked out rear window of the Secret Service Chevrolet SUV. It was now 2 p.m. but it already felt like the longest day ever. The president seemed keen to assign blame for the King's assassination at the foot of two other nuclear powers. This strategy had the potential to escalate quickly if Baqri decided to launch the other missile. The president would then be forced to seek retribution. McInnis did a quick calculation through his head.

Baqri stated that the first Avangard had only a small amount of polonium. Let's assume, say, ten percent of his stock. The total stock in his possession was, say, two hundred grams. So, ninety percent of the remaining stock would be one hundred and eighty grams. If a millionth of a gram could kill someone, then ...'

No further analysis was required. It was abundantly clear that Baqri could kill the entire population of any major US city that he wanted. McInnis assumed that the target would be New York, as the nation's financial heart, or Washington, to cripple the executive and administration. The impact on America and its economy would be disastrous and this would have a knock-on effect for the world. The last missile had to be captured. Russia needed to act.

The SUV turned left on to Massachusetts Avenue. Fortunately, the journey to the Russian Embassy was a fifteen-minute drive from The White House but McInnis got the feeling that his meeting with the ambassador would not be so brief. He had met him a few times before and thoroughly disliked him right from the start. A chubby little man who had mastered the art of smiling warmly and lying convincingly at the same time.

'Get down!' shouted the Secret Service driver.

McInnis instinctively looked forward. A large white van had pulled across the front of the SUV. He looked behind. Another van screeched to a stop. They were blocked in. Two masked men stepped out and levelled their sub-machine guns at the FBI vehicle. He snapped his head back to the front. Four other men were already out of the first van. Guns raised.

'Get down!' shouted the Secret Service agent again, opening his door and unholstering his pistol.

McInnis hid behind the front seat, peering out of the lower half of his window. His bodyguard had squatted behind his open door. A short burst of machine gun fire and the top of the agent disappeared from view. A terrorist almost casually walked towards the SUV, stopped by the open door, and then fired another burst towards the ground. McInnis looked around. There were now two terrorists on either side. They raised their guns.

Another burst of machine gun fire. But McInnis realised that the shots had not hit the SUV. Instead, all the terrorists were facing the rear. The one that killed his driver now appeared to be in a panic – shooting wildly. He turned and looked at the cowering McInnis and frantically tugged at the door handle. McInnis knew that the bullet proof glass and door armour were the only things stopping his immediate demise and instinctively grabbed the handle from the other side – even though he also knew the door was still locked. The terrorist raised his sub-machine gun. Another burst of fire from the rear and the terrorist staggered back and dropped to the ground. McInnis peered out the other window. Only one terrorist was still standing immediately beside the SUV with one more a little further back. He watched as the remaining two terrorists retreated to behind the first van, firing behind them as they ran.

Four figures dressed all in black tactical gear, emblazoned with 'FBI', were advancing around the van to the rear. They stopped next to the SUV, as one of them leaned down – presumably to check on the Secret Service agent – before throwing stun grenades under the other van. In a matter of minutes, the nightmare was over.

The tactical team returned to the Secret Service SUV and positioned themselves to provide protective cover as the sounds of police sirens now became audible in the distance.

One of the FBI agents knocked on the window. Their head and facial features mostly covered by the tactical helmet and goggles.

'Mr McInnis, we need to get you away. Right now, sir,' the agent shouted. A female agent from the sound of her voice.

He stepped out of the SUV, straight into a large pool of blood.

'Oh, God!' cried McInnis, briefly staring down and then across to one of the terrorists, who was lying on his back, adjacent to the vehicle.

'Mr McInnis,' the agent repeated.

'Yes, sorry,' McInnis replied, running with the agent towards the FBI vehicle. 'Is my driver alive?'

'I'm afraid not, sir.'

McInnis looked behind at the motionless, blood soaked, body lying by the driver's door.

'We have instructions to take you directly back to the White House.'

'How did you get here so quick?' asked McInnis, climbing into the rear of the FBI SUV.

'My name is Luna Rivers, Mr McInnis. My husband Tom asked us to follow you. He thought your life might be in danger.'

For the duration of the journey back to The White House, McInnis considered his close escape. The mystery was why he would be targeted for assassination at all. And by whom. His question would shortly be answered as he was taken to a meeting room. A few minutes later, the door opened and Tom Rivers hobbled in, with the aid of a crutch.

'Glad to see you alive and well, James,' said Tom, sitting down on the other side of the table.

'What on earth is going on, Tom? Who were those people that tried to kill me.'

'I believe they were assassins sent by The Collective.'

'Why is The Collective trying to kill me?'

'Because they think that you're giving away critical information about them to the FBI.'

'How would I know any information about them? And why the hell would they think that?'

'Because I told them.'

CHAPTER TWENTY-FOUR

'*You* told them? What do you mean *you told them*?' asked McInnis incredulously.

'Not directly, of course. I just made sure that there were enough whispers going round.'

'Saying what?'

'Suggesting that the chief of staff to The President had been discovered to be a member of The Collective but, having cracked under interrogation, was now helping the FBI by providing evidence against them.'

'Why the hell would you do that? Are you joking? Is this some weird British humour or something?'

'No joke. The Collective now believe that you are spilling your guts about every little thing you know about them in exchange for protection. You know, relocation to the *little house on the prairie*, in the middle of nowhere for you and your family with a permanent security detail, and to live out the rest of your days. That sort of thing.'

'You're nuts. What the hell is wrong with you? You're absolutely nuts. I thought Baqri was the madman but you … well. I'm the chief of staff, you moron. I'm going to have you arrested for this,' said McInnis, banging his fist on the table.

'Oh, and your family are probably next on their list by the way,' said Tom, ignoring McInnis's threats. 'You see, I'm pretty sure that The Collective will do anything to stop you from talking. I imagine that within the next few hours, your family will be kidnapped and then tortured. Unlike what happened to you, I haven't sent a team to protect them.'

McInnis jumped to his feet, and, in doing so, threw the chair on to its back. He strode towards the door and pulled it open – only to find the doorway blocked by a large Secret Service agent.

'Get out of my way,' ordered McInnis.

The agent responded by putting his hand on McInnis's chest.

'Don't touch me … get your hand off,' yelled McInnis in the agent's face.

Tom said, 'We have evidence by the way that you're a member of The Collective. I had your office fitted out with hidden cameras. I know you've been sending messages to them via the app that they hijacked.'

'You bugged my office? I want to see the president.'

'You will, Jim,' said Tom calmly.

'Who the hell gave you the authority to detain me? You're just an adviser that we brought in. You're not even an American, for God's sake. Well? Answer me! Who gave you the authority?'

'I did,' came a voice from behind the agent.

'Madam President,' said McInnis, as the agent stepped to one side.

'You're a traitor, Jim,' said Monroe. 'You've betrayed your president and your country.'

'Madam President, I don't know what he's told you but it's all lies. You've known me for years. I've always been loyal to you.'

'That's what upsets me the most. You had everything, Jim. The youngest chief of staff in the history of this country. A great family and a great future ahead of you. But it seems that wasn't enough.'

'Please, Madam President. This is a big misunderstanding.'

'Sit down.' Monroe shouted at point blank range into McInnis's face.

James McInnis stepped back, shocked by the unprecedented level of anger shown by the president.

'So, what to do with you,' Monroe continued, as McInnis complied with her instructions. 'Tom, please explain the options.'

'Well, we believe that there is enough evidence to convict you for treason. Sending you to the electric chair does have the advantage of sending a strong message to The Collective, of course. Politically, however, this may make life a little tricky for the president with lots of awkward questions.'

'But still. It's possible that the electric chair could work in my favour. A demonstration of strength. Cross this president and you get fried,' added Monroe.

McInnis visibly swallowed. The first beads of perspiration now beginning to form on his forehead.

'Well, that is a possibility,' replied Tom. 'The next alternative is, we just let you go. Kick you out of the building. I would be surprised if you actually made it home alive. That would be my recommendation.'

'But I did discuss a third option with Tom, you'll be pleased to know,' said Monroe. 'We assumed that you were likely to want to go with this one, given your other choices. That's why we sent Luna and her team to protect you.'

'Go on,' replied McInnis with a sense of desperation.

'You actually do exactly what I told The Collective you were doing. Tell us everything you know about them. Who the other members might be; what conversations you've recently had; and any other plans that have been discussed by the group. That sort of thing. Help us save American lives. You have a chance to do the right thing. In return, the president will pardon you for your treachery and you will be re-settled with your family in an area that has never heard of James McInnis,' Tom said, sliding a copy of the presidential pardon across the table.

'Why would you offer me that?'

'I don't want you to be under any misunderstanding, Jim,' Monroe said. 'I would like to see you go to the chair for what you have done. But one of the major reasons why Baqri has been so successful against both us and the British, is that he has the backing of that group. They are a threat to elected governments around the world – the very fabric of democracy. And they must be stopped.'

'Tell us about them. Have you any idea how big this group is? Who might be involved?' asked Tom.

For a minute or so, McInnis just stared at the tabletop.

'I can't tell you who the members are but I just get the feeling that there's a lot of powerful people around the world. They seem to know things which you think they couldn't possibly know unless they were at the top of the food chain.'

'And nobody has accidentally given away their name or even a hint of who they are?' asked Tom.

'No. Everyone has a codename taken from a mythical person or being. The Collective seems to have some AI system which monitors and filters any messages to check for anything that might compromise the members.'

'If you want immunity and the whole re-settling package, then the president expects you to assist the investigation that will be set up and identify other members of The Collective. I'll also be wanting your phone, so that I can go through the messages. Make sure any security is switched off.'

'I will help as much as I can. I don't really have a choice, do I?'

'Good. So, you can start by telling us about any other plans that they're working on.'

'I really wouldn't know. Each project works in isolation. Only those members who are signed up to it get to know what's going on.'

'Project?' barked Monroe. 'Is that what you call killing thousands of Americans?'

McInnis looked up at the president sheepishly. 'It's just what it's called, Madam President.'

'And what was your involvement in *this* project? Do different members of The Collective have different jobs on a project?' asked Tom.

'Yeah, they do. You see when a project is proposed, then members have the chance to put themselves forward to be involved. But you have to be able to contribute. And that's how you earn the big money. It could be contributing finance, resources, information, influence or anything like that. The AI system considers each member's application and then selects who will be included.'

'Tell me more about this app they use. The AI controls that too, right?'

'Yeah, the AI system hijacks an app for each project. The members involved in that project get given login details that sends them to a private messaging page within the app. The app developers won't even be aware of it. All done by the AI.'

'So, do you think we are talking about some world leaders being in The Collective?' asked Tom, trying to keep the questioning focussed.

'I would put money on it.'

'We need to deal with Baqri as the priority but, as part of your deal, we will then want you to help us infiltrate the organisation itself.'

McInnis simply nodded in reply.

'Good. Now tell me about their relationship with Baqri. How do they feel about him.'

'He makes them nervous. They consider him to be a very clever man who is one of only a few people with the ability to pull off certain missions. But they also feel he is unpredictable and mentally unstable.'

'No kidding,' said President Monroe.

'And what's their objective with the current attack on the US?'

'They've got what they want. The objective was to destabilise the Democratic Republic of Congo, to facilitate a regime change. The assassination of King Edward, with a finger pointing at America, will result in a withdrawal of support from friendly African countries who would have prevented it. Members of The Collective have large shareholdings in the companies that will be given the licences for mining cobalt, once Colonel Banza seizes power.'

'So, I imagine they wouldn't actually want Baqri to launch another, even more powerful weapon, at a major US city?'

'Absolutely not. The decimation of, say New York, would destroy the American economy. The Collective's sole purpose is to make its members huge amounts of money. Destroying the biggest economy in the world would be a disaster for us all. They are keeping a careful eye on Baqri.'

'How? I mean, how do they know what he's up to and thinking?'

'They've been cultivating a relationship with someone close to him.'

'And Baqri. Do you think he trusts them?'

'I think he trusts the information that they give him. They've proved to be reliable.'

Tom looked at President Monroe. 'Interesting. I think we may have just been thrown a bone.'

CHAPTER TWENTY-FIVE

The president had now returned to the Oval Office. The revelation that her chief of staff was a member of The Collective was still swirling around her head. Unusually for Jane Monroe, she started questioning her own judgement. *How on earth could she not have realised that McInnis wasn't what he seemed? She saw him every day and had done for many years and so how the hell did she not pick up on anything that might have given her a clue?*

'Come in, Rachael,' said Monroe with a beckoning motion of her hand.

'Madam President, I regret to inform you that Colonel Banza has started his coup in the Democratic Republic of Congo. His troops have engaged in active warfare with government troops and intelligence reports suggest that he is likely to be in power by this time tomorrow,' said Secretary of Homeland Security Rachael Goldberg.

'What? Where the hell are our African allies?'

'They're refusing to assist.'

'Why?'

Goldberg picked up the remote control from the central coffee table and switched on the television. The news flash headline banner read *America complicit in King's assassination.* The president watched on as the reporter regurgitated stories that had started to spread on the internet. Her head sank to her chest as phone recordings followed. Recordings proving that she not only agreed to demands to supply the King's motorcade route to terrorists but also that she would provide a safe building and even the military equipment to enable the assassination.

'Surely everyone knows that we would only do that under duress?' said Monroe.

'Well, not really. We haven't been able to give them the full story because of the outstanding threat of the last Avangard HGV. Baqri demanded that it was kept under wraps, didn't he? Plus, you didn't want to create panic in our major cities, if you remember.'

'Perhaps that was a mistake. Maybe we should consider telling the truth.'

'Actually, I don't think that was a mistake at all.'

'Really?'

'Yes, really, Madam President. Even putting Baqri's threats to one side, can you imagine the reaction if we make it known that the attacks in Ohio and Arizona were not accidents at all but were, in fact, terrorist attacks using an unstoppable and undetectable missile system containing the deadliest element on the planet? *Oh, and by the way New York, the biggest one could be coming your way and you are all going to die.*'

'I know, Rachael. I know. Millions of New Yorkers all desperately trying to get out of the city at the same time. It would be carnage.'

'Not just New York. Every major city in the US would be panicking that the missile will hit them. Baqri hasn't said which one he would go for.'

'So, what do we do?'

'I'm really not sure Madam President. I'm afraid we also have an even bigger problem. One which we had predicted with the assassination of the King.'

'Our allies?'

'Yes, ma'am. Many of them are just in a state of shock that this administration appears to have backed a terrorist group.'

'We didn't back any terrorist group. We had no choice. Surely, they can see that?'

'Unfortunately, that simply isn't how we are being portrayed by the media on the world stage. You have to understand that their trust in this country has been completely undermined.'

'Have you managed to get through to Prime Minister Hatcher?'

'We're not getting any response from the British, I'm afraid. A source that we have near to him has told us that the prime minister said … and I quote … *I would go to the US to discuss it with the president but she would probably have me killed as well.*'

President Monroe stood up with some urgency that was quite out of character for her normal relaxed style. She turned around and looked out the window across the White House lawn. Nothing was said for over a minute.

'Dear God, Rachael. This is madness.'

'It is, Madam President. And I'm afraid we are already starting to see the effects on the flow of information from our allies.'

'So, are you saying that holes have already started appearing in our intelligence network?'

'Yes, Madam President. There are some countries that have actively cut us off – like the British – and then there are others that seem paralysed while they work out what to do. But however you want to look at it, we are now a sitting duck for other terrorist organisations. We can pretty well only rely on our intelligence agencies with a very limited flow of information coming into us now from outside.'

'We need to work hard on getting them back on side then.'

'Easier said than done. The Russians have just added fuel to the fire,' said Goldberg placing the tablet that she had been carrying in front of the president.

'What's this?'

'This, Madam President, is the confession of American servicemen to a black ops mission.'

'What black ops mission?'

'Where we illegally attacked a Russian convoy of Avangard HGVs, captured them and have then been launching them at our own cities.'

'What?' said Monroe incredulously. 'What the hell are you talking about? I haven't authorised any black ops missions! And why the hell would I want to fire them at ourselves?'

'It's a complete fabrication, of course. In their so-called confessions, the servicemen say that their mission was to make it look like Russia had deliberately allowed the terrorists to take the weapons. Another deliberate act by America to undermine and frame Russia. They're claiming that this would then give the US the material to call for international condemnation and recrimination.'

'Oh, good God. That's the most ridiculous thing I've ever heard.'

'And it gave us the opportunity to assassinate King Edward and blame it on the same terrorists.'

'And why would we want that?'

'Because he was interfering in American plans to take over a number of African countries by stealth and steal their resources.'

'I can't believe what I'm hearing.'

Rachael Goldberg started the video on her tablet as President Monroe watched on in complete silence and with the occasional shake of her head. Eventually, the president resumed her place behind her desk and leaned back in her seat to stare at the ceiling, once again.

'Well, Rachael. I could never have imagined that America would find itself in this position. I need to make a call. We'll have a catch up again later.'

As Goldberg left the Oval Office, Monroe reached for her cell phone from inside her blue suit jacket.

'Hello,' said the voice on the other end of the phone.

'It's Jane. I just wanted to check that you were ok.'

'I am. I can't believe what has happened.'

'It's getting pretty bad.'

'And I gather from Tom that this lunatic Baqri has one of these weapons left? One that could kill hundreds of thousands or maybe millions of Americans.'

'He has, yes.'

'What are you going to do?'

'I'm not sure. I would normally have all the might of every government agency at my disposal but my administration has been corrupted and I really don't know who to trust. We are very much in the hands of Tom Rivers. All I can do is pray that he's as good as I hope he is.'

'With all the sacrifices that have been made today, Jane, I would just like to express to you my deep and sincere gratitude.'

'I'm just so glad to hear your voice, Edward.'

CHAPTER TWENTY-SIX

With the aid of his walking cane, Tom stepped out of the room holding McInnis to be greeted by a very familiar voice behind him.

'Hi, honey.'

'Hey! I was told you were on your way,' said Tom spinning around.

'Wow! You're out of your wheelchair! I thought the doctors said it would be at least another month?'

'Yeah, they did. But you know.'

'No, I really don't.'

'I was bored. I need to get back into active service.'

'Do you ever actually do what you've been told to do? Ever? One day you might actually take heed of the advice that you're given,' said Luna, crossing her arms.

Tom tried to change the subject. 'Would it be acceptable for the president's special adviser to kiss an FBI agent?'

'Only if it's this FBI agent,' Luna grinned.

'Well, you better come into my office then.'

'You have an office?'

'Yep. Your husband has his own office in The White House.' Tom theatrically threw open the door. 'Dan-aaah!'

Luna stepped into the very beige room, its blandness only broken up by various generic wall prints of the Washington skyline and a small corner dedicated to photos of a random selection of former presidents. A very sparsely furnished and unremarkable space. In fact, the only thing that really stood out in the room was a Union Jack planted front and centre on Tom's desk.

Luna looked at the flag and laughed. 'What the hell's that doing there?'

'The staff found it following the King's visit. They thought it would make me feel more at home. Little Britain they call this office.'

'Oh, good God,' said Luna, spotting an open box by the desk. 'Is that what I think it is?'

'Yes, ma'am. One box of Murray mints – especially imported for me.'

'You know we do have butter mints in the US, don't you?'

'Yes, but it has to be Murray mints. As if I would compromise on my favourite sweet! I told the president that I think better with them and the next thing I know, this box arrives with another nine waiting in storage.'

'I swear that if it wasn't for your superior genetics, you would have died by now, or at least developed diabetes, with that sweet tooth of yours.'

'Yeah, I know. But just think, if it wasn't for your incessant nagging, then I would be way worse than this.'

Luna shook her head. Tom's sweet tooth had always been his Achilles' heel. Not that he had regarded it as such. The best that she could ever do was to try and moderate it.

'Any other demands on my countrymen?' asked Luna, sitting herself down in one of the chairs opposite the desk.

'Well, you should have seen their faces when I asked them to try and find me a gypsy tart! I did eventually explain that it was a local dessert from my home county in England. They looked quite relieved.'

Luna's head dropped back and she roared with laughter. It was Tom's sense of humour that she had found so attractive when they first met and, even after so many years of marriage, she still did.

Just for a minute – one brief minute – Tom had made her forget the awful tragedy that had just befallen her homeland and the countless lives that had already been lost. A brief respite from one of the worst days in American history. A day that would haunt so many people for the rest of their lives.

'So, what's the latest?' she asked.

'The latest? Well, I'm pleased to report that James McInnis is *shinging like a canary.*'

'Was that supposed to be some sort of Chicago gangster impression?'

'Pretty good, huh?'

'Pretty awful, actually.'

'Well, you got it.'

'Only because I've lived with you for so long.'

'Moving on then,' said Tom with a feigned look of hurt. 'McInnis is currently our best asset. I think we can make good use of him.'

'Does anyone else know you're holding him?'

'No. As far as anyone knows, we are having a private meeting with the president. The Secret Service agent present is long serving and has proved his loyalty over the years – as far as we can be sure of anyone right now. He's sworn to secrecy. It's a risk but one we had to take.'

'I still can't believe that the president's chief of staff is a member of The Collective.'

'I know. President Monroe is determined to break that organisation.'

'That's dangerous. It's not like she's just taking on some drugs gang or something.'

'I agree. The problem is that she doesn't know who the good guys and who the bad guys are. But she's a good woman and wants to do the right thing. I have to admit, I'm worried for her safety. President or not.'

'What about that last missile. Did McInnis know anything?'

'McInnis believes that The Collective would not support an attack on a major US city. Especially somewhere like New York, which would be devastating to the economy.'

'Devastating to their personal fortunes, you mean.'

'Correct, my little piranha,' said Tom, popping a Murray mint into his mouth.

'Do you think that they will try and stop Baqri from launching that last missile?'

'Yes. I'm sure they would. But this is where I'm a little confused.'

'Go on.'

'Baqri claims that this one contains the bulk of the polonium that he has acquired. In fact, enough to wipe out the population of New York City and anywhere else near it. Right?'

'Right.'

'So, my question is, why have they not acted immediately to ensure he doesn't launch that last missile?' They've got what they want now with the coup starting in the Congo, so why would they take the risk? McInnis told me earlier that The Collective consider Baqri to be mentally unstable.'

'Perhaps there's another part to the plan.'

'Maybe. But they must know that they are running a huge risk.'

'Do you really think Baqri would actually launch that missile at a major American city? I mean, the threat of that last HGV is the only thing protecting him from being hunted down for everything that he's done so far. Not just by our government either. The Collective would turn on him as well.'

'To a normal person, that rationale would make perfect sense. But we're talking about Baqri and this guy is a sandwich short of a picnic.'

'You think? At Baqri's picnic, you'll find him sat between the Mad Hatter and The March Hare!' said Luna.

Tom smiled at his wife and chuckled. It was good to have Luna there. She had always been a great sounding board for his thoughts. He was just not used to seeing her wearing an FBI jacket.

'We really shouldn't be laughing about this, should we?' said Luna.

'Some things are just so terrible that you have to laugh or cry. I'll save my tears for later.'

'What about the King? What happens if Baqri or The Collective find out that he's still alive?' asked Luna.

'Difficult to say. My guess is that Baqri will want to punish the US. I mean what could make him any happier than potentially wiping out millions of Americans? But for The Collective, the King's re-appearance could de-rail their Congo initiative. I imagine they will want Baqri to find another way of dealing with the King and painting America in a bad light.'

'One that condemns America in the eyes of the world?'

'Yeah. They won't want the King standing up and saying how great America has been at protecting him. I would expect they would have some sort of back-up plan for just such an event. The question is whether they have enough influence over Baqri to get him to refrain from launching that last weapon.'

'I've still heard nothing on the news to say that the attacks earlier on Arizona and Ohio were terror related, by the way,' said Luna.

'So far, the president has successfully managed to keep a lid on it. She's worried that there would just be mass panic – which there would be, of course.'

'It will get out soon though, surely?'

'Yes, I'm certain it will. Just a matter of time. So, we've got to move quick.'

'Have you got a plan?'

Tom pulled open one of the drawers in his desk and took out what was clearly a very well-read book.

'*The Art of War*,' said Luna, raising her eyebrows. 'He left one of those at the Waldorf for me.'

'Indeed. Ironically, this copy was left for me as a present by Baqri during his recent attack on Britain.' Tom opened the book up to a page that had been dog-eared. '*War has lies as its foundation and profit as its spring*. That's my plan.'

'So, lies then. That's your plan.'

'I would prefer to call it deception.'

'I guess I've been called in as part of your plan then.'

'I'm afraid so. It feels so strange … and really not right … that I'm sending my wife out on dangerous missions. Don't get me wrong. I know you're the best at what you do. But it still feels wrong.'

'Yeah, not really how a good husband goes on,' replied Luna. 'Look, Tom. I was specially selected and trained for this all those years ago, just like you. A level of training that no other agent has ever gone through. Trust me. I'll be fine.'

'I know. Sorry, I can't help it.'

Tom looked on as his wife stood up, smiled and walked towards the door. She turned to Tom who was now standing behind her. 'Anyway, look, I've got a meeting to get to. But before I go, I believe my husband still owes me something.'

Tom held his wife's hand and looked intensely into her eyes, before sweeping back her blond hair with his fingers and delivering on his offer with a long, passionate kiss.

Tom said, 'I'll join you soon. I've just got to have another chat with our friend down the hall.'

CHAPTER TWENTY-SEVEN

While the rest of his team were watching the news headlines that were dominating all the main television channels, Baqri was sat in the corner of his living room and perched on the edge of his chair – staring intensely at the laptop.

'Are you still watching that video?' asked Brigid, walking over to him. 'I didn't think that even you could get so much pleasure from watching the King get blown up again and again and again.'

'Well, I just can't quite believe that it's all gone to plan. Especially as they have the British bloodhound working for them. I expected more from him, I guess. A clever plan to get Monroe out of her predicament. But I have to say, that it does look like we've done it. Have a look, Brigid. That is the King, is it not?' said Baqri, freezing an image of King Edward waving out of the window, just seconds before the explosion.

'Does look like him to me,' sighed Brigid. 'Can we move on now? I assume we're going to get ourselves off to a friendly country?'

'Maybe.'

'What do you mean by *maybe*?'

'Well, we have the Americans by the short and curlies. Why give that up? Think what else I could force them to do.'

Baqri rewound the video clip to the moment that the King walked out of The White House.

'There he is, right?'

'Yes, Mohammed. There he is.' Brigid rolled her eyes as Baqri continued playing the video.

'Now he gets into his Rolls-Royce and it sets off. But it stops shortly afterwards. The royal protection officer, who had got in the back with him, now gets back out. Why?'

'Who knows? Perhaps the King didn't like the smell of him or something. Or maybe the King didn't feel that anyone else should be in the back with him, apart from the Queen.'

'The Queen who was conveniently ill that morning.'

'Do you know something? You're too suspicious. Sometimes things are simply what they appear to be.'

'Yes, you're right, Brigid. I should have more faith in my genius. I should follow the advice of Sun Tzu. He did say that you have to believe in yourself, you know.'

'Of course, he did,' replied Brigid mockingly.

'I had asked The Collective to confirm that it was definitely the King that got into that car. And they did. You should never assume Brigid. It's the mother of all cockups.'

Baqri replayed the clip again of the King getting into his Rolls and the protection officer getting out.

'Do you know what? Something is bugging me about this but I can't work out what,' Baqri continued, scratching his goatee.

'Or perhaps you're just looking for an excuse to send that last missile?'

'There it is!' Baqri exclaimed, jumping up from his seat. 'Look Brigid.'

Brigid stared at the laptop screen as Baqri played and then quickly rewound it. The King got in and the protection officer got out. She frowned at Baqri.

'You still can't see it? Look here at the King waving at the crowd. He uses his right hand. He then gets into the back of the Rolls. When the Royal Protection Officer gets into the back with him, he opens the door with his left hand. But when he gets back out again, he closes the door with his right hand.'

'You've lost me.'

'I think that the royal protection officer who gets back out of the Rolls is actually the King.'

'That's pretty thin, you know. He could have been ambidextrous, you know.'

'Maybe. But I'm going to ask The Collective to check the security personnel register again,' said Baqri, tapping away on his phone.

'Why?'

'Because if someone did take the place of the King, then they knew that they would most likely be killed.'

'But we saw the King waving out the window just before the explosion.'

'Did we? It looked like him, I agree – from a distance. But with modern facial prosthetics, I could even be made to look like you. Don't forget they have the finest people in Hollywood at their disposal.'

It was less than half an hour before Baqri was alerted to a message on his phone.

'There you go. A last-minute change of personnel. Oh, clever …'

'What?'

'It seems that all those *so-called* royal protection officers, who were killed in the bomb blast, had terminal illnesses. All of them. And … get this … none of them had served in that unit before. They were all ex-police or armed forces. And had nothing to lose.'

'Willing to die for their King. The chance for a heroic exit from this world.'

Baqri paced from one side of the room to the other before finally stopping at the window and staring out.

'So, it seems that the King may be alive after all.'

'Bet you didn't expect that?'

'That bloody president! What is wrong with her? I've killed thousands of her people to show my resolve and told her that my last missile has enough polonium to kill millions. And yet she still doesn't do as she's told.' Baqri banged his fist on the window.

'What are you going to do?'

'I'm not sure. But if I want to stay on-side with The Collective, then I guess I better find a way to get their plans back on track. The reappearance of the King would be a disaster.'

Baqri walked over to the middle of the room and picked up his sat phone.

'Who are you calling?' asked Brigid.

'The world's most belligerent woman, President Jane Monroe. Looks like we need to kill the King again. And this time he needs to stay dead.'

CHAPTER TWENTY-EIGHT

'Well now, Jim,' said Tom hobbling back into the meeting room. 'It's time for you to complete part one of the deal that will get you a step further to that rural idyl with your family and a new life.'

Tom walked around the back of James McInnis, who was still sat at the table, and placed his phone down in front of him.

'What do you want me to do?' queried McInnis.

'I want you to get into that app of yours and contact The Collective.'

'And say what?'

'Tell them that the Americans have discovered where the last Avangard HGV is being hidden and are sending in Special Forces in to capture it.'

McInnis's face changed from slightly puzzled to completely baffled.

'Why on earth would they listen to anything that I say now?'

'Because you're a member of The Collective.'

'Well, I was. Right up until the point that you told them that I had betrayed them. You do remember that they sent a hit squad after me, don't you?'

Tom put his hands on McInnis's shoulders before giving him a pat on the arm.

'Ah, yes. About that. Do you remember anything about that hit squad?'

'Not really. It all happened so quickly and they were masked.'

'Yes, I realise that. But if you think back, some of them might have had accents, for example? Or maybe, despite them being masked, you could see their skin colour? Have a think.'

For a minute or so, McInnis stared at the table and thought. He closed his eyes and tried re-living that harrowing experience.

'Actually, thinking about it, I'm sure the guy who appeared to be their leader was black. Does that help?'

'Did he have a very deep voice? Did he perhaps have an English accent?'

'Yeah, he did,' replied McInnis, with a hint of excitement. 'Do you know him?'

'Indeed, I do. That man is Aaron Jax. Captain Aaron Jax to be exact, of His Majesty's SAS.'

'The Collective have got members of the SAS working for them?'

'Errr … no. Most of the participants were very much loyal members of the British Special Forces. Ironically, the only Americans present were you, your Secret Service driver and my wife, Luna. The President personally vouched for the Secret Service agent, whom she has known for many years. He's very much alive and well, by the way. They all are.'

McInnis tried standing up but a firm application of pressure to his shoulders by Tom ensured that he stayed sat down.

'What the hell is going on?' McInnis protested.

'Well, you see, The Collective didn't really try to kill you. It was … what's the word? Oh yes. A ruse. That's the word I was looking for.'

'A ruse?' repeated McInnis.

'Yes, Jax and his team were on loan to us. We can thank MI5 Director, Iain MacGregor for sorting that one out. Before you ask, the president authorised their use on American soil. In fact, she made a formal request to the British.'

'She allowed British troops to be used in Washington? She's gone too far.'

'Desperate times call for desperate measures. Difficult for her to know who to trust in her own military and security services at the moment, of course. She simply couldn't take the risk. So, I suggested importing trusted people that I know. Technically, of course, it wasn't a case of British troops on US soil. They were seconded to the American military, so their use was quite lawful. And they were under direct orders from the commander in chief of the United States, at the end of the day.'

'So, what happened to me was all just a show?'

'Indeed, it was. We needed you to think that The Collective were hunting you down to get you to co-operate. And now, of course, we have recordings of you saying that you're going to spill your guts about them and help track down the other members of the organisation. Obviously, they will hunt you down if those recordings ever got out.'

'You bastard.'

'Now, now, Jim. The good news is that nothing has changed for you. You just need to do as I ask, and then enjoy that very generous deal offered to you by the president.'

McInnis stared back down at the table – the realisation hitting home that he had been expertly manoeuvred into a corner.

'Come on, Jim. You really don't have big range of options here, do you? But you do still have a great opportunity for a new life. Take it.'

'But you can't guarantee my safety, can you? Or my family? Not a hundred percent? Not against these people.'

'Tell me something that you can guarantee a hundred percent?'

'The love of my family.'

Tom placed his hand on McInnis's shoulder again.

'I'm not even going to try and understand why you have done the things that you have done, Jim. Why you would betray your president and your country. Perhaps you never imagined it would go as far as it did. Perhaps you thought that just giving a bit of information away here and there couldn't do much harm and the reward at the end would be worth it? I don't know. I'm sure you had your reasons at the time. And no, I can't guarantee your safety a hundred percent. But what I can guarantee a hundred percent, is that if you don't cooperate, you will go to the electric chair and your family's final memories of you will be that you were executed for being a traitor.'

McInnis looked back at Tom with a furrowed brow.

'Oh, God. What have I done?' he sobbed, with his head in his hands. 'I had everything. And I've just ruined it. What was I thinking? How I wish that I could turn back time, Tom.'

'I can't help you with that but you do have the opportunity to try and do the right thing.'

'I will. I'll do whatever I can, of course. Just tell what you want me to do.'

'That's good, Jim. First thing that I want you to do is send that message to The Collective. Tell them that US Special Forces are moving on the location of the last Avangard.'

'I assume, we don't actually know where it is?'

'Not a clue.'

'So, what are you hoping is going to happen?'

'Well, first thing is that Baqri will be forced to try and move it. We should then be able to find it on satellite as it appears from the cave or wherever it's being kept in southern Russia.'

'But the Russians won't take kindly to American boots on the ground in their country. This could lead us into a war.'

'I don't think we will get to that stage. I believe that President Petrov will take action to ensure the retrieval of his new weapon system rather than risk it falling into American hands. Once we have confirmation that he has taken it back then the crisis will be over.'

'Then what?'

'Well, first we have the architect of the catastrophe from the last few days to track down. Then we need to get ourselves a bright lamp.'

'Sorry? What do you mean?'

'The best way to find something lurking in the shadows, is to turn a light on it. And I think The Collective have been hiding there long enough.'

CHAPTER TWENTY-NINE

'Oh, for God's sake!' said Baqri looking at his phone.

'What now?' asked Brigid, who was sat on the sofa with her feet up on the coffee table.

'I'll tell you what. Apparently, the Americans have found out where we are hiding the last Hyper-Glide Vehicle. They're sending in a Special Forces unit.'

'Well, just tell them to back off or you'll launch it at one of their cities.'

'I'm going to. But you're missing the point.'

Baqri clenched his fists and flung himself into the nearest armchair – behaviour more like a spoilt child, than the most infamous terrorist on the planet.

'Arrrghhh! That bloody woman.'

'Who?'

'President pig-headed Monroe. That's who.'

'Oh, right.'

'Don't just say *oh, right,*' snapped Baqri. 'Why can't she just do as she's told. She's ruining my plans.'

'Sorry but what point am I missing, Mo?'

'The Americans aren't the threat. The Russians are.'

'Why?'

'Because if the Russians think that the Americans are going to capture their amazing new Avangard weapon, then they're going to be sending their own forces to get it first.'

'Do you think the Russians know where it is then?'

'Absolutely. They've been letting it play out. Pretending they don't know where it is. Just sitting back and watching America suffer.'

'What are you going to do?'

'I've got no choice,' replied Baqri tapping a contact on his phone.

Baqri walked over to the window and looked out at the twinkling lights over the Washington skyline. A place that he had recently found to be a source of solace when life threw up its inevitable challenges.

'It's me. You need to move the HGV. Take it to position B on your map. Stay alert. Is the good doctor behaving himself? Good. The Russians will now be coming for you, so make sure Doctor Farooqi is kept out of harm's way. His safety is critical,' said Baqri. 'Now put Alexei on.'

'I've done all that you've asked of me,' said Alexei Nevsky, after a short pause. 'Now I want to see my family again.'

'Nearly, Alexei. You will be with your family again very soon. I have to say that your piloting of the first two Avangards was very impressive. I may, however, have one more mission for you before we can reunite you with your wife and children. Further instructions coming to you soon,' said Baqri ending his brief call.

'You're going to let him go and see his family again? Well, I never saw that coming.'

'I've no more need for him if we end up sending the final Avangard. Anyway, I didn't say that I was going to let him see his family.'

'Yes, you did.'

'No. I actually said that he would be reunited with his family.'

'And the difference is?'

'He doesn't need to be alive for that.'

Brigid lifted her feet off the table, moved to the front of the couch, and perched on the edge.

'You're going to send his body back to his family?'

'Yeah. But they won't care.'

'I think they will.'

'No, they really won't.' Baqri looked at Brigid unabashed and shrugged his shoulders. 'They were a drain on resources.'

Brigid thought that she had become accustomed to Baqri's extreme behaviour but, this time, even she sat in silence and just stared at him.

'You don't approve?' asked Baqri.

'Killing a whole family? An innocent family? Of course, I don't. At least I only kill people who deserve it.'

'Like the King? You tried to kill him, don't forget. Did he deserve it?'

'That was a necessity. I only agreed to do that because you promised to help me kill Tom Rivers.'

'You seem very flexible with your definition of someone who *deserves it*.'

Brigid dropped back into the couch and exhaled heavily. She knew that this was an argument that she was never going to win.

'So, now what?' she asked. 'It looks like the King is still alive and you've got both the Americans and the Russians after your last missile. Hey, I'm not a great strategist like you, but it looks to me like you're screwed.'

'Thank you for your extraordinary insight, Brigid.'

'Just saying.'

'Well, don't.'

'I do agree, though, that Monroe's actions were quite a surprise,' said Brigid. 'I mean you demonstrate your capability by sending two HGVs which she knows will result in the deaths of thousands of her citizens. You tell her that if she doesn't assist in killing the King, then you'll send one that will kill millions more. And yet she still doesn't comply.'

'Because she knew that if she did then America would lose its allies and become the prime target for every organisation like ours around the world.'

'And because she has Tom Rivers advising her. You should have helped me kill him when we had the chance.'

'Perhaps. I always thought of him as a worthy adversary but now he's really starting to hack me off.'

'Hate to say it but for every plan you come up with, he's got a better one.'

'So, it seems. And thanks again for pointing that out. But I'm not beaten yet.'

'Why don't you just fire that last HGV at somewhere like New York. Be done with it. You'll fall out with The Collective but you'll go down in history.'

'As I said before; I've got my reasons.'

'OK. Fair enough.'

'And anyway, we're not screwed, as you so eloquently put it. As far as President Monroe knows, I still have the capability to decimate one of her major cities. Time to make my demands before they find the last HGV.'

'So, The Collective still want the King dead, I guess?'

'They clearly don't know yet that he's still alive. I'm going to rectify our little issue before they do. Time to call the president.'

CHAPTER THIRTY

It had already felt like a very long day for President Jane Monroe. It was now 9 p.m. and her national security team had reconvened in the White House Situation Room.

'I believe that you have some good news for us, Admiral,' said Monroe.

'Indeed, I do,' replied Womack, glancing at Tom. 'We have received some important intelligence as to the whereabouts of the last Avangard HGV.'

'That's fantastic!' exclaimed Secretary of State Walt Houston. 'So, what's the plan?'

'We're sending a Special Forces detachment into southern Russia to capture it. We're going to put an end to this nightmare,' Monroe replied.

'Whoa! Surely if Baqri gets a whiff of this, then he'll just launch it. Are we really going to risk the lives of millions of Americans? Because if that's the plan, then, with the greatest of respect Madam President, it's nuts,' said a flabbergasted Vice President.

'Not sure we have an option, Jed. We can't carry on with this threat hanging over us. At some point we have to deal with it,' replied Monroe.

'And has anyone considered the fact that we will be sending US troops into Russian sovereign territory?' continued Stone. 'This is tantamount to a declaration of war!'

The tension in the room was broken with the ringing of the Situation Room phone. James McInnis answered.

'It's Baqri, Madam President.'

'Put him on speaker.'

'Madam President, you continue to defy me,' Baqri said scoldingly. 'I've decided that your country must now pay the ultimate price. So, sit there and watch as I kill millions of your citizens. The blame must lay entirely at your feet.'

'Mr Baqri, this is Vice President Jed Stone. I don't get why you're so angry? We complied with your wishes regarding the assassination of the King. At great cost to this country. So, why are you doing this?'

'Firstly, because I know that you are intending to send a Special Forces unit to try and capture the last HGV. And secondly because you *didn't* comply with our agreement regarding the King.'

'You've lost me.'

'Oh, I see. It seems that your President didn't include you in her plan. The King is still very much alive, isn't he Madam President?'

'I don't know what you're talking about,' said Monroe. 'The King was killed in your rocket attack.'

'Are we really going to play this game?' growled Baqri. 'You're lying. You say he's already dead – then prove it. But if I'm right, and he's still alive … well, you know what you will have to do.'

'Mr Baqri, you fired a high explosive missile through the roof of the King's car,' said President Monroe. 'What do you think happened to the occupants? There isn't a body as such that we can provide you.'

'I don't believe you. You can't provide it because he's still alive. But you can always prove me wrong, of course, and send me what remains of the King. His head will do. But we both know you can't. Anyway, if you're going to maintain this lie, then I will give you just thirty minutes to deliver his remains to a place of my choosing.'

'That's not enough time.'

'Thirty minutes, Madam President. That should give you just long enough to scoop him up and put him into a bag. But if you miss your deadline or I'm not convinced that it's the King, then I'm going to launch the last HGV. There is, however, another option.'

'Go on.'

'You can drop the false pretences. I will then give you a little extra time to deal with the King and deliver his body to me.'

'What do you mean?'

'What I mean, Madam President, is that you're going to have to execute him. But I appreciate that you might experience little issues such as dealing with his security detail. So, I will be generous and give you a whole hour from now to do that – plus a further half an hour to deliver his body. But there is one extra condition to this.'

'What?

'To prove that you have met your extended deadline to execute him, I want you to send me immediate video proof of the King's demise.'

'I don't know what to say.' Monroe closed her eyes and exhaled.

'You can do it Madam President. An hour to execute him and then a further thirty minutes to deliver his body. Oh, and I expect the video to show his certain death. So, chop his head off or shoot him in the head – I really don't care. But I expect to see him dead. I'll send you the details of where to send the footage. Again, if you miss either of these deadlines, then the HGV will be launched. I assume you understand your options?'

'I do.'

'So, to summarise, I will expect a video of the King's execution within the hour. I will shortly send over the location for where to then deliver his body. You could always prove me wrong, of course, and deliver a King-in-a-bag within the next thirty minutes – but we both know that's not going to happen. I would also strongly suggest that you don't drag this ridiculous charade out any longer. Time is a precious resource and you don't have much of it,' said Baqri, ending the call.

Monroe looked around the table at the mix of facial expressions from those present – which was mostly bewilderment.

'What the hell is going on?' asked Vice President Jed Stone.

'It's a bit complicated, Jed,' Monroe said.

The president looked across at Tom Rivers and then back to the Vice President.

'I'm sorry, Madam President. I don't get what you mean,' said Stone.

'What I mean, Jed, is that Baqri is correct about the King. He is still alive.'

Audible gasps and mutterings followed from around the room. The president raised her hand.

'Ladies and gentlemen. Ladies and gentlemen,' said Monroe. '*Ladies and gentlemen*,' she repeated for a third time – but now raising her voice.

Jed Stone said, 'Madam President, I am, along with my colleagues I assume, completely stunned by this revelation. We all saw the King being assassinated – as did the whole country. How on earth can he still be alive?'

'Because the person that was killed was a body double. The King is alive and well and in a safe house.'

'With respect, Madam President, are you saying that this was planned? That the King was never in any danger of being assassinated?' asked Secretary Houston.

'That's correct, Walt.'

'Sorry,' said Stone, 'I think I must be misunderstanding this. It sounds like you're telling us that you decided to ignore what we previously agreed to here? Am I reading that right?' added Stone.

'I'm the president, Jed. As much as I appreciate the opinion and advice of everyone here, I am the one who will make the ultimate decisions.'

'I'm sure we all appreciate that, Madam President, but I remember being told earlier that alpha particles emitted from polonium were the most lethal things on the planet. I distinctly remember Rachael saying that a millionth of a gram of polonium could kill someone,' said Walt Houston.

'And we believed that Baqri had enough to wipe out the entire population of one of our biggest cities,' added Stone.

'Ladies and gentlemen,' said Monroe, knocking the tabletop with her knuckles, until the chatter in the room subsided. 'You have all seen the reaction around the world to what was believed to be the King's assassination. Allies have already shunned us and we have found ourselves much more isolated.'

'In addition,' said Rachael Goldberg, 'I can confirm that our intelligence has started receiving reports that terrorist organisations are planning attacks on this country, as a result of our weakened state. This has been confirmed by our remaining allies.'

Monroe said, 'And all this, while non-friendly nations look to take advantage. This is a glimpse at what our future would have been, had we agreed to Baqri's demands.'

'So, you thought we should try and trick him? Risk countless American lives?' asked Stone.

'Be mindful of your tone, Jed. My plan was that we would have Baqri in custody by now and then we could triumphantly announce that the King is still alive. Instead of disengaged allies, we would have ones that would have owed us a huge debt of gratitude. Instead of destroying our relationships with them, it would have cemented them into something much stronger than ever before. It was a risk, yes. But there is no doubt in my mind that it was worth it.'

'Yes, it's so much better now,' muttered Stone under his breath. 'Thank goodness we decided to go down that route.'

'So now we are going to be forced to execute the King – and video it? For Baqri to play again and again over social media?' said Houston.

'God, this is a complete disaster. It's way worse than him being assassinated by terrorists!' exclaimed Stone. 'This will be the biggest media frenzy in history. I can see the headlines now – *America executes the British monarch*!'

'I assume that there is no chance that our Special Forces will intercept that HGV within the next half an hour?' asked Goldberg.

Admiral Womack shook his head. Even though communications with British intelligence had officially been severed, Womack was surprised to receive information from MI5's Director, Iain MacGregor, on the whereabouts of the remaining HGV. He guessed that he had Tom to thank for that.

'The current ETA of the Delta Force team is just over an hour and half, Madam President,' said Womack. 'They won't get there before Baqri's deadline to execute the King but we are confident that they will capture it when they do arrive – unless the Russians get there first.'

'You're very quiet, Jim,' said Houston. 'What's your take on this?'

'Well, I'm as shocked as everyone else, of course. Given the current timescales, I don't see any other option but to comply with Baqri's demands,' said McInnis, trying to look confident and not like his world had just fallen apart.

'Tom?' said Stone.

'I agree, Mr Vice President. We will need to do the unthinkable.'

President Monroe slowly rose from her seat, put both hands on the Situation Room table and looked up at her advisers.

'Then it's agreed,' said President Monroe. 'I will speak to the King. Knowing him as I do, I imagine he will simply accept his fate rather than see millions of people killed. It is clear that we are going to ask him to make the ultimate sacrifice.'

CHAPTER THIRTY-ONE

'I can confirm, Mr President, that the information that you received is correct. The last missing HGV is on the move,' said Viktor Gorsky, standing to attention in front of the Russian President's desk. 'Your source is clearly very well connected.'

'Please, Colonel,' said President Petrov, indicating with his hand towards one of the red leather chairs opposite his desk.

As Gorsky made himself comfortable, President Petrov walked over to his drinks cabinet in the corner of his office. The bottles mainly consisted of vodkas with two bottles of whisky sat in the back row. He reached for the half-full bottle in the middle of the front row and two tumblers.

'Would you join me in a glass, Viktor?' asked Petrov rhetorically, pouring the vodka. 'Did you know that Tsarskaya was the favourite drink of Peter the Great?'

'I think I have heard that before somewhere, sir,' replied Gorsky, knowing full well that Petrov was the person who had originally told him. And not just the once.

Petrov placed one of the glasses in front of Gorsky and returned to his seat.

'We have a couple of problems, Viktor.'

'Sir?'

'I have received information that the reason why Baqri is moving the HGV is that the Americans have managed to locate it. They are expected to intercept it in just over an hour. So, I have instructed General Volkov to take possession of it before they do.'

'The Americans are sending troops into Russia?'

'They'll be covert Black Ops. The Americans will say that it was an unsanctioned operation by a group of mercenaries. At any rate, Volkov assures me that his units will intercept it shortly and so the efforts of the Americans will be futile.'

'That is good, sir. Isn't it?' said Gorsky, frowning at his president.

'Yes, of course!' replied Petrov throwing his hands in the air and laughing. 'It's very good news. We've successfully managed to help the Americans humiliate themselves on the world stage as well as witness them losing allies and influence along the way. What's not to love about that?'

'So, why do I get the feeling that there's something else, Mr President?'

'Well, the other problem that we have is that my source tells me that the integrity of the HGV has been compromised and polonium is escaping.'

'How did that happen?'

'That's not clear but we need to adapt to how we deal with it.'

'Of course, sir. What would you like me to do?'

'I want you to call General Volkov and tell him that the FSB has received reliable intelligence that the last Avangard is leaking polonium. Tell him that you have taken this to me and that his orders are, once he has secured the HGV, to set up a cordon. It will need to be half a mile radius from the weapon to ensure the safety of his troops. His main priority will be to ensure that no one else can access it – especially the Americans, of course – and to wait for the special radiological team to arrive.'

'I see,' said Gorsky hesitantly. 'But could I ask why you want me to say that the information came to the FSB and not to yourself?'

'Because I don't want Volkov asking questions about my source. As I'm sure you realise, my contact is close to the terrorist cell and I don't want their cover to be compromised by the general poking his nose in.'

'I understand Mr President.'

'I knew you would Gorsky. Just think, the FSB – and you in particular – will get all the credit. You will have prevented the deaths of many Russian soldiers who would have got too close to the polonium.'

'Thank you for that, sir.'

'You know that your boss is due to retire soon, Gorsky?'

'I do, sir.'

'Good. Just checking,' said Petrov with a nod.

The pinging of an alert from the president's phone abruptly ended the conversation.

'Thank you, Colonel. That will be all,' said Petrov, still looking down at his phone.

Viktor Gorsky glanced at his glass – which still sat on the president's desk untouched. As much as he was tempted to throw the contents down his neck in one go, he wasn't sure if that would be appropriate behaviour in front of his commander in chief. He rose to his feet but, in an unusually reckless move, decided that he was going to do it anyway and disposed of the vodka in one swift move. He was sure that his boss would have done the same in his position. *It was, at the end of the day, a vodka that was far too good to waste*, he thought, as he walked out of the president's office.

Petrov never looked up but just smiled. Gorsky reminded him of his younger self.

'I would agree, Odin - whoever you are. *Farsight* is definitely now an issue. I will second your motion,' Petrov whispered, tapping on his phone. 'Time for a vote.'

President Petrov watched intensely as green ticks started appearing on his phone screen one after another and finishing with a flurry. Just the odd red cross dissented to the proposal. He placed his phone on the desk and turned his chair around to look out through his window at the rooftops of the Russian capital.

Petrov considered the momentous decision that had just been taken.

So, it is agreed. The die is cast.

CHAPTER THIRTY-TWO

Tom Rivers had returned to 'Little Britain', deep inside The White House, accompanied by James McInnis and his chaperone from the Secret Service. As soon as he walked in, McInnis looked uncomfortable – his eyes darting around the office.

'If you're worried that The Collective may have managed to bug it, then you shouldn't. This is my inner sanctum and it's swept for devices so many times a day that I lose count. In addition, that little camera in the corner automatically activates if anyone enters the room and sends the images to my phone in real time. Trust me, no one else will find out about your current position.'

'That's good to know,' said McInnis, sitting down in one of the chairs opposite Tom's desk.

'In this humble little office, I discuss with the president – and other people that we trust – what is really going on and our strategy in response. Out there, it's just smoke and mirrors.'

'By the way, are you going to have him follow me everywhere?' asked McInnis, pointing at the closed door with the agent stood outside.

Tom said, 'That's generally what happens when you're under arrest, Jim. I don't want you to be under any misunderstanding as to your position. Despite the normal appearance that you are being allowed to convey to everyone, you're still facing the death penalty for treason.'

'But I've done everything that you've asked.'

'So far. But there's more for you to do before you can disappear and wave goodbye to the electric chair.'

'Like what?'

'That's what we are here to discuss.'

'Can I ask you something?'

'Go on.'

'How the hell did MI5 manage to find out where the last HGV was when our intelligence hadn't got a clue.'

'They didn't.'

'Sorry?'

'MI5 didn't have a clue either. We made it up.'

'You made it up?' repeated a baffled James McInnis.

'Yeah. We picked a location inside southern Russia that American special forces could get to in just over an hour and then Iain MacGregor at MI5 passed it on to Admiral Womack like it was confirmed intelligence.'

'And Womack didn't check the intelligence.'

'Sworn to silence by the president. She told him that MacGregor had gone out on a limb for us and we wouldn't want it getting back to the British government that he had provided unsanctioned intelligence. Womack was told to keep shtum and not discuss it with anyone until the meeting we just had.'

'But why would you share false intelligence with the US National Security Council?'

'Because the president's administration is leaking information like a sieve. In some ways this is a good thing. I'm sure you're not the only person who sided with The Collective, Jim. Admiral Womack's confirmation has just backed up the message that you sent back to them earlier. Again, you have supplied what is believed to be reliable information. It will force the Russians to take immediate action and retrieve the last HGV.'

'And the King?'

'I'm sure of two things. Firstly, had we not gone down the route of deciding to execute the King, then Baqri would have immediately launched the last Avangard and any minute now we would have been facing disaster on an apocalyptic scale. Secondly, if we just give the Russians a little time, they will capture the weapon. Let's be honest, they're properly incentivised now with US Special Forces closing in.'

'And Baqri?'

'I think we need now to force Mr Baqri out of his little hiding hole. Which brings me to your next assignment. Look at it as another big step towards your happy retirement.'

'Go on.'

'Shortly, I want you to send out another message via the app that The Collective have hijacked.'

'Saying what?'

'Saying that Benny Erikson has sold out Baqri and provided tracking details for a tiny divice that's installed in his sat phone. You remember Benny, don't you? Has the nickname of *Benny the Bomb*.'

'The arms dealer. He supplied Baqri with the phone and other bits – if I remember correctly.'

'That's the one. Say that the FBI have now pin-pointed Baqri's location and are moving in. Then suggest that Baqri's position is now untenable and he should be extracted to a country that … should we say … is not America friendly. Propose that he makes his way to a small private airport just outside Washington.'

'Where you'll be waiting, I guess.'

'Not me personally, of course. Not sure I'll be much help with my walking cane.'

'Do you think he will bite?'

'I'm sure of it. He trusts the information from The Collective and as far as they know, you're still a member.'

'And I imagine that Baqri will be forced to ditch or destroy his sat phone.'

'He will have to.'

'That's going to make it a whole lot more difficult for him to communicate,' said McInnis.

'And way more risky,' added Tom.

McInnis looked down and started twiddling his thumbs. The James McInnis that Tom first met seemed to be a shadow of his former self. Gone was the confident – almost cocky – demeanour that McInnis was famous for and, instead, a quiet, sombre, and more reflective person had emerged.

'Something on your mind?' asked Tom.

'I've just realised just how much I'm sticking my neck out. The Collective will hunt me down for ruining their plans and turning on them.'

'They can try. I've been assured that you will just disappear off the radar.'

'I bet you really despise me, don't you? A traitor to my country and my president. I'm surprised you've stayed so calm.'

'I'm calm because, firstly I've been conditioned to stay calm, and secondly because I'm not an American. My wife Luna, who is American, of course, would like to slice you up like a chunk of salami.'

McInnis raised his eyebrows and started fidgeting in his seat, knowing that Luna was somewhere in The White House. She already had a reputation for being significantly less restrained than her husband.

'Don't worry. She knows the score. You won't become deli meat if you continue to cooperate,' said Tom.

'You said you've been conditioned?'

'I was. Many years ago, the British Secret Service had started a new programme where they would identify people with superior genetics and, if they were suitable, recruit them. Through MI5 sorcery, those genetics were enhanced to allow the new agent to be the best that they could be. Once training was complete, the agent was then put into a type a sleeper state and returned back to the community until needed. But the other thing that they did was to condition your mind. And this is what allows me to still think clearly under extreme pressure. Don't get me wrong, I'm not devoid of emotion. I'm easily irritated but full anger is usually kept under control.'

'Wasn't Luna also a sleeper. Didn't she get the same conditioning?'

'Yeah … she did. What can I tell you? Let's just say that when it came to restraint and control, her starting point was at a different level to mine.'

'Tom … I just wanted you to know that I'm not a bad guy. I'm really not. The thing is, I've got a daughter. She has leukaemia. It's an incurable disease.'

'I'm sorry to hear that.'

'What I'm trying to say is that the doctors have given her a year at most. The Collective told me that they can save her. They said that they have access to special treatments. New drugs that aren't available to the health service. I didn't join The Collective for the money.'

'I understand that, Jim. And if all you had done was something like a bit of minor fraud, then you would have my complete sympathy. But your actions have helped Baqri murder thousands of Americans – including children. Other people's children. There's no justification for that.'

McInnis hung his head and nodded. The silence that followed was broken by a brief knock on the door, as President Monroe entered the room. After a contemptuous glance at McInnis, the president turned her attention to Tom.

'All organized?' asked Monroe.

'We're ready to go, Madam President. And I have some interesting news for you.'

'You can go now, Mr McInnis,' said Monroe. 'Agent Williams will escort you back to your office.'

As McInnis closed the door behind him, President Monroe sat herself down in the now vacant seat. Tom took a deep breath.

'As agreed, we monitored any use of the app used by The Collective before, during and immediately after your National Security meeting,' said Tom.

'Have the techies managed to break their messaging system then?'

'Not yet. It's protected by all sorts of firewalls and safeguards but they're working on it. But I do have something. It's not conclusive, as it's a popular games app that they are currently using to communicate with each other.'

'Go on.'

'Well, you're probably aware that the CIA have hackers who have for some time now been able to get into Apple and Android devices. I think this was made public in some Wikileaks reveal.'

'Yes, they kindly briefed me on it *after* it had become public.'

'Oh, right. Well, I asked the CIA to monitor the phones of every person who attends your national security meetings. Even down to the people that bring in the refreshments. We were hoping to see if someone would open up that games app.'

'And?'

'Someone did. Within five minutes of the conclusion of one of the most important meetings in American history.'

'Someone logged in? Someone who was at the National Security Council meeting?'

'Yes. Just one person.'

'Who?'

'You're really not going to like this. It's Vice President Stone.'

CHAPTER THIRTY-THREE

The 9.30 p.m. 'King-in-a-bag' deadline had been and gone and, since then, Baqri had been pacing around the apartment relentlessly, only interspersing it with the occasional stop at the window where he would quietly grumble away to himself.

'Well, that's time,' announced Brigid. 'One hour and still no sign that they've executed the King.'

'Unbelievable,' replied Baqri spinning around. 'What is wrong with her?'

A 'ping' alerted Brigid to a new e-mail. She grabbed the laptop from the glass-topped coffee table in front of her and opened up the new message.

'Hold up, hold up,' she said, with a hint of excitement in her voice. 'We have a video.'

'Really?' said Baqri, genuinely surprised and striding over to join her.

The unexpected news brought Zane and Idris swiftly to the coffee table as well, where they squeezed around the small screen. The image was unmistakably that of King Edward sat in large high backed green leather chair. To his right was a small side table with a glass of water sat on it. Another figure that both Baqri and Brigid recognised approached the King.

'Turn it up, turn it up,' barked Baqri at Brigid.

Brigid complied and the voice of Luna Rivers could distinctly be heard, as she held out a small silver salver with what appeared to be two white pills sitting on a napkin in the middle of it.

'Your majesty,' said Luna, with a bow of her head.

The King simply smiled gently, said, 'thank you' and picked the pills up off the napkin. He then looked directly at the camera.

'I would like to make a statement. I, Edward, by the Grace of God, of the United Kingdom of Great Britain and Northern Ireland and of other Realms and Territories, King, Head of the Commonwealth and Defender of the Faith, do declare that I freely and willingly agree to forfeit my life in order to preserve the lives of others.'

With little further ceremony, the King reached for the glass of water, placed the pills into his mouth and swallowed a large gulp of water. It was just a matter of minutes before the King's head dropped and he slumped to the side of his seat.

'Don't you wish you could come out with a title like that?' said Brigid looking around at Baqri.

'So, is he dead then?' asked Baqri, ignoring her quip. 'I mean all I've seen is a lot of drama followed by a very posh man falling asleep in a chair. He could have just nodded off as far as I know.'

Any doubt that Baqri had, swiftly evaporated as Luna approached the King with a pistol by her side. Having placed her fingers on the side of the King's neck for a pulse, she lifted her pistol and aimed for the centre of his forehead.

'Please forgive me, Your Majesty,' said Luna, before pulling the trigger.

For once Baqri was temporarily lost for words and the silence extended to everyone else in the room. The shocking image of the King slumped in his seat, with a bullet hole in the centre of his forehead, felt unreal and impossible. But there it was and there seemed to be little room for doubt that a shot had passed through the King's head and out the back of the chair.

'Holy Maloney,' said Baqri breaking the silence. 'They've really done it.'

'They really have,' agreed Brigid, with her hand over her mouth. 'I can't believe it.'

'Me neither.'

It took another minute or so before Baqri broke the silence once again.

'OK, so what we need to do now is make sure he's dead.'

'You did see a bullet go through his brain, didn't you,' replied Brigid. 'I'm no doctor but I'm pretty sure that would kill him.'

'As Sherlock Holmes said, I presume nothing. We need to make sure it was him and positively identify the body first hand. Not that I don't trust the Americans … well, I don't, of course. They managed to fool us once with the use of prosthetics. I'm not going to be made a fool of again. I've already told Monroe that I want the FBI to deliver the body to a disused industrial estate. Brigid and Zane, you will go and check. Take some photos. The King in a body bag. That's not going to be an image that the Americans will enjoy all over the media.'

An alert from his phone drew Baqri's attention to a new app message from The Collective.

'What the hell!' bellowed Baqri. 'Are you kidding me?'

'What?' asked Brigid.

'Apparently Benny *the Bomb* has sold me out! My sat phone has some sort of tracking device in it apparently and Benny has just made a deal with the Americans to allow them to find me.'

'He's sold us out?' repeated Brigid.

'Have you turned into a parrot, Brigid?' Baqri mocked. 'Hey, no need for that.'

'Yes, OK then. Sorry. I'm never in the best of moods when people ruin my plans – you know that.'

'You should be grateful that you have an organisation like The Collective watching your back,' said Brigid, slightly taken aback by Baqri's unusually conciliatory tone. 'Do you not think we better get going then?'

'You're right, of course. Hang on. There's another message. They want us to make our way to a small private airport just outside Washington where a plane will be waiting. And we need to ditch the sat phone.'

'What about the King?'

'Forget that. If we can't communicate then it's too much of a risk. For all we know it could be a trap.'

'Can we not just use our cell phones?' asked Idris.

'Oh dear. That's why I'm the brains and you're the brawn,' replied Baqri, rolling his eyes. 'Cell phones are much easier to track. That's why I had a specialist sat phone that scrambled my calls. So, no Idris, we are not going to use cell phones. Instead, we will all go to the airport and leave the country.'

'I just thought …' Idris started saying.

'Please don't try doing that again. Just do what I tell you and we'll be fine.'

'But what about the last Avangard HGV? Are you just giving that up to the Americans or the Russians?' asked Brigid.

Baqri walked towards the kitchen and threw his sat phone into the bin. He turned and faced Brigid.

'Oh, no. That one has always been destined for something very special.'

CHAPTER THIRTY-FOUR

President Monroe looked over her lap-top at Tom, who was sat in one of the two leather chairs opposite her desk. It was difficult for her to comprehend the video that she had just watched. But the evidence was there. Probably not enough for a criminal conviction, but it was enough to convince her. An arrest and criminal prosecution were not really what the country needed right now. Not of a senior member of her administration anyway. With so many people killed and so many more likely to die from Baqri's attack, what the country really needed to see was a strong government. If the general population were to discover the existence of The Collective, and just how much influence they had over world governments, then their belief in the system would just crumble. *What would be the point of electing Presidents and those meant to represent the people, if the real power laid with a secretive organization?*

A knock on the Oval Office door interrupted the President's train of thought. James McInnis entered the room. 'Madam President, Vice President Stone is here to see you.'

'Please show him in, Jim,' replied Monroe, trying hard to keep a lid on her growing anger. 'Take a seat, Jed.'

Jed Stone was certainly an impressive looking man. Facially, Baqri's description of him having an uncanny likeness to Major Chip Hazard, from the movie *Small Soldiers*, was amusing but pretty accurate. A former army colonel in the 75th Ranger Regiment, Stone was famous for his relentless fitness regime and was widely respected for his straight talking and no-nonsense attitude. With short cropped dark hair, athletic build and average height, his rugged good looks and immaculate appearance had also resulted in quite a popular following. Always immaculately dressed, often in the finest tailored suits that money could buy, he had adorned the cover of many a magazine. Stone was well educated too and proved to be a strong and reliable running mate at the last presidential election. The president knew that dealing with Jed would be a lot harder than her chief of staff.

'Thank you, Madam President,' said Stone, complying with the instruction and settling himself into the empty chair by Tom. 'I have to say that I was a bit surprised to be told that you wanted to see me. I thought we had a Security Council meeting coming up? I'm guessing something can't wait?'

President Monroe clenched her fists and gritted her teeth. Every ounce of self-control was being utilised to prevent herself from getting up and punching her vice president. She was, after all considerably bigger than him, and he wouldn't be the first man that she had ever hit. The betrayal by those close to her – people that she had worked with and trusted – had cut deep. James McInnis and now Jed Stone. Both of them, she had also regarded as good personal friends.

'We have got some traitors amongst us, Jed.'

'Some traitors?' repeated Stone. 'How do you mean, Madam President? Working for the Russians?'

Monroe shook her head.

'The Iranians? North Koreans?'

'No, Jed. Working for themselves is probably more accurate.'

'You've lost me.'

'You remember the report that we received after the attack on the UK? The one where MI5 had discovered a secretive organisation called The Collective? And that they were supporting the terrorists?'

'Yes, I do. Are you suggesting that they are behind the attacks on us?'

'We know they are, yes. Though the British will officially deny it, the CIA believe that the then director of MI5, Sir Nicholas Meads, was a member of The Collective. And it has become clear that we also have people in powerful positions over here who are working against us.'

'Do you know who?'

'We do, yes.'

'Who?'

'You.'

'What?' asked Stone incredulously.

'You, Jed. You're a member of The Collective.'

'You're crazy! What evidence could you possibly have to support this ludicrous accusation?'

President Monroe glanced at Tom.

'Well, we know that The Collective hijack an app when they have one of their projects on the go. Sir Nicholas Meads had told MI5 that. Now with Baqri's attacks on the United States, we discovered that the app used this time was a specific games app,' said Tom. 'One of those ones where you can play various card games.'

'And?' interjected Stone.

'And immediately after the National Security Council meeting, one person logged into the app. That person was you.'

'Is that it? That's your evidence? You come out with a completely outrageous accusation based on that?'

'What sort of person logs in to a game straight after witnessing the biggest terrorist attack in America's history? Thousands of people killed and the first thing you do is play a game on your phone?'

'Madam President, this is completely ridiculous,' asserted Stone, turning to the president. 'I can only imagine that the recent pressure which you have been under, has made you susceptible to the words of Grima Wormtongue here.'

'Do you know one of the things that I found to be so quirky about you?' asked Monroe rhetorically. 'Your habit of talking to yourself.'

'Most people do, I believe. And you've never talked to yourself?'

'There's more,' said Monroe. 'A little earlier, Tom came to your office, didn't he?'

'He did.'

'He told you that the National Security Council was reconvening soon. He also mentioned that there was some exciting news. Specifically, that Baqri's location had been identified and the FBI were closing in on him. And, in addition, that our Delta team had visibility on the HGV and were awaiting confirmation to move in.'

'Yes, he did. And what is your point, Madam President?'

President Monroe tapped on the laptop in front of her and spun it round on the desk. 'This is a surveillance video taken from inside your office.'

'What the hell? I'm the Vice President. You can't just go bugging my office.'

'Just watch and listen, Jed,' said Monroe, ignoring the outburst.

Stone started watching the video. As Tom leaves his office, Stone can clearly be seen opening up the games app on his phone.

'OK, you got me,' ridiculed Stone, raising his eyes to the ceiling. 'I'm addicted to playing that game. I will tender my resignation immediately and call a press conference, so that I can beg for forgiveness from the American people.'

'The interesting bit comes next, as you tap away to send a message in the app. Listen.'

FBI confirmed as identifying Baqri's location. US Special Forces in position to capture HGV.

'All I can see is me playing a game and talking to myself – which I do a lot, which you've already pointed out.'

'You're clearly sending a message,' said Tom.

'The game allows you to message other players. This is how people interact. Can you see what I'm typing?'

'Unfortunately, your hands are obscuring the text box.'

'This isn't looking very promising for your witch hunt, is it Tom?'

'So, what you're messaging in the app is something completely different to the words coming out of your mouth? Is that what you're saying Jed?' Monroe asked.

'I can walk down the street and chew gum, Madam President. Despite popular modern thinking, some men can multi-task.'

President Monroe rose from her seat and leaned forwards over her desk.

'I don't believe you, Jed. I know you're Collective. You're a traitor to this country and I would dearly love to see you prosecuted. The problem I have is that I don't believe a public trial of the vice president would provide the American people with the confidence in their government that they need right now. So, I want your resignation instead. You can cite ill health, family issues – anything you like – but I want to see you out.'

'I'm not going anywhere. Your accusations are preposterous. The evidence that you have is circumstantial at best.'

'What I've offered you is far better than you deserve. If you didn't hold the position that you do, I would happily see you executed. So, I guess as you clearly have no honour, we will need to treat you like the criminal that you are. I have decided that in the meantime, you will be detained. At least you won't be able to cause any more trouble.'

Tom said, 'Madam President, I have been assured by our tech teams that it is only a matter of time before they crack the messaging system that The Collective are using in this app.'

'Good. Then, Jed, you will be one step closer to being the first American Vice President in history to be charged with treason.'

CHAPTER THIRTY-FIVE

TUESDAY 11 JUNE – 10.45 p.m.

It was obvious to Luna that FBI Assistant Director, Hayden Marshall, was not feeling his usual controlled self – the constant humming had started to become annoying, as was the tapping on the centre armrest with his fingers. She could only assume that the pressure of knowing that the president would be anxiously watching the operation was getting to him. He had already confided in her that there had been hints from the director, based on the outcome. If the operation went well, then he would be formally announced as successor for the top job. If it went wrong … well … the best that he could hope for would be early retirement.

Luna looked down the road from the Potomac Airfield towards the junction with Glen Way and checked her watch. Outside it was pitch-black. No airport lights and, in fact, no light of any sort – even the moon was hidden behind a heavy cloud covering. Just the dimmed, muted glow from nearby houses at the top of the road. A single light aircraft sat on the runway – empty.If Tom was right, then Baqri – the man responsible for the deaths of thousands of Americans – would be arriving any minute, in the belief that an aircraft was going to whisk him away to a safe haven. If he was wrong … well, Luna was sure Marshall would be comforted by the fact that the finger of blame would be pointing elsewhere.

The FBI tactical team, which had been carefully positioned by Marshall along the fringes of the landing strip, remained completely hidden from any approaching traffic.

To ensure that Baqri couldn't leave the small airfield road once entered, two large SUVs were placed at the very top of Airport Drive – discretely parked on private driveways. Everything was in place and it was time to see if Tom's tactics had paid off.

The silence in Luna's SUV was abruptly broken. 'All units. All units,' repeated the radio call. 'Dark grey Ford Expedition now approaching the junction to Airport Drive. Members of the target terrorist team have been positively identified. I repeat, terrorist team identified.'

They had a bite. Headlights were visible in the distance – about two hundred and fifty yards from their location.

'Will you walk into my parlour?' whispered Luna. ''Tis the prettiest little parlour that you ever did spy.' Noticing that Marshall had turned his head to stare at her, Luna felt compelled to explain. 'The Spider and the Fly. It's a poem.'

Marshall nodded in reply, looked forwards once again and placed his finger over his radio's call button. Once Baqri's vehicle had entered the main tarmac, then he would close the net.

At the top of the road, Luna could now see Baqri's grey Ford starting to turn into Airport Drive. But instead of accelerating towards the airfield as she had expected, it seemed to be slowing down instead.

'What's going on?' asked Marshall.

'Not entirely sure,' replied Luna hesitantly. 'Do you know what? I think they're going to turn around.'

Luna's prediction materialised almost immediately, as the Expedition spun a hundred and eighty degrees and raced off in the direction that it had come.

'What the hell!' cried Marshall.

Luna's reaction was immediate. Her right foot pedal was floored within seconds of starting the engine and switching on the headlights, throwing the black Chevrolet Tahoe out on to the road.

'Pretty sure they just got tipped off,' Luna shouted over the strained sound of the engine.

With the majority of the Tactical Team positioned around the airport itself and just the two FBI vehicles – designation Foxtrot Charlie Two and Three Zero – on private drives near the highway, it came as no surprise to Luna when the message came through that Baqri's team had escaped the trap. But she also knew that they had something in place which would save them – satellite cover for the whole of the area.

'You can run Baqri – but you can't hide,' Marshall muttered under his breath, looking at the satellite picture in front of him.

***

Meanwhile, in the rear of the Ford Expedition, Baqri was revelling in his lucky escape.

'Well done, Zane. Good bit of driving that.'

Brigid said, 'That was close. What happened? Is that because of the message that you just got?'

'It was,' replied Baqri. 'Get this. Looks like the FBI have been trying to hack into The Collective's messaging system, inside that app that they're using. It has, therefore, been deemed as an unsafe method of communication and previous messages may have been compromised. Hence, we were advised to abort. They are now in the process of shutting it down.'

'So, just to summarise, we've got no sat phone and can't talk to The Collective anymore either?'

'Well done, Brigid. Correct. We are very much on our own.'

'So, how the hell are we supposed to escape now?'

'Not clear. All they said was they will find a way. We are to head back into Washington, over the Woodrow Wilson bridge and towards the city.'

'Back into the city?'

'As they believe that we're being tracked by satellite – this gives us the best chance of disappearing into the general population.'

Baqri turned around in his seat and looked out of the blacked out back glass. *Still no sign of the FBI*, he mused. He turned back and sighed.

'What is it?' asked Brigid.

'Hate not being in control.'

'You're going to have to trust them, I guess.'

A sudden jolt from behind sent everyone in the Ford lurching forward. Brigid immediately had a horrible feeling of déjà vu. She looked around. There staring straight back at her from the driver's seat of the black FBI SUV was Luna Rivers. A menacing grin and steely wide eyes; Brigid's nemesis had returned.

'Look! Now she's waving at me!' exclaimed Brigid.

'Stop freaking out, Brigid,' said Baqri also turning back around. 'She can't even see you through the glass. She's messing with you.'

'Stop freaking out? This is like a re-run for me of when her husband was chasing us through London … and you remember how that ended don't you? With the execution of my fiancée in the middle of the street!'

'Where the hell she came from, I've no idea. But don't worry, Zane will get us out of this. Won't you Zane?'

A single nod from the man-mountain driving the car was followed by a sudden lurch of the vehicle to the side. The Ford swerved back and forth across on-coming traffic in attempt to lose the pursuers. But every time Zane tried to shrug them off, Luna managed to regain any lost ground until she was again within inches of the rear of the Ford.

The junction from Old Fort Road and the Indian Head Highway was looming up quickly and Zane saw his opportunity. The lights were red and he pressed down hard on the accelerator, shooting the Ford across the middle of the junction, and somehow managing to miss every single vehicle. He spun the SUV to the right and then immediately back to the left, leaving complete chaos behind to the extent that even Luna could not stay with him and was forced to come to a stop.

***

'Arrghh!' shouted Luna, slamming her hands down on the steering wheel.

'Don't worry. We'll follow them on satellite,' said Marshall, staring at the mass of tangled metal that was now strewn across the junction. 'We've also got a helicopter that will be over them shortly. They can't escape.'

CHAPTER THIRTY-SIX

'Good evening, everyone. Please sit,' said President Monroe, entering the Situation Room. 'The Vice President will be unable to attend, I'm afraid. He has, unfortunately, been otherwise … detained.'

It was clear to everyone around the table that the president's demeanour had changed. Despite the long and very challenging day, Monroe had stridden into the room with the appearance of someone who was definitely on the front foot.

'I appreciate the lateness of the hour but I'm delighted to say that we have a positive update on the capture of the last HGV. Rachael?'

'Thank you, Madam President,' said Rachael Goldberg. 'I can confirm that approximately fifteen minutes ago, the Russian army took control of the last HGV. It is no longer in the hands of the terrorists. This was witnessed by our Black Ops unit in the area.'

There was an almost synchronised sigh of relief from everyone in the room with many just uttering 'Thank God.' Secretary of State Walt Houston even punched the air.

'That's fantastic news, Rachael,' gushed Houston. 'So, the threat to this country is now finally over?'

'It would seem so. I can also confirm that thanks to Tom's sting operation, Baqri's terrorist cell have been forced into the open and are on the run. The FBI are confident that they will all shortly be in custody,' added Goldberg.

'That needs to happen, Rachael,' demanded Monroe. 'I want the American people to see this son of a bitch on trial. I want them to see him publicly executed for the murder of innocent civilians. This will be the start of the healing process for them.'

'Understood, Madam President.'

'What is the latest casualty report for the two attacks?'

'We're now up to nearly eight thousand dead already, I'm afraid.'

'Good God,' said Secretary Houston.

'I assume that that's really the thin edge of the wedge?' asked Tom.

'I'm sorry to say, it is, yes. The local hospitals have become overwhelmed with casualties who have ingested the polonium. We're now having to utilise other hospitals further out. The National Guard are assisting with transportation.'

'I guess most of those people will die?' asked Walt Houston.

Goldberg replied, 'The vast majority will, I'm sorry to say. They're getting the best care possible but their likelihood of survival will depend on a number of factors. Not least, how much polonium they ingested.'

'I need to go and visit them. Jim, please make the arrangements for me to take Airforce One tomorrow morning. I'm going to visit all the hospitals in both states. Starting with Arizona and then to Ohio, before returning to DC,' said President Monroe.

James McInnis nodded in acknowledgement with just a fleeting look at the president – still unable to make full eye contact for any length of time.

'I've seen some of the news reports and the American people seem to be really confused out there. Actually, the media seem to be confused as well.'

'They are Madam President,' Goldberg replied. 'They're all still stunned by the assassination of the King and the suggestion that we were complicit. And the media have been building on speculation that America has been subjected to some sort of terrorist nuclear weapons attack. There's a genuine fear out there that we are going to get hit again.'

'It's about time that I addressed the nation. Jim, call an emergency press briefing. Our country needs to be re-assured now that the threat has been eliminated.'

'I will, Madam President.'

'And what's the latest in the Congo, Walt?' asked Monroe.

'Colonel Banza and his army have pushed the government forces back and are now just over thirty miles from the capital, Kinshasa. We are not expecting President Mwamba to still be in power by this time tomorrow.'

'Can I ask if Baqri has managed to upload the execution of the King on to the internet yet?' asked Admiral Womack. 'That may even quicken the pace at which Banza gains power. The Congolese people will be outraged.'

'I don't think he will have had time, Admiral. We've been pushing Baqri around non-stop since we sent the video, and at the moment he has the FBI chasing him,' Tom replied.

Houston said, 'Madam President, I assume we are going to talk about the King? His execution by us will be considered as completely abhorrent by the whole world. Particularly if that video gets out. Then I think we will be pretty well isolated. I mean, what sort of country executes the monarch of their closest ally? What does that mean for every other country out there?'

'Actually, Walt, as Colonel Banza hasn't reached the capital yet, I think we have a good chance of stopping him seizing power. And the video we can declare as fake,' said Monroe.

'How's that going to work? When the King never appears again, then the world will conclude that it's real. We can't exactly brush this under the carpet, can we?' said Houston.

‘I think I can help with that, Madam President,’ said Tom, retaking his seat after having received a call on his phone.

‘Go on, Tom.’

‘I have just received confirmation that a combined African force from Tanzania, Kenya, Uganda and Zambia have just started assembling a task force. They will start flying troops into the DRC’s capital, Kinshasa, tonight. Other units from the task force are expected to advance on Colonel Banza’s forces from the rear. He will be vastly outnumbered by much better trained and equipped troops.’

‘I don’t understand,’ said Houston.

‘Me neither,’ Admiral Womack agreed.

‘Why would they do that? What’s suddenly changed?’ asked Houston.

‘What’s changed is that the last Avangard HGV has been retrieved and Baqri can no longer threaten to kill millions of Americans with it,’ said Monroe.

‘No, you’ve still lost me. Why would they suddenly change their mind and support an American backed government?’ asked Womack.

‘An American government who was responsible for executing someone that they considered to be a living saint?’ added Goldberg.

Tom looked at his phone and sent a single message. A ping indicated the receipt of a reply.

‘Now, about that,’ said Tom, reaching for a remote control and switching on one of the main wall monitors.

‘Good evening, everyone. I’m so delighted to see you all,’ said the familiar voice.

Secretary Houston’s mouth dropped open as he stared at the screen. He managed to mutter just two words.

‘King Edward.’

CHAPTER THIRTY-SEVEN

'Not sure that having almost all of our units located around the airfield was the best idea,' said Luna, glancing at Marshall with a look that expressed her feelings perfectly. 'Perhaps you should have involved local law enforcement?'

'I couldn't take the risk. From the information that we've started collating, it seems likely that every part of the government has been infiltrated by The Collective. To think that they haven't got people in the police would be naïve, to say the least. So, my decision was to involve as few people as possible.'

'How do you know that the other FBI agents in this operation haven't been compromised?'

'I don't … but they're all hand-picked. People that I've worked with and trust.'

Luna glanced up at the sea of flashing red and orange lights in her rear-view mirror. Once again, she pushed her right foot down hard as the FBI SUV raced away from the crash scene and towards the bridge.

'They've already made it across the Woodrow Wilson Bridge and into Alexandria,' said Assistant Director Marshall, looking at his satellite screen. 'I'm going to instruct local police to block off all of the main arterial roads going north, west and south. Cat's out the bag now, so I might as well use them. I'll get two of our units to block off the bridge in case Baqri decides to double back.'

'They got there quick,' said Luna, swerving between the occasional vehicle.

'The result of lower night-time traffic, I guess.'

'This is Aerial One,' came the voice over the radio. 'Now over target vehicle. Travelling west along King Street.'

Luna turned onto the Woodrow Wilson Bridge and continued accelerating. The red tail lights of other vehicles were flashing by so fast that Marshall was now the one pushing his foot down – on an imaginary brake pedal. Luna looked up. She could see the FBI helicopter's searchlight beaming down in the near distance.

'You know, Tom smashed the previous record around MI5's vehicle pursuit track during his training. Until I came along, of course,' Luna shouted over the screaming sound of the engine.

'I believe that,' said a wide-eyed Hayden Marshall.

'Foxtrot Charlie One Zero,' came another voice over the radio. 'Alexandria PD have confirmed that roadblocks are now established on all major routes. They're also starting to close down others - street by street.'

'Thank you, Control,' replied Marshall.

'This is Aerial One. Subject vehicle still proceeding west and heading under King Street Metrorail bridge.'

The black FBI Tahoe slid sideways onto South Patrick Street - smoke bellowing from the tyres. With Luna expertly compensating for the Chevy's over-steer, the Tahoe re-gripped the tarmac and charged on once again.

'Subject vehicle has now turned around and is heading the wrong way up Sunset Drive and on to Callahan Drive.'

'Where the hell are they going?' asked Marshall.

'Beats me,' Luna replied. 'But we should be able to intercept them shortly.'

'Subject vehicle has crossed junction with Duke Street and now heading east.'

'What the hell? They're heading towards us!' exclaimed Luna.

'All units. Subject vehicle has turned on to Dulany Street and heading south towards John Carlyle Street,' said Aerial One.

'Copy that. We're just coming up to John Carlyle Square, so we're nearly on them,' Marshall replied.

'Foxtrot Charlie One Zero, please be advised that your support units are currently about four minutes out.'

'Copy that.'

As the FBI Chevrolet approached the Square, Luna found herself having to slam on the brakes. Facing her were swarms of people all over the road. Many of them were in Georgian fancy dress and most of them appeared to be very drunk.

'What the hell's this?' said Luna.

Marshall pointed at some banners hanging off the side of the buildings. 'Looks like some sort of festival. Now we know why they came this way.'

'Hoping to get lost in the crowds,' replied Luna, honking the horn.

'Not going to work when we have satellite coverage. They've turned into the East Parking Garage – coming up on the right.'

Luna drove the Chevrolet Tahoe into the entrance of the garage before turning ninety degrees and partially blocking both the entrance and exit barriers. Jumping out of the driver's seat, she looked back at Marshall.

'We need to keep them bottled up in here. When the rest of the team arrive, get them to block off all other ways in and out of here.'

'What are you going to do?'

'Go hunting.'

'I should come with you.'

'With respect, sir, you're better off here – co-ordinating and controlling. And to be honest, you're gonna slow me down. This is what I'm meant for.'

Luna made her way up the exit ramp of the car park – side arm already drawn. With only two storeys above her, she knew that proceeding with caution was more important than speed. She was also sure that Baqri's group would avoid leaving the car park, if possible, where they could be seen by the helicopter hovering overhead or by the satellite or by any of the ground teams that had started arriving.

Baqri would surely have known that he would be tracked by satellite, wouldn't he?

What wasn't so clear was why Baqri had adopted such a poor escape strategy. A man renowned for his careful planning had managed to trap himself in a car park with no real prospect of getting away without being seen.

Stealthily advancing behind the parked cars – which were numerous thanks to the festival – Luna rounded the corner to the first floor. She looked down to the end. Not one spare parking space. Her eyes darted from one side to the other.

So far, no grey Ford SUVs but they could now be on foot, of course. High potential for an ambush.

'Luna, all exits secured. Can confirm that no one has left the building. Just to advise, there appears to be parking on the flat roof as well. Be aware that other FBI tactical units have now entered the car park,' said the calm voice of Hayden Marshall over the radio. 'Two Zero are behind you.'

'Copy that,' she quietly replied.

Luna looked around. The four-man unit, dressed in black tactical gear, was quickly moving towards her position. Luna stopped and silently indicated to the team behind her to do the same. The familiar sound of a vehicle engine coming from the floors above was getting louder. Kneeling down behind the front of a parked convertible, she looked over the hood as the flash of headlights appeared near the top of the ramp. An old station wagon turned the corner and trundled downwards. As the vehicle got closer, Luna could make out an elderly couple sat in the front. She stepped out with her FBI badge raised in one hand and her Glock 9mm handgun in the other.

The terror on the face of the old lady in the passenger seat, who saw her first, was clear and genuine. The tactical team followed Luna's lead, edging out with their MP5s raised as the car shuddered to a halt. The driver, a terrified looking senior, raised both his hands.

'Check it over,' said Luna to the Tactical Team leader, before again proceeding carefully up towards the second floor.

Rounding the next corner, Luna squatted down and looked towards the end of the floor. Brighter wall and ceiling lights highlighted the final ramp to the roof. She moved slowly forwards, knowing that contact with the terrorists was imminent. She looked behind. The Tactical Team had now caught up again.

Still no sign of their Ford, thought Luna. *Where the hell are you?*

The sound of a large V8 engine grabbed Luna's attention and she looked towards the roof ramp. The area quickly became flooded in light, and a pickup truck, fitted with an array of rooflights, drove slowly down onto the second floor and stopped. Such was the blinding brightness emanating from the truck, none of the FBI team were able to see the occupants. The team cautiously advanced anyway. A squeal of tyres and the truck lurched forwards, hitting an FBI agent, flinging him into the windshield of a parked car. The rest of the Tactical Team opened fire as the pickup raced past, peppering the rear.

'Hold your fire,' shouted Luna, noticing the terrified young couple in the front.

Luna raised her Glock and squeezed the trigger three times. A bang from the rear wheel sent the vehicle into a spin, crashing into more parked cars and finally finishing across the middle of the lane. The far-side rear passenger door opened and Luna could make out two people exiting.

'Everyone out of the vehicle and lie on the floor,' shouted Luna.

The driver's door, which was facing the FBI team, opened and a man almost fell out of the cab and onto the ground.

'Please don't shoot, please don't shoot,' he repeated hysterically, at the same time as lying flat on the ground.

Near the front of the pickup, Luna noticed movement. A head appeared over the hood. She recognised the face. It was one of Baqri's team – Idris. He raised a rifle and fired – the distinctive 'clacking' sound of an AK47. The FBI Tactical Team took cover before returning fire – forcing Idris to duck back down behind the pickup and just returning the occasional shot.

The exchange of fire continued for several minutes – until a voice yelled out from behind the vehicle.

'FBI. Lay down your weapons or I will shoot her,' came the deep voice of an exceptionally large man, walking out with a young woman held in front of him. Bald, black and with a scar down the right side of his face, Zane was certainly an intimidating sight.

'Oh God. Please don't … Please don't kill me,' the woman begged, tears streaming down her face.

Zane shouted, 'I'll give you five seconds to do what I've told you or she will die. Five … four … three … two…'

'One,' said Luna, who had moved unseen behind the parked cars and was now standing at the rear corner of the pickup.

A single shot rang out and Zane fell to the ground like a sack of potatoes but now with the addition of a hole to his temple. The girl that he was holding screeched like a banshee – her face now splattered with the blood of her captor. A shocked Idris looked over and tried twisting around with his AK-47. Luna fired one more shot, disabling the arm that Idris was holding the weapon with.

As the FBI Tactical Team moved up and secured Idris, Luna opened the blacked out rear doors.

'Director Marshall,' said Luna, pressing the button on her radio. 'We have one in custody. However, Baqri and Brigid Doyle are gone.'

CHAPTER THIRTY-EIGHT

'Your Majesty,' said Secretary Houston, staring at the large overhead screen – with his mouth still open. 'We thought you were dead – though I'm delighted, of course, to see you alive and well.'

'Thankyou Walt. There's no one more delighted to be alive than me. That's twice now that your president has saved me,' King Edward beamed.

President Monroe said, 'Well, it was Tom's plans and he's the one who made them happen.'

'Yes, of course. Thankyou Tom. But it was your risk Madam President. If Americans had died as a result of you not following Baqri's instructions, then you would have been the one held accountable by the people of this country.'

'We're Americans, Your Highness, and we don't negotiate with terrorists.'

'I'm very grateful for that!'

'I know that the huge loss of American lives is tragic, Madam President, but you are not responsible for any of it. Baqri launched his attacks before there was even a mention of the King,' said Tom.

'I would agree,' said Walt Houston. 'And I would also add that your actions have, in fact, prevented further loss of life. If you had conceded to Baqri's demands regarding the King, then we would have lost many of our allies. Subsequently – and there is no doubt in my mind about this – America would have been subjected to terrorist attacks on an unimaginable level.'

'I think you'll find that your relationship with your allies is now stronger than ever,' said King Edward. 'I just came off the phone with the British Prime Minister. I think you can shortly expect a phone call from a very contrite Bob Hatcher, Madam President.'

'That's good to hear. Seems like a good time to ask him for a favour.'

'Difficult for him to say 'no', I would suggest. By the way, that was a great video, Tom. I think I even checked myself for a pulse at one point.'

'Thank you, sir,' replied Tom.

'Anyway, I better crack on. I've got a long list of world leaders still to call. And then I've got a press conference, where I need to lavish praise on the American President.'

As the call with the King ended, Walt Houston turned his chair to face Tom.

'I'm sure you know what I'm about to ask you, Tom. How did you fake the King's death?'

'Something called *deep fake*, Walt. It's an AI program. Anyone can appear to do anything. I had some of the best people on the planet working on that.'

Houston sat back in his seat and sighed. 'I have heard of that. Madam President, I have come to the conclusion that I really don't understand the world we live in today. In the old days, you could have faith in what you saw. Now, you can't even believe your own eyes.'

'It's your experience and wise council that matters to me, Walt.'

'Well, I've been around long enough to give you a little bit of that.'

Rachael Goldberg said, 'I can't believe you managed to get that done so quickly, Tom.'

'I got them started on it as soon as Baqri first mentioned his plan to kill the King. We were then in a position to tweak the video, depending on what Baqri came out with,' replied Tom. 'A critical part of playing chess is being able to predict your opponent's moves.'

'Sorry, Madam President. Do you mind if I take this? It's Hayden Marshall – hopefully with an update,' said Goldberg holding up her phone and then walking to the back of the room.

'But if you had reached Baqri's deadline without delivering the body of the King, then you would have been in trouble, surely?' Houston continued.

'Yes, I would have. But I took the gamble that Baqri's need for self-preservation would trump anything else. When he received a message saying that the FBI were moving in on him straight after getting the video, I knew that his priority would be to run for cover.'

'So, *you* gave him that information. How did you manage to send him a message he would believe?' asked Houston.

Tom Rivers, President Monroe and James McInnis exchanged glances with each other, before Tom cleared his throat.

'Well, Walt, let's just say that we managed, very briefly, to find a way to get into The Collective's messaging system in an app that they were using. They've subsequently deleted everything,' said Tom.

'Did you manage to get any other information before they did that?' asked Monroe.

'Not much, I'm afraid. Our tech team were able to grab just a few lines apparently, but it doesn't seem to mean anything. The messages were using code words. They're sending it over to me. I will be having a look at it shortly.'

Monroe looked over at Homeland Secretary Goldberg, who had just re-taken her seat.

'I'm eager to hear your news, Rachael. Your face isn't telling me that we've caught Baqri.'

'Unfortunately, not, Madam President.'

'He's escaped again?'

'He has.'

'Unbelievable! What the hell happened this time?'

'It looks like he was tipped off again. The trap was set; he was on his way; and then suddenly his car just stopped and turned around. By the time that the FBI caught up with them, Baqri and Brigid Doyle were both gone.'

'You need to get to the bottom of this, Rachael.'

'There's a full investigation already underway, Madam President. We do have one of Baqri's cell in custody, by the way, and he's being interrogated as we speak. The other member of his group was shot dead by Luna Rivers, Ma'am.'

'Do you think that you'll be able to track Baqri down?'

'We're tracing the route that his vehicle took, to see if he had the opportunity to decamp somewhere.'

'Keep me updated.'

'I will, Madam President. I do have some other interesting news which has just come through.'

'Go on.'

'Our intelligence reports that the last HGV recaptured by the Russians had no polonium in it.'

'What?' said Monroe incredulously.

'It seems that Baqri's threat was a bluff.'

'So, the last Avangard HGV was … just that? Nothing more?'

'Well, not nothing more,' said Goldberg. 'It was still fitted with an EMP.'

'That doesn't make much sense to me. He threatens the United States with what he claimed was the majority of his polonium. But it was actually fitted with an EMP instead?'

'Perhaps he felt that the threat of a large amount of polonium was more likely to illicit your co-operation in executing the King?'

'Even though the detonation of an EMP over, say New York, would still have been a disaster for the country? Frying every electrical circuit in America's financial heart?'

'Still not as persuasive, I would suggest, as the threat of showering American civilians with the most lethal element known to mankind,' Goldberg reasoned.

President Monroe looked over at Tom Rivers, who had remained unusually quiet throughout the debate.

'OK, Tom. I'm getting used to that look now. What's running through your head?' asked Monroe.

'This EMP thing doesn't sit well with me,' said Tom, closing his eyes for a few seconds of meditative thought.

'In what way, Tom?' asked Walt Houston.

'My problem is this. He's got one of the most advanced weapon delivery systems in the world and he's equipped it with an EMP.'

'Well, he was gambling that we would believe his claim that the third Avangard HGV had the bulk of the polonium.'

'No, you're missing my point, Walt. If it was all a bluff, then why fit an EMP at all? From what I have been told, Baqri went to the trouble of kidnapping Dr Alim Farooqi's mother in order to get his co-operation. It's now clear that it wasn't just to get him to work on polonium HGVs but to create an EMP version as well. Why?'

'Maybe he wanted some sort of back-up device. In case the polonium Avangards failed in some way?' suggested Goldberg.

'At the end of the day, it's pretty academic, Tom. Baqri's running for his life and the Russians now have control of the last Avangard,' added President Monroe. 'I don't know about anyone else, but I'm sure as hell pleased that this nightmare is now over.'

'You can say that again,' said Secretary of State Walt Houston.

'I guess that's all true, Madam President. Perhaps Baqri has just made me a little paranoid,' said Tom.

'Just to let y'all know, I'll be leaving early morning on Airforce One to visit the casualties in Arizona and Ohio,' said Monroe. 'I want to be in the position to tell those people that we've caught the person responsible and I'm going to make him pay.'

'I understand, Madam President,' said Goldberg.

Jane Monroe leaned forward and looked intensely at her Secretary for Homeland Security. She paused briefly before speaking again.

'No more mistakes, Rachael. Make sure you get him this time.'

Tom sat back in his chair and looked around the table. Everyone else seemed so calm – even relaxed – about the current situation. So, why was he the only one that felt like Baqri was down but not out?

CHAPTER THIRTY-NINE

WEDNESDAY 12 JUNE – 1 a.m.

Idris Flint blinked repeatedly as the black hood was pulled from his head. He tried focussing his eyes. A man holding the hood left the room. Idris looked around. White walls and minimalist – just the chair that he was sitting on, a table in front and another chair on the other side. The bright lights from the ceiling above adding to the antiseptic, clinical ambiance.

Though Idris was of a similarly impressive size to his former colleague, Zane, he was otherwise very different in appearance. Fair skinned with crew cut ginger hair and an instantly recognizable tattoo on his right arm. Square jawed and muscular, he was the epitome of a US Marine.

The door opened and Tom Rivers entered the room.

'Hello, Idris.

'Where am I?'

'Nowhere. Well, nowhere that you'll be able to find on a map. My name is Tom Rivers, by the way.'

'I know who you are.'

'Good. You've got an unusual first name, haven't you Idris. I always thought that Idris originated from north Africa and Arabia?'

'It's also Welsh. My Dad was from Wales.'

'I've been to Wales a few times. Got some lovely parts there, hasn't it?'

'I wouldn't know. Never been.'

'Well, that's a shame. You've got kids haven't you, Idris? Take them on holiday there.'

'So, you're going to let me go then, are you? Tell you everything that I know and you'll let me walk out.'

'If I said that, you know it would be a lie. But I'm pretty sure that the President could be persuaded to intervene and commute the death penalty that you'll certainly receive, down to a prison sentence. Depending on your level of cooperation, of course.'

'How tempting! I get to spend most of my life in prison and if I ever get out, then I can take my children for a holiday. And they get the pleasure of pushing their frail old father around in a wheelchair. I think I'll pass.'

'It's better than them having to live with the pain of knowing their father was executed as a traitor who didn't have the courage to do the right thing when he had the chance. All I want is a little bit of cooperation and information.'

'Such as?'

'Where did Baqri get out of the car and where was he going?'

"I'm not saying anything without my lawyer present.'

'Oh dear. You think that you're in some sort of federal custody where we have to respect your rights? Is that it?'

Idis nodded.

'I've got some bad news for you. This facility comes under Special Operations. We don't really do people's rights and all those fluffy things. It's more like you tell me what I want to know, and we don't hurt you too much.'

'You can try,' replied Idris defiantly.

'Actually, it would be my wife, Luna, not me. I believe you two have already met. And she was sort of hoping that you were going to say something like that, by the way. She's eager to get started.'

'I've been trained to resist interrogation techniques.'

'Yes, I know. Everyone has a limit though. And Luna has received interrogation training that would be considered so extreme that it would be classed as illegal in all but a very few brutal countries. Anyway, you're a brave man and you obviously feel that Baqri is such a great person, that it's worth going through the unimaginable horror of what is about to happen to you.'

'I'm prepared.'

'Trust me, you're not.'

Idris stared straight ahead and folded his arms.

'I don't think you're a bad guy, Idris. I've read your file. Previously a highly decorated Sergeant in the Marine Corps. But you feel let down by your country. Abandoned after being discharged on medical grounds. A downward spiral in your mental health, sending you into that dark desperate void called depression. You left the family home and even slept rough for a while. Then along comes Baqri. Charismatic and uplifting. Promises you a way of getting back at those that caused your misery. But here's where I think you are conflicted. You were a loyal soldier of great integrity. Dedicated years of your life to the honourable protection of your country and its people. Does it sit well with you that thousands of those people have died and there's many more still to come?'

'Justice had to be served.'

'That sounds like Baqri speaking, not you. Do little children deserve to die for your justice?'

'There are always casualties of war.'

'I know you don't mean that. Not really. Let me show you something.'

Tom placed a tablet in front of Idris. On the screen was the static picture of a little girl. About the age of six, with black hair tied up in pigtails and dressed in a school uniform.

'This is Jessie Winters. About the same age as your youngest daughter, I believe. Look at that smile. She wants to be a nurse when she grows up. This was taken less than a week ago.'

Tom pressed the play button.

'And here's Jessie, ready for her first day at school,' said the male voice behind the camera. 'Are you excited, Jessie?'

'Yes,' came the short reply, followed by a broad grin.

'What are you looking forward to most?'

'Making friends. And play time.'

'Not lots of hard work in the classroom?' said a female voice.

The camera jogged up and down with laughter.

'No … You're silly, Mommy,' said Jessie.

'I know, sweetheart. But don't you think Daddy's even more silly than me?'

Jessie giggled and pointed at the camera.

'Daddy's pulling funny faces again!'

'That's his normal face, darling.'

'Hey!' said the voice behind the camera.

Tom pressed the pause button.

'Let me show you Jessie now. Her parents wanted you to see this.'

The video started again but this time from a hospital room. The camera zoomed in on the occupant of the bed. Barely recognisable under the layers of tubes and wires was a little girl. Her eyes were closed and on one side of her head she was completely bald. Scraggly tufts of black hair were all that remained on the other side. The girl briefly woke up, just in time to vomit into a receptacle that was being held by a woman who was sat beside her bed.

'That's Jessie's mother. She's been sat at her daughter's bedside for the last twenty-four hours. But it will all be over soon. By this time tomorrow, Jessie will be dead. You see those weapons that you helped Baqri launch at your own country, contain the world's most deadly element. It's highly radioactive and releases things called alpha particles. Jessie's body has been destroyed from the inside. They go through the body like a wrecking ball, destroying DNA and causing mass cell suicide. For the tiny amount of people that initially survive this … well they can look forward to lung cancer and a slow death.'

Idris looked up at Tom. For the first time, his face conveyed a hint of regret.

'You haven't been abandoned, Idris … not by everyone anyway.'

Tom tapped on the iPad until a video screen came up.

'What's this?' asked Idris.

'Your wife and daughters want to tell you how much they love you.'

CHAPTER FORTY

'Hey,' said Luna, placing a mug of coffee on the table in front of Tom. 'Thought you could do with a caffeine boost.'

'Thanks, my love.'

'That was amazing, by the way.'

'What was?'

'Getting Idris to spill his guts so quick.'

'Everyone has a vulnerability. It's just a question of working out what it is.'

'So, do you think Baqri is at this derelict mansion that he mentioned?'

'Possibly. The question is how long he will wait for Idris and Zane to turn up.'

'Neither of them had phones on them, so they couldn't have stayed in contact with Baqri.'

'I guess Baqri didn't trust them enough to let them keep their phones. The risk being that we might track them. I think we have to assume though that The Collective will have supplied Baqri with another sat phone by now.'

'But with their app messaging system now inoperative, The Collective's internal communication must be shot. So, I don't imagine any instructions are going out to Baqri at the moment?'

'Not yet. I imagine that they will have left some standing escape plans with him though. But I also think they will be looking to hijack another app very quickly. Can't see them wanting to be out of contact with Baqri for too long.'

'Baqri's getting good at this escape business. Idris and Zane drop him off with his little sidekick, Brigid, under the bridge by the Metro. Out of view of our surveillance. They get on a train and somehow disappear into the population?'

'I assume that his Collective friends left them some sort of disguise. Probably on the train. Then they melted away into a mass of late-night revellers.'

'Still shouldn't have got past transport police – but there you go,' said Luna, pulling back the seat that was formally occupied by Idris and sitting down.

'I thought that you would be getting ready to move out, now that we've got a lead on Baqri?' said Tom. 'Not that I don't like a visit from my lovely wife, of course.'

'Very smooth. We've got the mansion under satellite surveillance now, so if Baqri is still there we'll be able to track him if he tries leaving. Hayden Marshall is going to do a briefing in a minute. We can't afford to mess it up again – obviously. So, he wanted to remind us of a quote by Thomas Edison.'

'Go on.'

'*Good fortune is what happens when opportunity meets with planning.*'

'That's a good quote and I get where Marshall's coming from. But why do I get the feeling you've got something else that you want to say?'

Luna briefly looked to the ceiling and grinned. She had hoped that she would be able to deliver her news with a solemn face. The awaited news that, despite all that they had just been through, was never far from their thoughts. But one thing Luna had never mastered was to lie to her husband without him spotting the tell-tale signs. She decided that she couldn't keep it to herself anymore.

'I have some good news. On the personal front.'

'Go on.'

'The girls phoned. Their results have come in from university. And … they've only both got themselves first-class honours degrees!'

'You're kidding? Really?' Tom replied excitedly. 'They both got firsts?'

'Yep. Both our daughters.'

'Wow. That's amazing news. I'll call them when I get a chance. Well, this is a cause for celebration. And self-congratulation, of course.'

'Self-congratulation?'

'A pat on the back for us as parents, I think, is quite well deserved.'

'Does it involve champagne?'

'Absolutely.'

'Oh, go on then. You forced me into it.'

'As soon as this is over, then I suggest dinner at that posh restaurant which Vice President Stone keeps going on about and a nice bottle of fizz.'

'Sounds perfect. Speaking of Stone, has the president decided what to do with him?'

'Yeah, she's letting him go. Lack of evidence.'

'Really? That's not what I expected. How do you feel about that?'

'She's right. I mean, on my recommendation, the Vice President of the United States was detained for playing a game on his phone! Let me say that again. I had the vice president detained just for playing a game. And since he was detained, up until The Collective deleted their messaging system in that app, only three people messaged him. And they all appear to be legitimate games players. Not sure what I was thinking.'

'What are you going to do?'

'Apologise, I guess. Going to have to face him at some point. Seeing shadows where there weren't any. I was so sure he was Collective. Perhaps my instincts aren't as good as I thought they were.'

'Tom, does he seem like the sort to play games on his phone? Seriously? This is the most boring and serious guy that I've ever met.'

A knock on the door and a member of the FBI tactical unit poked his head around the corner.

'Sorry to disturb you ma'am. Assistant Director Marshall is about to give his briefing.'

'OK, thanks,' replied Luna, 'I'll be there in a minute.'

'Well, I better nip back to The White House,' said Tom standing up. 'The President believes that the threat is all over, so it's time to return to my office and box up *Little Britain*.'

With the aid of his crutch, Tom hobbled towards the door along with his wife. He stopped and turned around to face her.

'Be careful, Luna. Expect the unexpected. We know that The Collective has at least one person in the FBI. They'll be trying to find out what you know.'

'Hey, don't worry,' Luna replied, holding her hand to Tom's face. 'We've deliberately kept this to a small team. I can handle anything that they try.'

CHAPTER FORTY-ONE

Tom had just started on his boxing up of 'Little Britain' when there was a brief knock on his office door. His visitor was the person that he was least looking forward to seeing again – Vice President Jed Stone.

'Good morning, Tom,' said VP Stone. 'I heard you were back.'

'Good morning, sir,' replied Tom, in an unusually quiet tone. 'Only briefly. Last day for me here at The White House. I've got a new office back at FBI headquarters to go to. Look, I just want to apologise for your detention. It was my recommendation and, in hindsight, it looks like it was the wrong call.'

'Tom, don't worry about it. The President explained everything to me … and graciously apologised, of course. To be honest, I would probably have made the same decision, if I was in your shoes. This Collective organisation seems to have infiltrated all aspects of our government.'

'They have, sir, I'm afraid.'

'I gather from the president, that she has got Prime Minister Hatcher to assign you to us for the foreseeable future. And you will be completely dedicated to defeating The Collective.'

'Yeah, I don't think the Prime Minister was in a position to do anything else but agree to a long secondment.'

'Good job, by the way, with the King. Instead of dividing us from our allies, we are now closer than ever.'

'Thank you, sir.'

'Talking of The Collective, have you made any progress?'

Tom picked up a piece of paper from his desk. Information that had been hand delivered to him just fifteen minutes earlier by the FBI's special tech team.

'Some progress. Maybe. I'm not sure yet. We've managed to grab the last few messages that were sent before they deleted their messaging system. Not much to go on because they wiped it so quickly. Most of it just seems like gobbledegook but there's a few interesting words and phrases in there.'

'What words?'

'Well, there's a referral to *making sure that Aslan has been neutralised.* There's also another one that says *Farsight should be terminated immediately* and asks for a vote. Not sure what that means. Could possibly be the name given to this 'project' of theirs. Just about to Google it. Might go and see Jim McInnis to see if he can shed any light on it.'

'Well, you're clearly a busy man, so I'll leave you to it. You will let me know if there's anything that I can do to help, won't you?' said Stone.

'I will. Thank you, sir. And thank you for your understanding.'

As the office door closed, Tom looked at the piece of paper again. He tapped *Aslan* into the browser of his laptop.

Well, I'm pretty sure I know who Aslan is but, as I keep telling Luna, you should never assume. OK, well that's more results than I expected. Shops, sportsmen and, of course, Aslan the lion of C.S. Lewis origin. But the name itself is of Turkish origin. Interesting.

Tom opened up another browser window on his laptop and tapped in *Farsight.*

So, we have some shops and companies but by far the biggest result is Commander Farsight from the Warhammer games. What the hell has that got to do with Aslan?

After a further half an hour of reading about the Warhammer character, it became obvious to Tom that he was going to need help connecting the dots. Fortunately, just along the hall was a man who had some knowledge of The Collective and was all too keen to help.

Tom's train of thought was abruptly interrupted by the sound of people running and shouting outside his door. He got to his feet and hobbled as quick as he could out into the hallway. Secret Service agents had crowded around the doorway of the chief of staff's office.

'What the hell's going on?' asked Tom.

'It's Mr McInnis. I'm afraid he's dead, sir,' replied Agent Williams. 'Looks like he committed suicide.'

On the face of it, the Secret Service agent's deductions couldn't be faulted. There was James McInnis slumped over his desk with blood still pouring out of his opened wrists. On the floor, directly below his right hand, was a knife. The only thing out of place on an otherwise very tidy desktop was a framed photograph, lying flat. Tom took a closer look. It was a photo of the McInnis with his family. Bloody streaky fingerprints ran across the glass and it looked like he had tried touching the faces of each member of his family.

'I'm sorry, sir,' said Agent Williams. 'We need to seal off this room until investigators get here.'

'I don't get this,' Tom replied. 'Why would he suddenly decide to kill himself?'

'I really couldn't say, sir.'

'When did you see him last?'

'About half an hour ago. I took a briefing pack in for him. The president left instructions that I should check anything that the chief of staff receives.'

'Yeah, I think that there's a bit of a trust issue there. But how did he seem to you then?'

'Unusually distracted. His mind seemed to be preoccupied. Very sombre and sort of disconnected. Not like his usual self at all.'

'And did anyone visit him before or after you?'

'No one after me. Just one visitor a quarter of an hour or so before me.'

'Who?'

'Vice President Stone.'

CHAPTER FORTY-TWO

Once more, Colonel Viktor Gorsky found himself standing to attention in front of the Russian President's desk. This time, however, his boss appeared to be in much more agitated mood – completely consumed by a press briefing on the television. A briefing by the one person that he never expected to see again – King Edward.

'Unbelievable!' President Petrov shouted at the screen. 'This guy has more lives than a cat.'

'Sir?' said Gorsky.

'I'm not sure how Monroe pulled this off but, with the King still alive, everything has changed. And not for the better. Not for us, anyway.'

'I understand that Colonel Banza's forces in the Congo are now surrounded.'

'Yes, President Mwamba gets to cling on to power and all those American companies get to keep their contracts. For the moment anyway.'

'Do you think that will change, sir?'

'One thing in life that I have learnt is that things always change. I'm pretty sure that this isn't the end of our ambitions in Congo.'

Sergei Petrov stood up and once more headed for his drink cabinet, grabbing a bottle of vodka and two glasses.

'I got the feeling that you rather enjoyed my Tsarskaya last time I saw you?'

'I did, sir.'

'So, tell me about the Avangard HGV that we now have control of, once again,' said Petrov as he poured out a large measure of the vodka into each of the glasses.

'Your biohazard team has arrived and are investigating the polonium breach.'

'And General Volkov's forces?'

'The army is keeping their distance, as I requested. I don't think the General is too keen on his troops getting anywhere near something that is leaking the most lethal element on the planet.'

'Excellent. And you have not mentioned me to anyone else?'

'No one knows about it, sir. As you ordered. As far as the army are aware, this is an FSB led operation.'

'Well done, Viktor. Your service to me and your country have been noted. Please feel free to finish your drink.'

Viktor Gorsky picked up his glass. As President Petrov was now just silently staring at him, Gorsky suddenly started feeling very uncomfortable. It was clear from the president's body language that the invitation to finish his drink had an unsaid part to the ending. 'Finish it now and then leave,' was the full sentence.

Once again, Colonel Gorsky threw the vodka down his throat in one go, before standing, saluting, and exiting the president's office.

***

As soon as the door closed, Petrov picked up the phone.

'General Orlov. This is the President. Where is that last Avangard HGV which we managed to retrieve?'

'Colonel Gorsky told me that our radiological team took possession of it and have taken it to a secure location to deal with the leaking polonium.'

'Except that it's not leaking polonium.'

'Sir?'

'Colonel Gorsky has just admitted to me that he has been conspiring with terrorists to seize back our remaining Avangard HGV. He's a member of that Collective organisation.'

'What? Are you sure, sir?'

'Of course, I'm sure, Orlov. The terrorists are impersonating one of our radiological teams. He lied about the polonium. The HGV is actually fitted with an EMP device. And now they have it back again. How did you not realise that your deputy was working with the terrorists, General? How did you let this happen?'

'I'm sorry, sir. I can't believe it. I'll have him arrested immediately,' said the flustered voice on the other end of the phone.

'This is likely to prove very embarrassing to us, Orlov. When I confronted Gorsky, he tried blackmailing me. He said that he would implicate me and the Russian government in this whole affair if we arrested him.'

'What would you like me to do, sir?'

'Make sure he's never seen again.'

CHAPTER FOURTY-THREE

The sudden suicide of the Chief of Staff had been occupying much of Tom's thoughts. *Why would a man who was on track to get pardoned and start a new life decide to kill himself? What changed? Had everything just become too much for him? He seemed a devoted husband and father – despite the treasonous acts that he had undertaken. It just doesn't make sense. But then you never know what's going on in someone's head.*

The death of James McInnis wasn't Tom's only concern either. There was still the little matter of capturing Baqri and then on top of that was the massive threat posed by The Collective. He couldn't help but feel that President Monroe's departure to the areas affected by the terrorist attacks was somewhat premature.

Tom had all but packed up 'Little Britain' – with just his Union Jack and laptop left on his desk. Having just decided that he should now have a go at walking unaided, Tom plodded slowly and with great deliberation to the side of his office. If Douglas Bader could fly Spitfires during the war with only metal legs, then he could bloody well make it twelve feet.

He looked again at his whiteboard. Two headings were written on it in black marker pen on either side of the top of the board – 'Aslan' and 'Farsight'. Underneath each one he had tried to do some brainstorming, but even he had to admit that it looked a little weak.

'OK, let's recap. So, what do we know about Aslan?' said Tom out loud, pointing his marker pen at each of the words written underneath that heading. 'He was a lion. A magical lion. Believed to represent Jesus Christ.'

Tom returned to his desk and tapped in 'Aslan' again into the internet browser.

Interesting. The word Aslan means lion. Sounds about right. Then there's C.S Lewis, The Lion, the Witch and the Wardrobe. *Not sure what Turkey has to do with it. Maybe Aslan really relates to Britain which has the lion as its symbol – probably from the medieval period of King Richard the Lionheart. Maybe the lion actually represents the King then, rather than the country. So, when* The *Collective's message said neutralising Aslan, they meant taking out the King? That makes sense,'*

He picked up his marker pen, returned to his white board and then, under the words 'Lion' and 'Jesus', wrote 'Turkish', 'Britain' and 'King Edward'.

'Does *The Witch and Wardrobe* have anything to do with it? Maybe they consider President Monroe to be the Witch?' Tom muttered, with a brief snort.

He looked at his heading of 'Farsight.' Just the words 'Commander' and 'Warhammer' were underneath.

'But this I really don't get. What the hell would the Warhammer game have to do with the assassination of the King? Not sure how that connects. And then who would Commander Farsight be? Maybe Farsight is the name for their project, as they call it.'

Tom returned to his desk once more. He was pretty sure that his decision to keep walking unaided would not be well received by his physical therapist. He tapped 'Commander Farsight' into the browser of his laptop.

Here we go. Crash course in Warhammer, he mused. *So, what have we got? Real name is O'Shovah, apparently. Came from the T'au world of Vior'la and led the T'au empire and was the bane of the Greenskins. Oh, right, they were Orks.*

'Well done, Tom. You've cracked it,' he muttered to himself, slamming the laptop shut. 'The Collective are, in fact, Orcs in disguise who are planning to take over the world! Bravo!'

A knock on the door and, without a pause, Rachael Goldberg was stood in the doorway. Tom was actually quite relieved that someone had broken up his misery.

'Talking to yourself, Tom?' asked Goldberg.

'Indeed, I am, Rachael. My father used to do the same thing. *Only way I can be sure of intelligent conversation*, he always used to say.'

'I'll try and remember that one. But I'm surprised to see that you have a bit of a temper. I thought that MI5 had conditioned you not to get angry, so that you stayed in control whatever the situation?'

'There's a difference between anger and frustration, Rachael. Full blown rage is highly unlikely but I'm quite easily irritated. Luna says I'm turning into a grumpy old man.'

'Well, I'm afraid any tantrums and discussion that you want to have with yourself is going to have to wait. We've got a problem.'

'More than the chief of staff topping himself?'

'Baqri's terrorist cell have recaptured the last HGV.'

'What? How? I thought the Russians had just got it back?'

'They had. Some Colonel in their FSB was working for The Collective and came up with a plan to allow the terrorist to recapture it, apparently.'

'And we're supposed to believe that President Petrov knew nothing about it?'

'That's what we're being told.'

'Rachael, Petrov is a control freak. Nobody farts at the Kremlin without him authorising it.'

'I know where you're coming from. But what we know for sure is that Baqri's group now has control of a huge EMP device that could devastate our country.'

'So, what now?'

'The president wants you back on the case. She's just boarded Airforce One and is about to chair another meeting of the National Security Council once she's in the air. That's where we're going next.'

'And there was I thinking I'd be going home to bed soon.'

'Now I know that's not true.'

'Yeah, complete lie. Rachael, I'm surprised that the president's still going ahead with her trip.'

'She feels that a visit to the affected towns and hospitals is very overdue. She's also betting on the FBI arresting Baqri soon. If not, then she'll consider returning.'

'What's our strategy, then?'

'We are assuming that Baqri will be directing the attack. So, Luna getting to him quickly is obviously critical.'

'I get that. I believe that she has just had her briefing with Assistant Director Marshall and is leaving now.'

'Tom, I'm sure that I don't need to remind you of what a massive EMP attack, on say New York, would do to our country's economy. What it will do to the world's economy.'

Tom stared at Rachael Goldberg for just over thirty seconds before he spoke again.

'That's the bit that I don't understand.'

'What do you mean?'

'The Collective exists for one purpose. To make its members money. So, to destroy the American economy and decimate other economies around the world – how does that help them?'

Goldberg shrugged her shoulders. 'Beats me. Come on. We've got a meeting to get to.'

CHAPTER FORTY-FOUR

The large monitor at the end of the Situation Room flicked on with the image of a very fatigued looking President Monroe. Her furrowed brow and angry scowl aptly conveyed her feelings on their current situation.

'Good morning, everyone. I know most of you expected to be tucked up in bed, after hearing that the last Avangard HGV had been recaptured by the Russians. But as they seem to have a habit of losing their weapons, here we are again. Clearly, this is now going to be an even longer day for all of us. Rachael, could you please briefly update everyone.'

'Ladies and gentlemen, I regret to inform you that, about an hour ago, we received word that Baqri's terrorist group had managed to re-acquire the last Avangard Hyper-Glide Vehicle.'

The relative quietness in the room was instantly elevated to a loud debate as the shocked members of the Security Council tried absorbing the news.

Rachael Goldberg tried continuing with her briefing but shortly stopped again.

Jane Monroe intervened. 'OK everyone. Quiet now please. 'I said QUIET!' she repeated in a raised voice, almost yelling.

'We confronted the Russian government when our Black Ops team noticed a group had been allowed access past their military's cordon,' said Goldberg. 'Originally, they claimed that it was some sort of radiological team to deal with a polonium leak from the HGV. But we identified a number of people in that group who were known Adalah terrorists. So, we challenged them again.'

'Polonium leak? But I thought it was only supposed to have an EMP fitted? And no polonium?' said Secretary Houston.

'And that was correct. But the Russians are saying that it was the Deputy Chief of the FSB, a Colonel Gorsky, who had falsely stated that the Avangard HGV contained polonium and that it was leaking.'

'Now, I'm really confused.'

'That's understandable, Walt. Apparently, this Colonel was a member of The Collective and his objective was to keep the Russian army away from the HGV. Hence, the change of advice to them. Bottom line is that the so-called radiological team were, as we thought, terrorists and have taken it.'

'That's complete bullshit. You know that right?' said Tom, then realising that his choice of words might be considered inappropriate in front of the President of the United States. 'Apologies, Madam President.'

'That's quite alright, Tom. You seem to be losing some of your famous English reserve. Now you just need to say it nice and slow like a Texan and it'll have some real guts to it,' she replied with a wan smile. 'Continue Tom. Tell me why you think that.'

'The Collective work from the shadows. This Gorsky guy blatantly attaches his name to the terrorists? That's not how they operate. Where is he now?'

'He's been arrested according to the Russian ambassador,' Goldberg replied.

Tom said, 'Of course he has. And will, no doubt, disappear forever, poor sod.'

'At any rate, we now have the threat of an EMP to deal with. An EMP that can be delivered to any American city without being detected,' said President Monroe.

'But I assume you have been using satellites to track the transporter carrying the HGV?' asked Vice President Stone.

'We were. But that area of Russia is covered in vast thick forests. We lost visual on the transporter when it entered one those forests,' replied Goldberg.

'OK. And so, what are the Russians doing to retrieve it?'

'President Petrov says that now he is aware of Gorsky's treachery, he is instructing his military to pursue. However, if we account for the delay in Russia admitting their loss to us, we believe that the terrorists have a two-hour head start.'

'So, they didn't send them as soon as they realised what had happened? They waited until they were forced to admit it to us. Not really the actions of a government desperate to stop an attack.'

'I concur, Jed. Petrov did agree that our Black Ops team could proceed as well, though.'

'Because he knows that they have no chance of getting to it in time,' said Tom. 'Petrov's behind all of this, you know.'

'I think you're right – but we have no proof of that. What I need to know is how we're going to stop that HGV being launched at one of our major cities,' said President Monroe.

Goldberg said, 'I believe that Tom's correct, in that our Black Ops team won't be able to catch up with the HGV before they are in a position to launch it. So, the only thing we can hope for, is that they won't do that without specific instructions from Baqri.'

'And that the FBI team gets to Baqri before he can give that order?'

'That's correct, Madam President.'

'And if they don't?'

‘Well, I’m working on a lead from a message we intercepted from The Collective. I’m hoping it’s a clue as to their targets. Might help us prepare and minimise casualties,’ said Tom.

President Monroe’s face loomed closer to the screen. ‘I really hope it doesn’t come to that. I’m sure I don’t need to remind you, Rachael, that turning somewhere like New York into a wasteland will be nothing short of catastrophic. Be under no misunderstanding everyone. The United States of America is now staring straight down the barrel of economic disaster.’

CHAPTER FORTY-FIVE

'Are you heading back to Little Britain?' asked Secretary of State Walt Houston.

'Ha! I can't believe you know that my office is called that,' replied Tom.

'Everyone calls it that. Even the president.'

'Well then, yes, I am on my way back to Little Britain. Do you fancy joining me? Could do with someone to bounce some ideas off – especially someone with a bit of life experience.'

'Is that code for *old*?'

'Not at all, Walt. The wisdom that comes from a wealth of experience. That's what I could do with.'

'Still sounds like *old* to me,' Walt Houston added as he held open the Situation Room door.

'Thank you for lending me this, by the way,' said Tom looking down at his newly acquired walking cane. He stepped out into the corridor.

'You're very welcome. When you get to my age, you may find that you have built up a collection of them. I have to say, though, I'm very surprised that you have decided to abandon your wheelchair so soon.'

'Yeah, I know. Haven't told my doctor or physio yet. Actually, I'm trying to do some unaided walking too. Build myself back up. Anyway, still glad my office is so close to the Situation Room.'

Tom looked over and smiled at Houston as they approached his office door.

'What?'

'Sorry, Walt. Just something Baqri said. Apparently, he said you could be a double for Morgan Freeman. Got to say, he has a point.'

'Yeah, I hear that a lot,' Houston replied with a smile and opening the door.

Tom hobbled back to his whiteboard with Walt Houston close behind.

'So, here it is. Two main names that we managed to get from an intercepted Collective message. Aslan and Farsight. The messages talked of *making sure that Aslan has been neutralised* and another one that says *Farsight should be terminated immediately.* What I managed to conclude, before the meeting, was that Aslan might refer to King Edward.'

'Makes sense.'

'Oh, OK. Good. But what doesn't make any sense is Farsight. What on earth has a character from Warhammer got to do with it? I don't suppose you've ever played Warhammer?'

'As it happens, I have.'

'Great! So, any thoughts?'

'Absolutely none. I can't see a connection either.'

'Oh dear.'

'I didn't even connect Warhammer, when I saw those two words on the board. I thought Chronicles of Nania.'

'*The Chronicles of Nania*?'

'Yes, one of my favourite series of books.'

'What's Farsight got to do with it then?'

'Well, Farsight was a character in one of the last books. Might have been the last one, actually.'

'And what sort of character was he … or she?'

'Oh, well Farsight was another talking creature. Like Aslan. An eagle, in fact. A talking eagle.'

'Oh my God,' muttered Tom, staring at Walt Houston.

'What?'

'The animal that represents Britain is the lion. Has been since the Middle Ages. And the animal that represents America is the eagle,' said Tom grabbing his phone from inside his pocket.

'So, if Aslan is the King …'

'Then Farsight the eagle …'

Secretary of State, Walter Houston, didn't need to finish his sentence.

CHAPTER FORTY-SIX

The four vehicle FBI convoy had reached the junction to the long private drive for Baqri's hideout – a large, sprawling, neo-Georgian style country house just outside Great Falls, Virginia, with white timber weather-boarding and an impressively ornate front door, framed by columns on either side. The property had, however, seen better days – having been abandoned and left empty for the last year, ever since the owners suffered a terrible family tragedy.

With both ends of the main road now blocked off, Assistant Director Hayden Marshall called a meeting with the three tactical team leaders in the Mobile Control Centre.

'OK, everyone. Just wanted to give you an update since the briefing back at headquarters. As you know, due to the length of the private drive and size of the building itself, we have not been able to get close enough to use radar or heat detecting equipment in order to identify the exact number and location of Baqri and his associates within the house. And we still haven't, I'm afraid,' said Marshall.

'So, we really haven't got a clue what we'll be facing?' said Luna.

'Well, we do have an update. A few minutes ago, we received some further intelligence on the sort of numbers that you are likely to be facing. The estimate is now between six and eight – plus Baqri and, we assume, his sidekick, Brigid Doyle. So, between eight and ten in total. I'm afraid that's the best information that we've managed to acquire in such a short space of time.'

'And has their individual positions changed?' asked Special Agent Steve Garcia, leader of Alpha Team.

'Still the same. Four of them are always based outside, with two of those being at the front. That leaves only two to four grunts inside plus Baqri and Doyle. One of the terrorists inside, patrols the first floor and keeps an eye out of the windows. He's a slow walker and it normally takes him just over five minutes to do a circuit. Always the same person and only occasionally gets replaced – for meal breaks, I guess. So, once he's moved away from the front window then that's when we'll go. Prepare your teams guys. Get ready to move in. May fortune favour the bold,' said Hayden Marshall, finishing with one of his favourite lines.

Luna looked across at Special Agent Steve Garcia and nodded. A very competent and experienced agent, in overall charge on the ground, who was also known for his extreme physical fitness. Alpha team and the operation itself was undoubtedly in good hands. Why she had been put in charge of Bravo team was a bit more of mystery to Luna – especially after the failure of her last mission to capture Baqri. She could only imagine that, with her enhanced genetics and conditioning, Marshall knew she would lead from the front.

Luna climbed into the passenger seat of Bravo team's BearCat. She looked at the driver and then around at the rest of her eight-man team sitting behind her. Six of the FBI's best. One or two seemed to be lost in their own thoughts and the others were just chatting. But it was a nervous chatter. The gravity of their mission was not lost on any of them. Their second attempt at capturing the world's most dangerous and infamous terrorist needed to be a success. Another failure was not an option.

Luna gazed out of the windshield. As beautiful as the moonlight was, she would have much preferred approaching the house in pitch black. *Mind you, as Baqri had generator powered flood lights around the perimeter of the house, then we wouldn't have got that close to it anyway without being seen,* she considered. The pressure was on the FBI snipers to eliminate Baqri's men outside before they could sound the alarm.

Spots of rain started appearing on the windshield and the wind was starting to pick up. This change in the weather was not unwelcome. Any background noise was going to be useful in masking the sound of their vehicles approaching. Her instructions from Marshall were clear – wait until Alpha team enters the house from the side. Then her team – Bravo team – would proceed through the front. Charlie team would remain at the foot of the driveway to cut off any possible escape or provide back-up if required. Snipers were already in place in the wooded perimeters of the grounds.

The lack of firm intelligence on the exact numbers that they would be facing was a little disconcerting, pondered Luna, but then the lack of preparation time due to the time critical nature of the operation was mainly to blame.

There was also, however, one added complication. Baqri needed to be taken alive. Orders direct from the president. Not only because he may be necessary to stop the launch of the last HGV but also for the goldmine of intel that he could provide on The Collective. If anyone could help them crack this organisation wide open, it would be Baqri. Whether he would co-operate, of course, was a different matter.

'This is Marshall. Alpha and Bravo units – move in,' came the calm and clear instruction over the radio.

Luna pressed the timer function on her watch.The two black FBI Bearcats accelerated off down the drive towards the house. The vehicles exited the wooded area of the drive and into the open grounds of the house. Luna could now make out the two guards at the front of the house. Both responded by attempting to raise their weapons but failing to get them further than chest height before the FBI snipers intervened.

So far, so good, thought Luna as the two terrorists slumped to the ground.

As had been anticipated, the two remaining outside guards raced around either side of the house to investigate, but they also then became easy prey for the snipers. Alpha team's Bearcat veered off towards the side door of the house as Luna's team pulled up to the front.

Luna looked at her watch again. Plenty of time before the guard inside was due to return to the front window. She decamped from the Bearcat, immediately followed by the rest of the team. Explosives were strategically placed around the white timber front doors and Bravo team stood behind the two columns on either side and waited.

A loud bang confirmed that Alpha team had blown their door and would be entering the building. *The one plus point in this operation*, Luna considered, *is that at least there are no hostages that could be killed. Anyone not in black FBI tactical gear is fair game. Except Baqri, of course. Disappointingly.*

Almost immediately an exchange of gunfire ensued, as Alpha team moved into the west reception area of the house. Luna looked across the front and, without hesitation, the member of her team holding the detonator pressed the switch. The controlled explosion ripped both doors from their hinges – one finishing flat on its back and the other on its side. Luna indicated to her team that they were moving in.

Three steps up and she was stood in an impressively large entrance hall. Black and white tiles adorned the floor and, overhead, a huge crystal chandelier. About ten yards directly in front – a magnificent sweeping staircase, which split into two at the first landing. With no sign of anyone on the stairs, Luna indicated to four of her unit to check the reception room on her right. The voice of Steve Garcia broke the silence over her radio.

'This is Garcia. West ground floor area clear. Little resistance. One hostile neutralised. Moving to main entrance hall to meet with Bravo team.'

'Copy that,' replied Marshall.

From her left came the sound of multiple footsteps. Even though expected, Steve Garcia and Alpha team were still a welcome sight. Garcia nodded at Luna and indicated, as per the mission plan, that he was moving his team to the stairs in order to secure the first floor. As the other half of her team returned, Luna responded by indicating that she was advancing on the reception rooms at the rear of the house. She watched as Alpha team advanced – ready to assist if needed.

Garcia's team proceeded cautiously up the stairs but, unexpectedly, finding no resistance. The absence of the first-floor guard was not the only thing that surprised Luna. Two members of Alpha team stumbled on their way up the stairs. And even Garcia himself looked shaky. Nevertheless, Luna watched as they moved up the second flight to the first floor.

With a hand gesture, Bravo team followed Luna to the right-hand side of the staircase and another door. Whereas the entrance hall had been flooded with artificial light through the windows, the same could not be said for the rest of the house. Luna approached the doorway leading into another reception room. A dim flicker of light came from half a dozen candles adorning the window sill.

Something caught her eye. A shadow from behind the door. A shadow that moved. She slammed the door backwards towards the wall and then grabbed the sub-machine gun which was now clearly in view. Luna pulled the guy on the end of the gun into the open and struck him hard in the throat. The man choked and gasped for breath, lowering his weapon, and grasping his neck.

Hurried footsteps came from the corridor that led off the back of the room. Another guy appeared in that doorway, but with a shotgun this time. Luna pulled the man that she was holding around to use as a shield and, before the second guy could react, she fired off a burst of rounds from her MP5. He dropped to his knees and then fell face down on to the floor. The guy that she was holding struggled to break free, which Luna obligingly did before firing a second burst into the middle of him.

Bravo team cautiously advanced towards the doorway to the long candle-lit corridor. One of Luna's team stumbled. The relative quiet was abruptly shattered by the sound of gunfire from the floor above. But not the sound of a fire fight. Sounded more like a single semi-automatic weapon being discharged. The radio opened as if someone was going to speak and then fell silent again.

'Special Agent Garcia, status please,' said Luna, into her mike. 'Garcia, respond.'

Luna stopped and crouched down. The sound of gunfire had ended.

'Alpha team, please respond,' said Luna. But no reply was forthcoming.

A series of thuds came from behind. Luna looked around. Her entire team was either lying on the floor or propping themselves up against the walls. It was less than a minute before even those, had joined their colleagues on the ground. Luna shook her head. She felt dizzy and disorientated. She tried standing up and, with an enormous effort – plus the aid of her MP5 – she struggled to her feet. She looked up. At the end of the corridor, in the flickering light of the candles, stood two men with semi-automatic weapons raised. She tried raising her MP5 but her strength had completely left her. Despite her genetic advantage, Luna now felt as weak as a toddler.

From behind the two men came a roar of laughter. It wasn't difficult for her to guess who was finding the situation so amusing.

CHAPTER FORTY-SEVEN

Tom Rivers had wasted no time picking up the phone to the president, whose flight was now somewhere over Missouri.

'Madam President,' said Tom.

'Hi Tom. Is everything OK?'

The urgent tone to Tom's voice was so unusual that Monroe immediately stopped what she was doing, put her pen down on the desk and picked the telephone handset off its speaker base.

'I don't think it is Ma'am. I'll get straight to it. I believe Air Force One is in danger.'

'What? Is this the reason why the aircraft has suddenly just started banking away?'

'It is Madam President. You're being re-routed to the nearest air force base.'

'What the hell's going on, Tom?' said Monroe, straightening her posture.

'The last Avangard HGV, Madam President. I don't think it's meant for a city at all. I think they intend to use it to bring down Air Force One. I believe that their target is you.'

'Me? I'm sorry, Tom, but that doesn't make any sense. That's a huge EMP. Our intelligence suggested that it is so large that it could take out not just the whole of New York but anything for miles around it. Why would he waste it on me? He could cripple the American economy with that.'

'I know – and you would be right if it was just Baqri. I'm sure that he would be delighted to bring down the US – but it's not him calling the shots.'

'You mean, The Collective.'

'Exactly. Baqri has only gained the infamy that he had so desperately wanted, because of their support. If he loses their backing then he becomes just … well, just another terrorist. And that would be the worst thing for him. He wants to be remembered. He wants to be revered. Mohammed Baqri – the most famous terrorist in history.'

'God, he is quite mad. And you don't think The Collective want to hit a major US city?'

'No, I don't. That's contrary to their purpose. Destroying the heart of America's financial system would have a knock-on effect across the globe. It would result in a disastrous hit to the whole world's economy.'

'Well, maybe Baqri will use it on a less critical city. Perhaps he's reached a compromise with The Collective?'

'OK, but what would be the point? This is their last missile. If it detonates over a city which isn't that important in the great scheme of things, then what's the result? There could be some loss of lives, of course. But as far as the infrastructure goes, everything destroyed by the EMP can be replaced or re-built over time. It doesn't really serve any purpose.'

'I get your thinking, Tom, but what makes you think that they're going after me?'

'Do you remember we intercepted part of a Collective message?'

'I do.'

'Two names were mentioned. Aslan and Farsight. We believe that these are codenames for important individuals. The names are both characters that are in a series of books – *The Chronicles of Narnia*.'

'Go on.'

'Aslan, is a talking lion.'

'Yes, I remember. From *The Lion, The Witch and The Wardrobe* – right?'

'Right. Now, we think that Aslan refers to King Edward. The lion has been the symbol for Britain for centuries. The message talked about neutralising Aslan. Which, of course, they tried to do.'

'OK. That makes sense. And the other name?'

'The other character, Madam President, is Farsight. And Farsight is a talking eagle.'

Monroe paused for a minute before she simply uttered, 'Dear God.'

Jane Monroe slumped back into her seat, put her hand to her mouth and looked out of the window.

'Madam President, the message talked of terminating Farsight.'

'I'm sure they told me that Air Force One has some sort of protection against an EMP attack. It seems like it does for everything else.'

'Whatever they told you, it won't be enough. You yourself just said that the EMP is so big that it could take out New York and for miles beyond. Madam President, Baqri is using a sledgehammer to crack a nut.'

'And you think that I was always the target? It really wasn't about crippling America?'

'I think that Baqri knew that, after attacking those towns with polonium, you would at some point go to visit those affected. He knew that you would be taking Air Force One.'

'But I still don't understand why me? OK, I get why Baqri would want to kill me, but why The Collective?'

'Because you're one of the good guys. You've made it clear that you intend to crack them wide open. You declared war on them … and they knew you would. Baqri gets the pleasure of killing the President of the United States and The Collective gets rid of the one person who could cause them serious trouble going forward.'

'And the King?'

'Well, by not dying, he cost them a fortune in the Congo. But you're the main target now. So long as you're in power, then any other plans that they have will be put in jeopardy.'

'All right. Say they manage to kill me. It doesn't mean that they get a free ride. Jed Stone will take up the gauntlet.'

'He might.'

'You don't think so?'

'I think he will follow his own agenda. He probably won't even want to try and do battle with The Collective. Especially if he sees that they were able to get to you. Will he want to stir up the hornet's nest? He seems like the sort of man who's into self-preservation, to me. And he won't know, of course, which other world leaders are on his side or are actually Collective.'

'Do you think Petrov's a member?'

'I do. But if he isn't, then he's done a great job of helping them.'

'So, what happens now?'

'Admiral Womack has despatched fighter aircrafts from various Air Force bases to join your escort detail. The hope is that they will be able to provide a protective bubble around Air Force One, until it is able to safely land.'

'How long till they get here?'

Tom looked at his watch. 'They should start arriving within the next twenty minutes or so.'

'Do you know what, Tom. From what I've learnt about this Avangard system, I really don't see how the fighters can protect me. We may end up losing a good many pilots as well.'

'I'll be honest. It's a chance. The main priority is to get you safely back on the ground. I understand that you're being diverted to Whiteman Air Force Base.'

'OK, thanks Tom.'

'Good luck, Madam President.'

President Monroe placed the handset back on to its base, stood up from behind her desk and ambled towards the glass door of her office and looked out. The level of activity by members of staff had definitely increased since she had been on the phone to Tom. Now, John Barratt, the director of her Secret Service, was stood facing her on the other side of the glass. Abruptly, he opened the door.

'Madam President, we need to get you seated and strapped in. Our Black Ops team in Russia have just reported a missile launch.'

CHAPTER FORTY-EIGHT

Luna dropped back down to one knee. She shook her head. Fog had overtaken her mind and physically she felt herself getting weaker and weaker. Her breathing had also become shallow and more laboured as if she was heavily asthmatic. She heard footsteps from behind and managed to turn her head in time to see a guy, with a P90 sub-machine gun, fire a burst of rounds into each of her team lying on the ground.

'I can't believe you're not on the floor,' said Baqri excitedly from the end of the corridor. 'Gentlemen … oh, and lady … sorry Brigid … here is a great example of what superior genetics can do. When every other member of the FBI team was incapacitated or dying, Luna here just kept on going. And she's way older than all of them. Oops! That was a bit of a faux pas, wasn't it? Mentioning a lady's age.'

'What have you done?' Luna managed to whisper.

'Oh, personally, I haven't done anything. If you mean, what's happened to you and your team, then the answer is a specially modified type of nerve agent. Slow start and then it just powers through the body. For mere mortals, like your colleagues there, then after complete seizure of their muscles, organ shut down will rapidly follow. My man there, Raul, actually performed an act of mercy by putting them out of their misery.'

Luna again tried standing up. *If she could find the strength to raise her gun, then it would all be over.* She again pushed herself up on her MP5 but after using all of her remaining strength, dropped back.

'Wow. Just wow!' exclaimed Baqri, frenziedly clapping away. 'I've got to give it to Sir Iain MacGregor, his MI5 Sleeper project has been an amazing success. First came your husband, Tom. Intelligent, perceptive, dogged and with an almost super-human constitution. Completely ruined my plans for London. But what a guy. Then comes you. Like some sort of terminator. I mean, if we hadn't poisoned you, then I reckon you would have gone through everyone here like a hot knife through butter. Am I right?'

'I'm still going to kill you,' Luna whispered.

'Actually, you're not. Even with your incredible gifts that's not going to happen.'

Baqri stepped forward into the light of the flickering candles. This was the first time that Luna had actually seen him in person. Exactly like the photograph that she had been shown back at MI5 headquarters. Medium height and build, shaved head, goatee beard and a tattoo of three tears underneath one eye. But there was something more that the photograph hadn't shown. His eyes. Bright, round brown eyes which almost sparkled. If Luna had not known him and met him for the first time, she would have imagined him as someone who had a good sense of humour and a zest for life. But what made his eyes sparkle, however, was simply having the power to take lives. She was in the presence of a true psychopath. Baqri was capable of killing thousands of men, women and children – and to not even contemplate that this was wrong. She had to kill him.

Raul walked up to Luna's side and grabbed her MP5. Though her breathing had become even harder and she was feeling more disorientated by the second, she managed to look down at the floor, move her weapon slightly to the side and pull the trigger. The bullets ripped through Raul's left boot. He screamed loud and hard before managing to pull the gun from Luna's hand and strike her in the face with it.

'Are you OK there, Raul?' Baqri laughed.

'Jesus Christ, look at my foot! Look what that bitch did to my foot!' said Raul, now sat on the ground and gripping the ripped boot which was pouring blood from the holes.

'Hello, Luna,' said Brigid walking over to Luna and then slapping her in the side of the head. 'Nice to see you on your knees this time.'

Brigid took Luna's radio off her and walked it back over to Baqri. Luna looked up. She managed a slight smile.

'You're on borrowed time, Baqri. Marshall will know there's something wrong soon when he doesn't hear from us,' she muttered.

'Doesn't matter,' replied Baqri.

'They'll be coming to get you, you know.'

Again, Baqri laughed.

'Do you think so?' said Baqri mockingly. 'Brigid, what do you think? Do you think that Hayden Marshall is going to burst into the house with another bunch of FBI guys?'

Brigid Doyle shook her head.

'Me neither. I mean, what did you expect, Luna? Did you think that you caught us here by surprise? That it was as a result of Tom getting one of my guys to talk? This was all by design. My design. I knew Idris, that weak-minded fool, would talk. In fact, it was essential that he did.'

'I don't understand. You wanted us here?'

'Wanted *you* here. By the way, did you ever get to the bottom of who the traitor was in the FBI? Embarrassing that I've slipped through your fingers twice before, isn't it? All thanks to someone tipping us off.'

'Jones.'

'Special Agent, Ed Jones? Poor Ed. A bit of circumstantial evidence and he's in the frame. Quite low down the pecking order, don't you think to be a member of The Collective? I don't actually know who's in that organisation – even they don't know who else is a member – but I can tell you that they are all people of power. And that's how I know that we're safe. The Collective want this to happen.'

'Want what to happen?'

'The death of Luna Rivers.'

CHAPTER FORTY-NINE

President Monroe had now moved from the Presidential suite to the VIP section - slightly further back on Air Force One. Buckled up in her seat, she looked across at her deputy chief of staff and communications director. Both sat in complete silence, staring blankly ahead and consumed by their own thoughts. Monroe tried giving them a comforting smile.

She looked out of the window. There, sitting between the clouds, she could see a flashing light coming from one of the escort fighters. She questioned in her mind how they could possibly help. What was coming their way was almost undetectable – no heat signature and so fast and manoeuvrable that it could be sat underneath them before her pilots even realised. None of the counter measures fitted to Air Force One were designed to defend against this – an EMP blast so big that it could take out a city. She looked back at the large monitor on the wall opposite her. Once again, her Security Council were convened in Washington DC.

'How long till that Avangard thing can reach us, Admiral?' asked President Monroe.

'Well, we estimate that there is about five thousand, four hundred miles between you and the area in Russia where the missile was launched, Madam President,' replied Womack.

'That sounds like a decent distance to me.'

'You would think so. But the problem is that the Avangard is believed to be able to travel at a speed of at least fifteen thousand miles an hour,' said Tom.

'Initially seems like you would have a lot at time,' said Admiral Womack.

'But I haven't.'

'I'm afraid not ma'am,' said Womack.

Monroe looked at the ceiling and performed a quick calculation. 'That means that it could be on us in, say, twenty minutes? Is that right?'

'It could, but there are a number of variables,' replied Tom. 'The Avangard is initially carried as a payload by an intercontinental ballistic missile. An RS-26 Rubezh in this case. The missile also travels at around Mach twenty. But it has to go about sixty-two miles up to the edge of space before releasing the Avangard. And that is likely to be a diagonal trajectory. So, what I'm getting at, is it's not a direct path to you. The Avangard is effectively a glider, so it needs the height.'

'And we also don't know exactly what speed it can achieve. It's too new for us to have any verified data on it,' added Womack.

'Well, try gentlemen!' shouted Monroe, slamming her hand down on her armrest. 'My apologies,' she quickly added.

'Completely understandable,' said Tom.

'Best case scenario is that the Russians have exaggerated, and it travels at more like twelve thousand miles an hour. So, with an indirect route that Tom mentioned, it could take just under half an hour. If the Russian propaganda is true, however, and it can reach twenty-one thousand miles an hour, then it could be with you in ten minutes or so,' said Womack.

'And how long till we reach the air force base?'

'You're currently just south of Branson. That's a flight of about a hundred and eighty miles to Whiteman Airforce Base. Air Force One is travelling at six hundred and thirty miles an hour, so you're looking at about seventeen to eighteen minutes.'

'Let me just try and understand this correctly. By the time Air Force One manages to get less than two hundred miles further north in this state that we're flying over, a weapon launched all the way from southern Russia, could have reached us?'

'That's correct, ma'am,' said Womack solemnly.

'And our other fighters?'

'The ETA of the first wing is about twelve minutes out, Ma'am.'

Monroe looked down at her hands, which were firmly clasped together. The feeling of being completely helpless and at the mercy of others, was an alien concept to her. She had gone through life as a strong, confident woman. She enjoyed the feeling that came with being intimidating to other world leaders, not just because of her physical size but also because of the power and influence that came with being the President of the United States. But right then – right at that moment – she realised that she had no more power to alter her fate than a member of her administration staff.

'So, take me through it, Admiral. How are those fighters going to stop it? What's your plan?'

'We'll be having to rely mainly on visual identification, Madam President. We've sent up as many aircrafts as we can. The idea is that there will be rings of aircrafts around Air Force One. So, even if the Avangard isn't intercepted at the outer ring, but is still spotted, information such as its current heading can be passed on to the inner rings, giving them a better chance at shooting it down.'

'But I don't understand why we can't track this thing with all the technology we have at our disposal. What about radar or satellite?'

'The problem is that the Avangard is travelling along the edge of space. At the moment, we have nothing that will detect that. We can track the ballistic missile that was carrying it. But when it releases the Avangard, that doesn't become visible again until it drops to a lower trajectory. And it probably won't do that until it's on a final attack course towards Air Force One.'

'Just on that particular point, Madam President, as we know the direction that the ballistic missile was travelling, it should give us an idea of where the Avangard will come from. Logically, they will want to take the most direct route to their target,' added Tom.

'To me, you mean. I get what you're saying, Tom. But it still doesn't mean that it can be stopped, does it? How long do we have from when it moves into visibility to reaching Airforce One?'

'Well, even with your pilot reducing his altitude slightly – which he's currently doing – the truth is that the Avangard is going so fast, we may only have a matter of seconds to respond,' said Womack.

President Monroe stared blankly at the screen before looking back out the window again.

'Seconds … Seconds,' she muttered, before turning her attention back to the monitor in front of her. 'So, with a window of just a few seconds, tell me how the hell you're going to be able to stop this thing, Admiral?'

'Ma'am?'

'How the hell are our fighters going to stop something that's travelling at eight times their speed? I mean it'll be like a prize racehorse blasting past a three-legged donkey! Even if they spot it and launch a missile, I assume that the missile wouldn't be able to catch it?'

'You're correct, ma'am. We will have to rely on intercepting it,' said Womack, demonstrating with his hands how fire from the fighters would hit the side of the Avangard.

'And you think that can be done in a matter of seconds?'

'Quite honestly, that's the only play we've got.'

'What about Baqri? He could stop it, surely?'

'The FBI teams have only just arrived at his suspected location, but it's highly unlikely that they will get to him in time,' replied Rachael Goldberg.

'OK, so let's assume the worst. The Avangard manages to get near Air Force One and detonates. There's a huge EMP blast. Then what? I assume it doesn't just drop out the air?'

'No, it won't just drop like a brick. It will still be able to glide for a while. I've checked and a 747 has a glide ratio of fifteen to one,' said Tom.

'In English, Tom?'

'Sorry, Ma'am. It means that it can glide fifteen kilometres for every kilometre it drops in height. I've done a quick calculation. So, you are currently just over four miles up or, say seven kilometres. That means that Air Force One can glide for about a hundred and five kilometres or sixty-five miles.'

'Which is only about a third of the way to Whiteman Airforce Base. But if we were higher up then, surely, we could have glided further?'

Womack said 'True, Madam President. But you would also be closer to the Avangard when it descends, and that would give us absolutely no chance of shooting it down.'

'Sorry to say this, Admiral, but I don't honestly believe you have a chance anyway. And my next question is whether the pilot will actually be able to land Air Force One after an EMP hit of that magnitude?'

'Air Force One has been hardened to an EMP attack in its last upgrade, Madam President. And it's also one of the most technically advanced aircrafts in the world, using the latest fly-by-wire technology.'

'But?'

'But fly-by-wire is an electronic system which replaces conventional manual aircraft controls. Its reliance on all those electronics is also its Achilles heel.'

'And we have to assume that this weapon is directional,' added Tom.

'Meaning?'

'Meaning, Ma'am, that instead of a wave that radiates out in every direction, all the force from the EMP is focussed into going one way.'

'Straight at Air Force One,' said Monroe. 'An EMP which has the force to take out the whole of New York and beyond, directed towards us, at point blank range.'

'The pilot will lose a lot of critical stuff but the aircraft does have some degree of mechanical back-up. Difficult to say how much control the pilot will end up with though. Having said that, he's one of the very best in the Air Force.'

President Monroe turned her attention to Tom Rivers who had an expression on his face that she had become very familiar with.

'There it is again. What's on your mind, Tom?'

'Well, I'm just thinking about the EMP that Baqri used on London. In order to create the EMP effect that was required, Dr Farooqi used an extremely high yield explosive. I think we can assume that he has used a similar but larger device here. The Avangard could carry, say, one or two tonnes of this explosive.'

'Your point?'

'My point, Ma'am, is that if I was Baqri, then I would want that explosive to not only detonate the EMP but also to physically damage Air Force One. Seriously damage it.'

'A double whammy. Just damaging Air Force One not being certain enough, the EMP destroys all the critical electronics just to make sure that the pilot has no chance.'

'I think that's the plan. It would have to get very close to be able to do that.'

'We'll get the inner circle fighters ready for that scenario,' added Womack.

'Thank you, everyone. I can't see there's much more that can be done apart from pray. As I may be on borrowed time, however, I think I need to call my husband and son now.

'I understand, Madam President,' said Tom.

'Family is important. There are a few things that I would like to say to them.'

CHAPTER FIFTY

The room was dark. Save for a few candles dotted around here and there in the impressively large and ornate drawing room, the main source of light came from the roaring fire. Beside the marble fireplace, and opposite each other, were two leather high-back winged Chesterfield chairs in antique tan. A small mahogany coffee table sat in between. On that was a bottle of Petrus 1982 and a half full glass.

'I thought that you would be a little more comfortable through here, Luna. Don't you think these chairs are just beautiful, by the way?' asked Baqri, leaning forward to pick up the glass. 'OK, I know they're looking a little … tired … yes, that's a nice way to put it … tired. But I think a few worn patches here and a little tear there, just adds to their character – don't you? They're pretty well all that was left in this house, along with the table.'

Luna was sat in the chair opposite, unable to move – incapacitated by a nerve agent which had somehow been delivered to every member of the two FBI tactical teams that had entered the house.

A huge explosion and the sound of gunfire could be heard in the distance. Baqri raised his head and smiled.

'I hope that you like all the candles and the lovely fire. Two of your favourite things you enjoy at home, I believe. I went to all this trouble, just for you. I could have just got in another generator, but I wanted you to feel comfortable.'

'I'm touched,' mumbled Luna.

'I would offer you a drink,' said Baqri, 'but unfortunately, I've only got the one glass. Very selfish, I know. Then again, you would probably waste it by dribbling out the side of your mouth. And for a red wine this good … well, that would just be criminal, wouldn't it?'

'You would just poison me … again anyway.'

'Sounds like you're struggling a bit now, Luna. Stay with me though – this is important. I want you to know that I had nothing to do with you being poisoned.'

'Pffff.'

'No. Seriously. It wasn't me. And I'm sure you agree that I am trying to treat you with the utmost respect and causing you no harm.'

'And why *is* that?'

'Because I want Tom to know that I had nothing to do with your death. But what I did do, was to try and make your last moments as comfortable as possible. Do you think I want your husband hunting me down for your murder? He's relentless enough when he's just working for a government. If I killed you, it would become personal. And he would become unstoppable. He could seriously hinder my future plans. As Sun Tzu said - *the wise warrior avoids battle*.'

'So, who then?'

'Difficult to say. But you know that The Collective have got someone in the FBI?'

Luna nodded. Her eyes were trying to close but she kept shaking it off.

'I think I know who now,' Luna mumbled.

'Not sure that the internal investigation has got anywhere yet, has it? But I just wanted you to know that The Collective are the ones that want you dead. I'm just the bait,' said Baqri, looking around as Brigid Doyle emerged from the shadows.

It was fair to say that Luna and Brigid were never going to be good friends. When they first met, Luna was at the family home in England, grieving the apparent loss of Tom who, according to the police, had been killed in a terrorist attack. Brigid had appeared on the doorstep, claiming to be one of the hospital nurses who had looked after him. But her real intention was revenge. An eye for an eye. In her mind, Tom had coldly gunned down her fiancé, Connor, on the streets of London – even though he was in the process of delivering Baqri's weapon of mass destruction to the centre of the city. Brigid vowed that there would be retribution for what Tom had done – and that included killing his wife.

At that time, however, Luna was still completely unaware of not just what Tom was but also what *she* was. As far as she knew, they were both just ordinary people - her husband was an architect and she was in marketing. Brigid's arrival would change all of that. Little did Brigid know that her attempt to kill Tom's wife would backfire so badly – inadvertently causing the activation of Luna from her *Sleeper* state. Her plan was to torture and eventually murder Luna, but the outcome could not have been more different. Luna had almost instantly turned into a relentless fighting machine, turning the tables on Brigid, and beating her so badly that she only just managed to escape with her life. Now, at their third encounter, the tables had turned. Brigid's nemesis looked weak, immobile, and helpless.

Luna watched out the corner of her eye as Brigid walked up to her and put a pistol to her forehead. She pulled back the hammer and pushed the gun harder into Luna's head.

'Now, now, Brigid,' said Baqri. 'You remember what we discussed? I do apologise, Luna.'

Brigid slowly lowered the gun's hammer, before giving Luna's head a push with her spare hand.

'Look at those eyes, Brigid. She can't move the rest of her body but those eyes! So much hatred. And not just for you. I think she hates me too.'

'I can … still … talk,' whispered Luna.

'Bravo … bravo!' exclaimed Baqri, grinning and wildly clapping his hands again. 'You see, Brigid. All the rest of the FBI team quickly succumbed to the nerve agent and died. Yet Luna's superior genetics, plus whatever witchcraft those MI5 nerds used when they conditioned her, have allowed her to keep going. Just astonishing! You've got to admit, this is pretty impressive.'

'You're easily impressed,' said Brigid.

'Oh, now, now. Don't worry, Luna, she's just jealous. I think you're awesome!'

'You're going … to … die,' Luna quietly muttered, her mouth stuck open like a ventriloquist.

Baqri laughed. 'You're right, of course. I will die. We all will. Well, one day, anyway. And that day will be a tragic loss to all those oppressed people around the world, who will consider me to be their saviour.'

'Ha!' whispered Luna, 'that's really … funny.'

'I'm glad you find it amusing because you, however, will die tonight along with all your FBI friends. Yes, all of them. That explosion earlier … did you hear it? And gunfire? Were you hoping that the cavalry was going to be galloping over the hill? What you heard was the sound of them all dying instead. Shall we call Assistant Director Marshall and see how he is? He's felt better, I imagine.'

Luna stared again at Baqri, with her hate filled green eyes. Even incapacitated, she could still look intimidating.

'So, I imagine you're now thinking to yourself *why the hell has* The Collective *gone to so much trouble to kill me*? A very good question, let me say. Well done. The answer is … wait for it … Tom!'

CHAPTER FIFTY-ONE

'Hey, Mom,' said the voice on the other end of the phone.

'Hey, darlin'. How are you?'

'Well, I'm not sure I'm ever going to get used to being told that the president is on the phone for me.'

'Sorry to call you at work,' said Jane Monroe.

'You know that we have a senior nurse, who I work with at the hospital, called Kim, and if you ever call then she enjoys shouting out on the Tannoy *Call from the President of the United States for Doctor Monroe.* Every time.'

'Yeah, I'm sorry, John. I know that I said I wouldn't do it anymore but I've got a few spare minutes and it's been so hectic. I can always have her killed, by the way.'

President Monroe looked out of her window. In the last few minutes, there had been a dramatic increase in the number of visible aircrafts. She also noted that the two F-35's, which Admiral Womack had insisted escorted Air Force One, had moved closer.

'Ha! If it wasn't for the fact that she's Colette's best friend, then I might have considered taking you up on the offer.'

'How is your lovely wife, by the way?'

'She's good. Finding being a surgeon now to be her perfect career. Absolutely loving it.'

'Oh, that's great. I can't believe that you two can work together as well as live together. If I had your father with me 24/7, well I reckon we would be talking divorce.'

'Now, I know that would never happen. Anyway, he's out on the golf course most of the time.'

'As he is at the moment. I've just spoken to him.'

'You've called Dad on the golf course? I thought that was something that you never did?'

'I don't normally, but I just wanted a chat.'

'Are you OK, Mom? I'm getting worried about you. You phone Dad on the golf course and then you phone me at work. Is there something going on that you're not telling me?'

'No. As I said, it's just been so crazily busy that I haven't had any family time. I've got a little time now, so I thought it would be good to have a quick catch-up.'

'Alright. Just checking.'

Monroe looked at her reflection in the window. The stomach-churning nervousness that she was feeling was being conveyed to her face. *Thank goodness this call isn't being done via video link*, she thought. *He would have definitely noticed.*

'And how's my favourite granddaughter?'

'Your only granddaughter, Mom. And she's doing well. Enjoying nursery but already getting a reputation for her belligerent attitude.'

'Hate to say it, but that might just come from her mother's French heritage.'

'It was that feisty attitude that attracted me to Colette in the first place! I think she would describe it as being passionate. But, yeah, I get what you mean.'

'I'm glad we had a chance to chat. I'm really proud of you. You know that don't you?'

'Thanks Mom. I do, yes … are you OK?'

Jane Monroe bit her lip. As hard as she tried to supress her emotions, she could not stop a solitary tear from rolling down her cheek. She immediately wiped it away, looked to the ceiling and tried to regain control of herself. She closed her eyes and silently inhaled and exhaled. On the other end of the phone, she could hear her son.

'Mom. Are you ok?'

'I am honey, thank you. I was just reflecting on how lucky I am to have such an amazing family. I don't get much time to do that.'

'And you're definitely alright?'

'Yeah, I'm fine. Just tired. Probably why I'm feeling like this.'

'Mom, I'm sorry. I've got to go. Looks like we've got casualties from a massive traffic accident coming into the hospital. Speak at the weekend?'

'Sure, darlin'. Love you.'

'Love you too, Mom.'

President Monroe pressed the end call button and placed the phone back on the table in front of her. She stared at it for a few moments. A feeling of helplessness and imminent doom had now taken hold. And then there was another feeling. One that was alien to her. Fear.

A rapid knock on the glass door to her room and her thirty-something acting chief of staff briskly walked in.

'Madam President. The Avangard has been spotted. It's on a sharp decent from the upper stratosphere. Our outer fighters are about to engage it.'

'Attempt to engage it, is probably more accurate.'

'Yes, Ma'am. But in our favour is the fact that it had come from the direction that we were expecting.'

'Well, I guess you better come and join me, Carly,' said Monroe, pointing to the seat opposite. 'Strap yourself in and tell me a little bit about yourself.'

'Ma'am?'

'Nothing we can do will affect the outcome. So, we might as well talk.'

'I guess that's true, Madam President.'

President Jane Monroe once more glanced out through the window.

'Our fate lies in the hands of our talented pilots and the Lord God Himself.'

CHAPTER FIFTY-TWO

'Tom?' Luna mumbled.

'Yes, Tom. You remember him. Your husband. The man who manages to wreck every plan that I conceive and frustrate The Collective's projects,' said Baqri. 'He's become a real pain in the ass, as you Americans would say. But don't get me wrong. I've got a huge amount of respect for the guy. Well, you can't not – can you? A bruiser of a man who is highly trained and proficient in weaponry, unarmed combat and pursuit driving plus a genius level IQ and the freaky ability to get inside the heads of others. I mean, I think he knows what I'm going to do next before I do. Oh, and not forgetting that he has an almost mythical status when it comes to survival and defeating death.'

'If a cockroach can ever be regarded as mythical,' said Brigid.

'Well, that's very rude,' said Baqri. 'I apologise again for my associate, Luna. Brigid is still sore that she failed to kill your husband, even when he was lying in a coma in a hospital bed. That's her bad, I would say, wouldn't you?'

'He murdered Connor.'

'Who? Oh, yes, yes. Your fiancé. Luna knows that already. That's why you tried to kill her last time,' replied Baqri dismissively.

'Wow. Just wow,' said Brigid.

'Anyway, getting back to the point. The latest project that The Collective had – they call them projects by the way – was to change the regime in the Democratic Republic of Congo. Their members invested eye-watering amounts of capital and resources to make that happen. Obviously, they expected huge returns when Colonel Banza took power and they then took control of the cobalt mines. But this has just been completely ruined by a combination of your husband and that great beast of a woman that lives in The White House.

'Calamity Jane,' added Brigid.

'Yes, I call her Calamity Jane, by the way. Now, my friends can't afford to let this continue, and Calamity has already declared war on them with a mission to root out all their members. So, The Collective have decided to act first. The first thing that they have determined is that President Monroe has to go the way of the dodo. Any minute now, Air Force One will get hit by an Avangard HGV fitted with an awful lot of explosives and one very large EMP device.'

Luna was now really labouring against the effect of the nerve agent. Still just about able to speak and with some minimal movement in her face, her brow furrowed and her nostrils flared.

'Yes, that good old country girl is shortly going to be spread all over northern Missouri,' crowed Baqri.

'Whoop, whoop,' cheered Brigid with her hands in the air.

'As Sun Tzu said, *the greatest victory is that which requires no battle.*'

'They won't give up,' Luna murmured.

'Oh right. You're thinking that the president's hunt for members of The Collective will go on without her? Well, they're pretty sure that it won't.'

'Why?'

'Come on, Luna! What? You thought that governments actually ran their countries? That's very naive, you know. This is the great illusion.'

'Great illusion?'

'Absolutely. The great illusion … or maybe it should be called the great deception. Maybe both. People have been brain-washed into believing that they get to decide who runs their country. And they actually think that their vote makes a difference. An unshakeable belief in something called democracy. But it's not real.'

'Oh my God! A conspiracy theory,' whispered Luna, mockingly.

'Not a theory. Most major governments only think that they run their countries. Sure, they get to deal with the day-to-day business but the big policies are decided by unelected shadows. The world's major governments are just puppets … and, like a great Punch and Judy show, the puppeteers operate from the dark.'

'They can't all be Collective.'

'You're getting quieter and quieter, aren't you? Well done for hanging in there, Luna. And the answer to your question is, that I really don't know. I don't actually have any better idea than you, as to who are members. I would assume that not all leaders are, no. But they probably have people in place who can influence the decisions made. That's my guess, anyway.'

'Don't think she's going to last much longer,' said Brigid.

'Yes, quite right. So, let's move on to the reason why we wanted you here. Your husband, Tom.'

'Tom? Why, Tom,' mumbled Luna.

'Well, The Collective have been trying to decide what to do with him. They can't exactly let him just carry on destroying their plans, can they? I mean even confined to a wheelchair, he's been a complete menace. And then when he becomes fully mobile again – which I gather isn't far away – well … they really don't need that, do they? So, option one is they keep trying to kill him. That task would probably be given to me to organize.'

'He'll kill you first.'

'Wow! She's ferocious, isn't she Brigid? And so defensive of her husband!'

Baqri took a sip of his wine, placed the glass back on the table and topped it back up again.

'As I was saying, you would think that we would succeed eventually, wouldn't you? Killing Tom, I mean. But the problem there is that for every time we try, questions are asked. Lighting up the darkness is something that The Collective doesn't enjoy. And of course, Tom's now high profile within Monroe's administration.'

A man entered the room. Luna recognised him. One of Baqri's henchman, Raul – the same guy who had tried taking the MP5 off her earlier and ended up having his boot ventilated in the process. He hobbled up to his boss, leaned over, and whispered in his ear, before turning on his heels and exiting the way he had come.

'I'm so sorry, Luna. Seems we have to start wrapping this up. The Feds have realised that something is wrong and have despatched more units. So, all I wanted to say was that The Collective came to the conclusion that there was another way to neutralise your husband. What's *the* most important thing in the world to Tom, would you say?'

'Family,' replied Luna, almost instantly.

'That was their conclusion too. And they believe that there is more than one way to break your opponent. In Tom's case, they felt that killing his family would … well … snap him in two.'

'Stay away from my girls,' growled Luna.

'Oh, you shouldn't worry about your daughters at this stage. MI5's finest keeps close tabs on them day and night. Far too risky and high profile. But *you* however … well they reckon your demise would still do the job.'

Luna's eyes closed. Her head dropped forward and rested on her chest.

'Is she dead?' asked Brigid.

'Not yet, I don't think. She will be very soon though.'

Baqri stood up and walked over to a small table. He picked up a single red rose and a letter and placed it on Luna's lap. The letter simply had the word 'Tom' written on the envelope.

'Goodbye, Luna. I'm glad we could spend this time together. And now it's time for you to rest.'

***

Baqri and Brigid walked through the open doorway - Raul now adopting the role of doorman.

Brigid stopped and grabbed Baqri by the arm. 'What's happened to you?'

'What do you mean?'

'Are you scared of Tom Rivers? I didn't think you were frightened of anyone.'

'Scared? No. But respectful, yes.'

'So, what's with all this *do you think I want your husband hunting me down* business?'

'Oh, that. Well, The Collective are keen that I don't become the focus of his retribution when she dies. If you think about it, there is an exciting possibility. If they play this right, then Tom could potentially turn against his masters. He goes to war against all those that completely failed him and allowed his wife to be killed. Now that would be something to behold, wouldn't it?'

'Won't happen.'

'Don't be so sure. A carefully drafted narrative from The Collective that perhaps shows how Luna was let down so badly. One that details how she died needlessly and all alone. Delivered to a man who is completely distraught with grief. A devastated man who then becomes consumed with anger. A man who wants someone to blame and make them accountable. You have to admit that the idea of a vengeful Tom Rivers, without the controls that normally keep him in check, would be a really useful weapon in their arsenal.'

'OK. I can see that.'

'Though they did also mention that they wanted their members to be on Tom's hit list too.'

Brigid stood and frowned at Baqri. 'They want Tom Rivers to go after their members?'

'That's what they said. Their exact words were *we want him to go after those people whom he believes are members. And, in particular, those responsible for his wife's death.*'

'I still don't get it.'

'I know. It doesn't make much sense but they don't tell me everything. Need to know basis, apparently. I do have a theory though. Let's discuss that on the way. Time to go, Brigid. We've got a boat to catch.'

CHAPTER FIFTY-THREE

'Madam President,' said Admiral Womack. 'I'm sorry to have to report that the Avangard HGV has passed through the outer ring of our Air Force fighters.'

Jane Monroe gazed at the screen in front of her. Her National Security team were gathered once again and their faces said it all. She briefly looked down at the floor.

'I see,' said Monroe after a pause. 'I assume there's nothing more that can be done?'

'We're doing everything we can, Madam President. This thing isn't following a fixed trajectory, like a missile. It jumps around and has no heat signature. Our pilots just can't get a fix on it. They can't even predict where it's going to be next.'

'And it's travelling at about seventeen times the speed of sound,' added Tom.

'I guess that Air Force One's defence system won't help,' said Monroe rhetorically.

'Not in this case, I'm afraid,' replied Womack.

President Monroe's attention was drawn to the frantic activity in the sky outside her window. She peered out, just about being able to make out numerous US Airforce fighters firing at something in the distance.

'I don't think we've got long,' said Monroe. 'I need to ask whether we are near enough to Whiteman Airforce Base to glide there if we get hit?'

'Our latest calculations are that you will, unfortunately be at least ten miles short.'

'There are emergency services positioned all along your approach path to Whiteman, Madam President,' said Tom.

'But this is a 747. It's not exactly a small aircraft, is it? Where the hell is it going to land?'

'We've been busy trying to come up with some possibilities with the pilot, Ma'am. I'm so sorry, Madam President.'

'Oh God, Tom. Please don't apologise. You cautioned me against taking this trip. I was just so damned keen to …'

President Monroe stared out of the window, once again. Something had caught her eye. One of her fighters had banked to its side. And there it was. So quick that it was just a fleeting glimpse. The Avangard tried veering around the fighter but it was not enough – clipping the fighter's wing with one of its own. The F35 pilot tried to regain control but the aircraft quickly descended into a sharp flat spin – like water going down a plughole. The Avangard also seemed to be out of control.

Even though the president was expecting it, the massive explosion still took her aback. Air Force One juddered from the blast and Monroe instinctively grasped the arms of her chair. Huge plumes of smoke were now bellowing from the side of the aircraft. She wishfully looked forward to the screen connecting her with the National Security Team – hoping that it was still functioning. It wasn't. Nothing was.

Monroe looked back out of her window. *Were the engines still working*? It was difficult to know. The sound of her coffee mug sliding off the table and on to the floor brought President's Monroe's attention back to the room. It was clear that Air Force One was descending both at a rapid rate, and at a sharp angle. She glanced up at her terrified Acting Chief of Staff Carly Johnson, who sat opposite.

A knock on the door and Secret Service Director John Barratt was once again standing in the doorway, leaning upwards and gripping the frame.

'Madam President, as I'm sure you realise, we're in a forced decent. At the moment, the pilot has limited functionality and none of the engines seem to be working. Not sure if that's due to the blast, or the EMP, or both. But he's currently trying to find somewhere to land.'

Air Force One violently shuddered again. The nose of the aircraft dipped and the president gripped her chair even tighter. She glanced across at the fresh face of Carly Johnson and was reminded that there were more people than just herself in danger of losing their lives. Monroe beaconed John Barratt to enter the room and sit beside her.

'I wonder if you would both join me in a prayer? You know, I've always been a church goer. Faith has been a big part of my life for as long as I remember. If ever there was a time to speak to God, then I guess it's now.'

CHAPTER FIFTY-FOUR

The National Security Team realised that the sudden loss of picture on the main screen meant only one thing. The attack on Air Force One had been successful and the President of the United States was now plummeting towards the ground. Whether the aircraft still had the ability to glide, or was dropping like a brick, was unknown.

'Commander, try and re-establish communications with Airforce One,' said Womack to his aide, Commander Graham.

'I'm trying sir, but there's absolutely nothing. No response from any of the close escort aircrafts either.'

'As expected, I think we have to assume that all of their electronics have been destroyed as well. I imagine they're also trying to work out where the hell they're going to land. Try the outer ring of fighters. They might still be operational.'

'But look at this,' said Tom, tapping the symbol for Airforce One on another screen. 'Looks to me like it's dropping at a controlled rate … albeit at a sharp angle.'

Admiral Womack nodded. 'Dropping quickly, by the look of it. I think we have to assume that the aircraft is not in a good way.'

'I think you could be right.' Tom turned to Graham. 'Commander, can you see if there's footage from any of the nearby fighters just before the detonation? I'd like to know exactly what happened. In the meantime, we need to try and establish the most likely place that Airforce One is going to attempt a landing.'

'Well, the good news is surely that there will plenty of big chunks of farmland over there. I mean, it's Missouri,' said Vice President Jed Stone.

'That would work for a light aircraft – maybe. But Airforce One weighs over four hundred and twenty-five tonnes. Its landing gear would just get shredded on the soft ground.'

'OK, then where?' asked Walt Houston.

'Route sixty-five,' Tom replied, running his finger along the road on the screen.

'You're kidding me, right?' Stone scoffed.

'Not at all. I've been busy making sure that sections of this highway have been cleared of traffic. Air Force One needs about a mile and a half of tarmac to land. In anticipation of the Avangard attack being successful, I previously discussed a number of possible landing points with the captain. Now, we just need to work out which one he's going for.'

'Sir, based on their current rate of descent and course, it looks like the pilot is heading for a section before Lincoln,' said Graham.

'That's sooner than I expected them to land. Again, might indicate a problem.'

'I'll make sure the ground units are prepared,' said Womack, picking up a phone.

'And, sir, I have that footage you asked for.'

Another screen in the Situation Room flicked on with recorded images from the helmet of one of the more central fighter pilots, far enough away to be unaffected by the EMP blast.

'OK, so there's Air Force One and right alongside it is one of the close escort fighters,' said Tom.

'What the hell was that?' asked Walt Houston. 'Did something just go past?'

'That must have been the Avangard.'

'Damn that thing's fast,' gasped Rachael Goldberg. 'I mean it's one thing saying that it travels at Mach whatever, but something else actually seeing it.'

'The close escort fighter then responded by banking to its side. Trying to shield Air Force One as much as possible.'

'The Avangard has clipped the fighter's wings …' said Stone.

The almost instantaneous explosion that followed, silenced the room instantly. Apart from ripping the tail off the fighter, it was clear that debris from the Avangard had peppered Air Force One itself.

'Freeze that picture,' ordered Womack, ending his call.

'Looks like damage to the wings, fuselage, engines … the lot,' said VP Stone.

Tom said, 'And no doubt every electrical system has also been fried, thanks to the EMP. I'm amazed that the pilot still has any control.'

'That's one hell of a pilot you have there, Admiral,' said Walt Houston.

'Sir, we now have live footage from that fighter, which has now caught up with Air Force One,' interrupted Commander Graham.

The National Security Team looked on as the F35 pursued the plume of smoke towards the ground – Air Force One continuing to plummet at a fiercely sharp angle. A road was now quickly looming into view.

'Route sixty-five,' declared Tom.

'And not another vehicle to be seen,' said Walt Houston.

'Well done, Tom,' said a contrite VP Stone.

Tom was slightly taken aback but, after a short pause, simply replied, 'Thank you, sir.'

'Well, now we can only hope that the plane's going to hold together and the pilot's as good as we think he is,' said Womack.

The room fell silent and, as Air Force One descended for its final landing approach, everyone held their breath. Just fifty feet from the road, Tom noticed something.

'I'm not sure,' said Tom, 'But it doesn't look to me like his landing gear is fully down and locked.'

'I don't think it is. And he's clearly struggling to maintain control,' said Goldberg.

'Not surprising when he hasn't got any working electronics. He'll be having to guess most of it,' added Womack.

'How the hell he's going to land without his landing gear locked down?' asked Stone.

Tom looked at Womack and then at Stone. Nothing needed to be said. The message was clear.

'I see,' said Stone.

'Are emergency services ready?' asked Tom.

'Yes, sir. Secret Service and FBI teams are also on standby. We can now give you images from ground level, by the way,' replied Commander Graham, switching over the screen.

Air Force One was repeatedly dropping and lifting, as the pilot tried 'feeling' for the ground. Everyone in the Situation Room stood, transfixed by the images. Tom could hardly imagine what the president was going through. And then finally it happened. The wheels touched down and, just for a minute, it looked like they were going to hold. Then came the inevitable. The belly of the aircraft crashed into the tarmac. Sparks flied and the first flames shortly followed. The aircraft starting disintegrating and parts were visibly being thrown behind it. Air Force One continued skidding along the road for half a mile. The flames continued to grow until eventually it came to a stop.

But the fire crews were ready. Every spare team that could be mustered from Kansas City and the surrounding area was there. And they had raced to the crash site in under a minute. The National Security team waited anxiously for an update.

'You know, the president's office and the VIP area on Air Force One have received upgraded protection,' said Admiral Womack, trying to sound optimistic.

Tom replied with a smile and a nod. They wouldn't have to wait too long to find out whether the expense had proved to be a good investment. The delay for the green light from the fire crews was excruciating for everyone looking on. The Secret Service team, kitted out with full breathing apparatus, stood ready to board Air Force One.

Finally, they were on the aircraft and making their way through the dense smoke towards the VIP room.

'We've reached the president,' said a muffled voice over the radio. 'Opening the door now.'

Tom clenched his fists.

'Ms Johnson is dead. Checking the president now.'

Rachael Goldberg closed her eyes and brought her hands to her mouth.

'She's alive.'

CHAPTER FIFTY-FIVE

The core members of the National Security team had now been awake for over twenty-four hours, and they were certainly showing physical signs of fatigue. Despite copious mugs of coffee, bleary eyes, and the occasional yawn – especially from Secretary of State Walt Houston – everyone was nevertheless acutely aware that their day was far from over.

'Tell me where we're at?' demanded Vice President Stone abruptly from the top of the table.

'Well, the president has already been airlifted and is on her way to the University of Kansas Hospital,' replied Rachael Goldberg.

'I thought St Lukes was bigger?'

'It is, but University of Kansas is a level one trauma hospital. It's one of the best in the country and has a helipad tested to take the weight of a military helicopter – like the Blackhawk that the president's being transported in.'

'And do we know what the president's condition is?' asked Houston.

Goldberg looked across with a solemn face. 'It's not good, Walt. As you would expect, she's suffered massive injuries.'

'What are we talking?' asked Tom.

'The primary survey at the scene indicated numerous fractures and possible spinal injuries but most worrying was a head trauma. The president has a suspected brain haemorrhage. She'll be going straight into theatre on arrival.'

'With the president incapacitated, I would say that the twenty-fifth amendment comes into force,' said Walt Houston. 'That would make you acting president.'

'You should be prepared, Mr Vice President, for the possibility of the president never recovering or at least not being able to fulfil the duties of her office,' said Tom.

'In that case, you will need to be sworn in as the new President of the United States,' said Admiral Womack. 'With your approval, sir, I'll make the necessary arrangements. Just in case. Hopefully, we won't need it and the president will recover. But we should be ready.'

Stone stared down at the table in front of him and tapped his pad with the side of his pen. He looked up again and, after a slight pause, nodded at Womack.

'And Baqri?' asked Stone. 'Have we managed to capture him yet?'

'Not yet, sir. All I can tell you, at this stage, is that further FBI teams have been deployed to the site where he was believed to be,' said Goldberg.

'Why?' asked Tom.

'It's not clear. We've lost contact with them.'

'And you were going to tell me that *when* exactly?' Tom fumed. 'My wife's in one of the original tactical teams. You know that!'

'Tom, I'm sorry. But I really didn't have anything to tell you. It could just be a technical fault for all we know. They'll be there any minute. I've instructed them to call me as soon as they arrive.'

It wasn't long until the anxious wait was over and the phone rang in front of Rachael Goldberg. Intensely, she listened to the report from the FBI ground commander with just the occasional words of confirmation repeated back.

'Well,' said Goldberg ending the call, and then pausing briefly. 'I'm afraid, the operation has been a disaster. It sounds like Baqri knew we were coming. Everyone from the two tactical teams that entered the building are dead – with the exception of Luna. The only other person to survive was Assistant Director Marshall, who was wounded but managed to crawl away and hide.'

'What happened?' asked Tom.

'It seems that the Tactical Teams who entered the building were all exposed to a nerve agent. They suspect it's Novichok. Hayden Marshall's units, which were waiting at the perimeter, were then ambushed. Looks like there was a brief firefight.'

'Where's Luna now?'

'She's being airlifted to Medstar Hospital, here in Washington. She's in good hands and perfectly safe. DC police are already cordoning off the area of the hospital where their rooms will be. And officers will be posted outside both Luna's room and Assistant Director Marshall's.'

'You know where I'll be if you need me,' said Tom, grabbing his walking cane from the side of his chair. 'I need to be with my wife.'

CHAPTER FIFTY-SIX

'What's the latest on the president's condition?' asked Vice President Stone.

Rachael Goldberg replied, 'She's already in theatre. The doctors initial report has confirmed that she has a significant brain haemorrhage and obviously her condition is regarded as critical. So much so that they're going to put her in an induced coma,'

'Will she make it?' asked Walt Houston.

'I pushed them to give me a figure on that one. They've estimated survival at just forty percent. But then she's a tough woman, so they're staying optimistic.'

'Did John Barratt survive, by the way?'

'He was breathing when they first found him, Walt. But I'm sorry to say that he died on the way to hospital. From what I gather, if it wasn't for the recent upgrading of the presidential areas on Air Force One, then they would all have been killed instantly.'

'Mr Vice President, I have spoken to the Attorney General,' said Admiral Womack. 'He agrees with our previous assessment of the situation and is of the opinion that it is now appropriate for you to formally adopt the powers of the President of the United States. Should the president recover … which we all hope for, of course … then power would revert back to her. Should the worst happen, and the president dies or is permanently incapacitated, then you would need to be sworn in.'

'I see,' said Stone. 'Suddenly, I feel a huge weight on my shoulders.'

'Sir, if I may,' said Rachael Goldberg. 'You've been awake for well over twenty-four hours now. As there's nothing more we can do, perhaps now would be a good time for a rest?'

'We've all been awake over twenty-four hours. I'm not sure for me to take a rest would be appropriate.'

'But we're not all in charge of the country, sir. I can always wake you if there's any news.'

'OK, Rachael. That's a fair point. But I think I need to be with the president. I've decided to fly out to Kansas City straight away. Maybe I'll get a little sleep on the plane.'

'I think a little nap, while we wait for news, seems like a good plan for me too,' said Walt Houston. 'I'll get them to sort me out somewhere here. I'm seventy-five now, for goodness' sake!'

As the door to the Situation Room closed behind Stone and Houston, Rachael Goldberg turned to Admiral Womack.

'Just me and you then holding the fort.'

'Indeed. With the adrenaline now dropping, I have to say I'm also starting to struggle a bit. I guess Tom will be at the Medstar hospital soon?' asked Womack.

'Yeah. I've asked him to just give me a quick call when he gets there on Luna's condition.'

The door reopened and Walt Houston walked back in. He looked around the table where he was sat and then lifted up his paper pad.

'I would forget my head if it wasn't screwed on,' he muttered to himself, grabbing the pen from underneath.

'Don't worry, Walt. It's been a long day,' smiled Rachael Goldberg. 'Oh, Walt, just one thing before you go again. Could you remind Jed that he should call his wife and let her know what's going on. She's such a worrier and Jed's so bad at communicating with her.'

'He's already done it,' replied Houston, reaching for the door handle.

'Really? That's great.'

'Yeah. I saw him sending a message outside in the corridor. He did say that if he didn't do it, then you would be on his case again.'

Goldberg grinned as Walt Houston stepped outside the room again. *Perhaps this is a new side to Jed Stone?* she thought. More caring and thoughtful. Qualities that both she and the American electorate had always felt were lacking.

Her thoughts were interrupted by the ringing of the phone on the Situation Room table. She stood half-up in order to reach it before slumping back into her seat. Tiredness seemed to be affecting everyone now.

'Oh, hi Julia,' said Goldberg.

'Hi Rachael,' said the woman's voice on the other end. 'I was just wondering if Jed was there?'

'I'm afraid, he's just left for Kansas City.'

'Kansas City? I guess he's going to see the president. I assume that means she is still alive. You don't have to answer that, by the way.'

'Julia, did you not get Jed's message?'

'What message?'

'He sent you a text message, I think. Maybe it still hasn't made it to your phone.'

'Why would he send a message? Why didn't he just call me?'

'Perhaps he didn't want to disturb you? I'm not sure.'

'Rachael, have you ever received a text from Jed? At any time since you've known him?'

'No, I guess not.'

'That's because he hates even the idea of messaging. Pretty sure he's never sent one in his life. The man's a technological dinosaur, Rachael.'

Goldberg pressed the hands-free button on the phone and closed her eyes. That sinking feeling had returned.

'Sorry, Julia. My mistake. He must have been doing something else on his phone.'

'The only thing Jed believes a cell phone should be used for, is making calls.'

'So, I guess he's not into playing any games on his phone?'

'Are you kidding me? He detests them, and the people that play them.'

CHAPTER FIFTY-SEVEN

Having requisitioned a black FBI SUV, Tom Rivers showed it no mercy. He had only one objective – to reach his wife as quickly as possible. This meant engaging his considerable skills and driving at such mind-blowing speed that it was more akin to a video game than real life. He dodged in and out of the traffic, with many drivers not even having time to react to the flashing lights and sirens from the FBI vehicle before Tom was on them, and then passed them.

In fact, Tom's hair-raising pursuit of Baqri around London previously, seemed like a re-enactment of 'Driving Miss Daisy' in comparison. At that time, he had two members of the British army in the car as passengers – Captain Jax and Sergeant Laing. He was pretty sure that if they were in the car now, one of them would have been sick. He was also pretty sure that person would have been Laing.

Tom raced on to Irving Street, pushing the SUV to such limits that, on the corners, the tyre rubber was close to losing its fight to keep touch with the road. Tom glanced out of the side window. The target destination, Medstar Hospital Center, was looming up quickly. A final dash up the approach road and the SUV came to a screeching stop near the Emergency Department entrance, it's lights and sirens now off.

An eager parking attendant, spotting the SUV from the other side of the road, decided to take issue with Tom's parking and briskly walked towards the vehicle.

'You can't park that there,' he yelled, crossing the road.

'FBI,' replied Tom, climbing out the SUV and holding up his FBI badge.

'I don't care who you are. You can't leave it there.'

Tom grabbed his walking cane and hobbled swiftly towards the man who was now starting to irritate him. The physical size difference was stark, as Tom stood directly in front of the diminutive attendant and straightened his posture to his full height before proceeding to look down at the top of the attendant's head. It wasn't just Tom's height that the man found unsettling, but he quickly realized that the FBI agent's jacket was concealing a solid, muscular frame underneath.

'I know that you believe you're just doing your job, but I've had a *really* tough last few days. So, I would be very grateful if you would personally look after my car for me,' said Tom, staring so intensely into the man's eyes that the guy felt like he had reached into his soul. 'Can you do that?'

The attendant was used to abusive and threatening people, but this FBI agent had a completely different demeanour. An ability to be polite and scarily intimidating at the same time. He furiously nodded in reply. 'Sure. No problem. Anything for our great law enforcers.'

Tom looked at the man's name badge. 'Thank you, Ed. I can't tell you how much I appreciate it. Now, I don't suppose you know where the ICU is?'

'I do,' he replied, still rapidly nodding his head. 'I've worked here for years. It's on the third floor.'

Tom patted the attendant on the side of the arm and started towards the hospital entrance doors. He noted the two cops just inside and stepped into the elevator – hoping that it didn't stop for anyone else on the way up. He nearly got his wish, but for just one brief pause as a couple of doctors got in on the second floor. The doors opened on the third floor and Tom made his way down a surprisingly long corridor towards the ICU. Having opened one set of double doors, he then continued a short distance further until it dog-legged off to the right and to another set of double doors.

With some relief, he could see ahead two more police officers. They appeared to be restricting access to the area. Tom had barely raised his badge before they parted in the middle with one officer saying 'Sir' and the other acknowledging him with a respectful nod.

'Shouldn't you be checking IDs properly? Especially, bearing in mind what has just happened?' asked Tom, somewhat perturbed.

'Don't worry, sir. I know who you are, Mr Rivers. We all do. Our guys at the entrance had spotted you and the chief had already told us that you were on your way.'

Tom looked at the officer quizzically. 'He did?'

'Yes, sir. I believe Homeland Director Goldberg had phoned him.'

And full points to the cops in the entrance, who were clearly on the ball, thought Tom. He looked ahead and noted that there were just two private rooms opposite each other. A cop outside each door stood guard. Just beyond them was another set of double doors with two more cops on the other side. Tom looked at the cop on the right. A short, stocky guy in his early twenties who had clearly been trying for some time to grow a moustache. Before Tom even opened his mouth, the cop said, 'It's that one over there, sir. I assume you're after your wife? Mr Marshall is in this one.'

Tom turned around to face the other cop. Ex-military he assumed. Late thirties with very short black hair. Lean and fit looking. Sharply pressed trousers and well-polished shoes. Name badge also nice and shiny. An appearance that inspired confidence.

'Good morning, Mr Rivers,' said the cop, in a gruff and slightly quiet southern accent. He opened the door and stood back.

Tom walked in and looked over at Luna. Driving to the hospital, he thought he had mentally prepared himself. He was wrong. It's one thing seeing someone you don't know lying in a bed motionless with seemingly countless tubes and wires sprouting from their limbs, but something entirely different when it's a loved one. After the initial shock subsided slightly, Tom realised that this was how he must have looked after the attack on the British capital. He was grateful that Luna never got to see him like that.

The door opened and a doctor walked in. Slim Caucasian, late forties he guessed, with the standard white coat and a set of stethoscopes around his neck.

'How's she doing?' Tom asked, pouncing on the doctor before he had the chance to get any further into the room.

'Mr Rivers, right?'

'Yeah. Sorry, doctor.'

'Well, thanks to the fact that she was airlifted straight here, we managed to administer an anticholinergic agent quickly into her. That was really important. We've followed that up with Diazepam and then a course of oximes.'

'So, she'll be ok?' asked Tom eagerly.

'We're not out of the woods yet, but I'm pleased to say that her condition has stabilised.'

'When will she wake up?'

'I'm afraid I can't tell you when or even if she will wake up. At the end of the day, her body is in a pitch battle with the nerve agent.'

'Fair enough.'

'Mr Rivers, I have to say that her recovery is nothing short of extraordinary. No one here has seen anything like it. The nerve agent should have killed her, as apparently it did the rest of her team. So, you'll forgive me when I say that I get the feeling that I'm not being told everything.'

'All I can tell you is that both my wife and I have some genetic advantages. The details are classified, I'm afraid.'

Tom looked behind him, aware that the door had opened again. The cop's head was peering round the corner.

'Sorry to disturb you, sir. There's an urgent phone call for you downstairs in reception.'

'Why didn't they just call my cell phone? Who is it?'

'I believe it's the White House. Couldn't tell you why they've called reception, Mr Rivers. All I know is that they said it was urgent.'

Tom could barely hide his irritation, as he made his way all the way back to the elevator. He pressed the call button on the wall and, while he waited, reminded himself of the doctor's positive comments. Luna's condition had stabilised and that she was getting the very best medical care. He looked up and noted that the elevator had passed the first floor. His phone rang. *Perhaps it was the person who had called reception,* he thought, *having now found his number.*

'Tom Rivers?' said the caller.

'It is.'

'It's Chief Dreyfus.'

'Oh, Chief. I gather that I have you to thank for all the security around my wife.'

'Least I could do.'

'Did you just call the hospital's reception, by the way?'

'No, not me. Sorry. But I just wanted to check that you're happy with the protection and there's nothing else that you need?'

'Nothing that I can think of. Much appreciate what you've done already.'

The elevator had now arrived at the third floor. The doors started to open. Tom moved to one side as three doctors and a nurse, deep in conversation, stepped out and walked off towards the opposite end of the floor.

'That's great. Just wanted you to know that I even assigned my nephew to your wife's room.'

'Your nephew?' Tom said quizzically, stepping inside.

'Yeah, Johnny.'

'So, he must be your sister's son then?' said Tom, pressing the ground floor button.

Chief Dreyfus paused briefly. 'Not sure what you mean, Tom. I don't have a sister. He's my brother's son.'

Tom stuck his walking cane between the elevator doors, which were now closing and then stepped back out into the corridor. 'But his name badge said *Giorgio*.'

A brief silence followed before Dreyfus spoke again.

'Tom, I've no idea who that is.'

CHAPTER FIFTY-EIGHT

Tom could feel his heart racing as he stepped back out of the elevator. The desperation he suddenly felt to get to Luna was overwhelming. He tried running back along the corridor but, frustratingly, this still ended up more like a fast hobble. He cursed his body for still not being up to the task.

He was nearly at the first set of double doors when his cell phone rang again.

'Tom, I've just made a quick call to my nephew,' said Chief Dreyfus. 'So, Giorgio is indeed an officer on his unit. Recently joined. Johnny told me that he had started feeling really ill when he was on duty at the hospital and then began throwing up. Giorgio, who was supposed to be on leave, happened to call in to his precinct to see if he could work instead. Needed the money, apparently. So, his captain then sent him over as a replacement.'

Tom slowed his walking pace. 'Well, OK. That's good.'

'You would think so. But then I phoned his captain. He said he never spoke to Giorgio.'

'Chief. You need to discreetly contact your other officers. Treat Giorgio, or whatever his real name is, with extreme caution. I think he may be ex-military. And Luna may be in danger,' said Tom increasing his speed again, and reaching under his jacket to draw his Glock M 19 from its holster.

The second set of double doors were promptly opened as Tom approached.

'Stay here,' said Tom to the two cops manning them. 'I don't want any civilian casualties. No one comes through. And tell the guys on the other doors the same.'

It was clear that Chief Dreyfus had wasted no time on his communication, as both cops nodded their understanding. No sign of Giorgio though. He approached the young cop who had been stood outside Marshall's room. Davis, the name badge said.

'Where's the other cop?'

'He's just gone into your wife's room.'

'Just?'

'Yeah, I mean like five seconds before you came through those doors.'

'What did he say?'

'Just said he wanted to check on her.'

Movement by the other set of doors caught Tom's eye. Through the glass he recognised the doctor that he met earlier. And beside him, another doctor. Tom looked at the cop again.

'Call Giorgio on your radio. Engage him in conversation.'

'And say what?'

'I don't really care. I need him distracted. Tell him your captain's arrived and he better get back out here. Just keep him talking. Oh, and you better tell those doctors that we may be needing them.'

Tom reached out and gently placed his left hand on the door lever. Davis started his chatter over the radio. With one seamless movement, the door was flung open and Giorgio was in the sights of Tom's Glock. Standing on the other side of the bed, with one hand on his radio and the other gripping Luna's ventilator tube, Giorgio stood exposed. Tom could see the conflict on Giorgio's face, as his mind wrestled with his next decision.

'Don't. Just don't,' said Tom. 'Let go of the tube and put your hands on your head.'

Giorgio paused. Tom repeated, 'Let go of the tube. And I mean now. If I see you squeeze that tube even a fraction, I'm going to ventilate your head.'

Giorgio had probably heard enough about Tom Rivers to know that he would make good on his threat. He complied.

'Now, take four steps to your side, so that I can see all of you, and drop to your knees.'

The young cop entered the room. Side arm drawn.

'Please liberate any weapons from Officer Giorgio,' said Tom.

'Sir?'

'Take his weapons off him.'

As instructed, Officer Davis walked towards Giorgio, holstering his weapon as he moved around to the side. But Giorgio had one last play. A swift punch to the young cop's junk gave him an opportunity. Giorgio took cover behind Davis and then pulled him up by the throat. Gripping the cop's neck with one hand, he pushed his pistol into Davis's back with the other.

'Sorry,' said Tom.

'Bet you are,' said Giorgio. 'Did you really think it would be that easy?'

'I wasn't talking to you.'

The bullet from Tom's Glock ripped through the young cop's shoulder, then Giorgio's, before smashing through the window behind. Davis dropped to his knees, as Giorgio staggered backwards – the shock on his face apparent. His attempt to lift his gun was abruptly ended as a further bullet punched through his forehead.

'Jesus,' said Davis, nursing his shoulder. He looked behind at the body of Officer Giorgio lying on the floor. Giorgio's lifeless eyes were, unsettlingly, staring straight at him and his head, with the addition of a hole, was now quickly pooling blood around it.

Tom shrugged. 'As I said … sorry. I'll grab those doctors for you.'

CHAPTER FIFTY-NINE

'Mr Marshall … Mr Marshall,' said the doctor softly, looking down at his patient. 'I need you to try opening your eyes now.'

Hayden Marshall struggled to comply. They told him before he went under the general anaesthetic that he may feel nauseous when he woke. As it happened, he didn't. What he did feel was a sense of complete serenity. Without doubt, that had been one of the best sleeps of his life, and he couldn't help but feel a little irritated that the doctor considered it necessary to wake him from it.

'OK, OK. I'm awake,' Marshall whispered, trying to focus through the small gaps between his eyelids at the man peering down at him.

The doctor smiled back. 'How are you feeling?'

'Very content. Shame you had to wake me.'

'Yes, I know. A lot of people say the same. My name is Doctor Mendez. I'm the senior doctor in charge of your care and also Mrs Rivers. And I'm pleased to tell you that the operation to remove the bullet was a success.'

'That's great. Thank you,' murmured Marshall, still fighting to keep his eyes open.

'You should make a full recovery. You were very lucky, you know. The bullet missed every major vessel.'

'Or maybe very unlucky to have got shot in the first place,' replied Marshall, trying hard to raise a slight smile. 'How's Luna Rivers doing?'

'Well, I'll let the others update you on recent events. But from a medical point of view, she's still in a critical, but stable, condition.'

‘What do you mean *recent events*?’

‘I’ll let the officer guarding your room know that you’re awake. He’s more qualified to give you that update,’ said the doctor, exiting the room.

Hayden Marshall leaned over the side, picked up the bed controller from its holster and pressed the button – adjusting the incline until he was sat upright. He looked down. Dressed in one of those patient gowns that never quite fit – even with his skinny frame – and an arm in a sling, he wondered how long he was going to be kept in and, more importantly, how long till he could dress in normal clothes. The door opened and a DC police officer stepped into the room.

‘Good afternoon, sir,’ said the officer. ‘I’ve been told that you wanted an update.’

‘What the hell’s going on?’ replied Marshall, getting straight to it.

‘There was an assassination attempt on Luna Rivers.’

‘What? Who?’

‘A cop from my unit.’

‘What?’ repeated Marshall incredulously.

‘We’re not sure what his motives were, but a cop on our unit by the name of Joseph Giorgio attempted to kill Luna Rivers.’

‘I assume he failed?’

‘Yes, sir. Her husband, Tom Rivers, calmly went into her room and shot him dead.’

‘Well … he would. Where’s Tom now?’

‘He’s still in there with her.’

‘Is she conscious?’

‘I don’t believe she is.’

‘OK, thank you. Would you let me know when Mr Rivers leaves? I would like to visit Luna, but I don’t want to interrupt their time together.’

The cop nodded but, as he exited the room, he briefly stopped and turned around.

'Forgot to mention, sir. You've had a delivery,' said the cop, pointing at the small wicker food and drink hamper, sat on a table in the corner of the room. 'Nice selection, by the look of it. From your office, I guess.'

As the door closed, Marshall pulled back the covers and swung his legs out of the bed. A distinctive but familiar tone from his cell phone on the bedside table, alerted him to a new message.

Did you know that, scientifically speaking, a banana is actually a berry? read the message. *Somethings aren't always what they seem, are they?*

Marshall stood up but immediately swayed towards the bed. He stretched his free arm out to support his balance and took a moment. A few deep breaths later and he staggered over to the corner table. He looked down at the hamper. There was something odd about it and it took him a few seconds to work out what it was. It was the banana. A single banana instead of the usual bunch that someone might expect. Removing the clear plastic wrapper covering the hamper, Marshall took out the banana and examined it. And there it was. A faint line running down its length. It was clear that the skin had been cut and then glued back together. A very neat job which no one would have seen, unless they were really looking hard. He prised it open with his fingernails to reveal a small, thin plastic bottle.

Sometimes ambition demands that you do whatever is necessary, thought Marshall. *The director's job should have been mine years ago. I got passed over. I'm not going to miss another chance. And that means finishing what I started. I'm sorry, Luna. I really am.*

CHAPTER SIXTY

Hayden Marshall considered his position. The risk that Luna might recover was one that neither he, nor the other members of The Collective, would wish to see. He had already put himself out on a limb once, by introducing Novichok to every member of the two FBI teams that went searching for Baqri. He didn't relish the fact that so many agents had to die in order to disguise the true target. Many of them had been his colleagues for years. Some, he even considered to be friends. *But it was a necessary sacrifice,* he rationalized. *Well, it would have been, had Luna actually died.*

The top job had been promised to him and he had no doubt that The Collective had the power to deliver. He deserved recognition for all the years of sacrifice that he had made. His job had cost him his marriage and, with the period of depression that followed, had a terrible impact on his health as well. It took years for him to get himself together again. But never, at any point, did anyone show that they really cared. Just a lot of disingenuous lip service from the Bureau. So, he decided that he had to decide his own destiny and take what was due.

But now, he was faced with a problem. The task that would deliver the position that he had always wanted was not complete. And there was also a further risk to The Collective. There was a real danger that Baqri had blabbed to her about what he knew and what he thought he knew. There was a man who unquestionably loved the sound of his own voice. Personally, Marshall felt that Baqri was a liability and The Collective would be better off without him as an associate.

But, unfortunately, most of the other members considered him to be a necessary evil.

So, now the question was how to get to Luna before she woke up. She might not, of course, and then the whole thing would be immaterial. But the recent hamper delivery left little doubt as to what was expected of him. By delivering an even larger dose of the nerve agent, even Luna's exceptional genetics would not be able to prevent her demise.

'Is Tom Rivers still here?' asked Marshall to the cop whom he had just summoned from outside his hospital room.

'He is, sir,' replied the cop. 'Since that attempt on his wife's life, he hasn't left her side.'

'That was three days ago.'

'Yes, sir. He has the odd meal brought to him and makes use of the ensuite bathroom. I think he's there for the duration. And the hospital has been told to give him anything he wants.'

'By whom?'

'The president.'

'The president? She's awake?'

'I believe she is. They woke her from the induced coma and that was one of her first instructions. Your office wanted to update you but you were resting and the doctors didn't want you disturbed.'

Marshall's brow furrowed. 'I should have been told immediately. Whether I was resting or not.'

The sound of a piercing alarm and frantic footsteps from outside the room, stopped the conversation dead in its tracks. Marshall sat up in his bed as the cop opened the door. Instead of the usual calm and controlled environment that he had become used to, Marshall could see instead something that bordered on mayhem. An unusually large number of doctors and nurses were outside in the corridor, and Marshall could almost feel an air of panic.

The centre of attention seemed to be Luna's room. Marshall, pleased to now be wearing his own pyjamas, climbed out of bed. Instructions were being shouted out from inside her room. He recognised the voice. It was the senior doctor who had been supervising their recovery.

'What the hell's going on?' said Marshall to another doctor standing immediately outside his door.

'I'm afraid Luna Rivers has gone into cardiac arrest, Mr Marshall.'

'What? I thought her condition was stable?'

'It was. But she's been exposed to one of the most powerful nerve agents ever developed. It's difficult to tell exactly what damage has been caused to the internal organs.'

Marshall watched on for another ten full minutes until a solemn faced Dr Mendez appeared in the doorway to Luna's room. He was staring at the ground and shaking his head. Like the calming of a mighty storm, the frantic activity around him came to an abrupt stop. Mendez shuffled out into the corridor, followed by another doctor and a nurse. He slowly raised his head and gazed at the other medical staff.

'Thank you everybody for your efforts. I'm sorry to have to tell you that I've had to call it. I'll let the president know.'

From inside Luna's room came a long, gut-wrenching scream of pure, deep, intense pain that only someone who suffered the ultimate loss could make. Marshall approached the doorway and peered round. There, lying in her bed, so perfectly calm and still, was Luna Rivers. All of the medical equipment that had been noisily supporting her since she was brought into the hospital, was now switched off and an eery type of quiet now prevailed. At her bedside knelt her devoted husband. Marshall watched on as Tom, with both of his hands, gently took one of hers and placed his forehead upon it.

CHAPTER SIXTY-ONE

Sir Iain MacGregor stood gazing out over the Thames from his office window and pondered the recent events in America. The remaining tea in his MI5 emblazoned mug hadn't been touched in the last quarter of an hour and was now stone cold. Nevertheless, he continued to nurture the mug with both hands – occasionally tapping it on the side with a finger.

Despite all the extraordinary things that he had seen during his thirty years in Britain's security service, he would never have imagined in his wildest nightmares such an attack on the United States. The world's most powerful nation brought to heel by a psychotic terrorist and a shady organisation. Told to commit a terrible atrocity to its closest ally or suffer terrible repercussions. Stolen Russian Avangards flying at incredible hypersonic speeds and delivering payloads of the world's most lethal element on American towns. And then, as if that wasn't bad enough, a final Avangard, equipped with not just conventional explosives but probably the largest EMP ever built, intercepts Airforce One and brings it down. To top it all, confirmation that The Collective have established themselves throughout the halls of power. The president's chief of staff, of all people, discovered to be a member. And he was certainly just the thin end of the wedge.

Mac couldn't help but let a feeling of hopelessness slip through. Unusual for him. Normally someone known for his positive attitude, for the first time in his life, he wondered whether they really were engaged in an unwinnable fight. Up until now, he had a good idea who his enemies were. Diligent intelligence work between friendly agencies saw to that. Now a large area of grey had developed between the black and white – an area occupied by The Collective. The important question of who to trust had just become much more difficult.

Then there was the tragic death of Luna Rivers. A loss that he felt deeply and very personally. Poisoned by some nerve agent. But poisoned by who exactly? The FBI's own internal investigations suggested that it had to be an inside job. Autopsies on the agents stated that the likelihood was that there had been physical contact with the Novichok rather than inhalation or some other method. Seemed unlikely that Baqri could have done that to all of them in one go. So, it must have been a Collective initiative. But then an assassin was sent to make sure Luna didn't survive. What was that all about?

In reality, of course, Mac was down by two 'Sleepers' not just the one. The death of Luna had, understandably, devastated Tom. Four days later and he was still holed up in his apartment, with the only person to have seen him being the guy who delivers his groceries. Surprisingly though, Tom did take Mac's call on the day that Luna passed. During their brief conversation, Tom asked him to investigate the background of Officer Giorgio. Few other men could have shown that incredible level of composure after losing their wives.

The whole saga has been an absolute, bloody mess, thought Mac, lowering himself back into his high back leather chair. Realising that his tea was now too cold to drink, he placed his mug back on its coaster in the corner of his desk. He looked at it and smiled. He couldn't even hazard a guess as to how many people had commented on his preference to that over a cup and saucer. *You're the head of Britain's intelligence service* said the home secretary, at a meeting the previous week. *Do you not think that a mug is a little out of keeping with your position?* Mac had made the point that something as simple as using a mug helped remind him of his working-class roots. Some of his favourite childhood memories were of when he used to sit in a greasy-spoon café in Glasgow with his dad, after he had finished a night shift on the docks. Full fried breakfast and a mug of tea each. *Never forget where you have come from*, his dad used to say. And he never did.

A triple knock on his office door and the assistant director of MI5 entered, marching towards his desk – paper file under his arm.

'Success?' asked Mac.

'Yes, indeed, sir.'

'Sit yourself down, Jason. Tell me the highlights.'

The assistant director pulled back one of the designer leather chairs opposite Mac, sat down and donned his round spectacles.

'We're still digging deeper into this but something came up which I thought you would want to hear immediately,' he said, opening the file.

'Go on.'

'Officer Joseph Giorgio only joined the Washington DC police department nine months ago. He was thirty-nine years old, by the way. Before that he was in the US military. Then Special Ops. Ended up working for the CIA.'

'The CIA? You're kidding me?'

'No, sir. And it gets better. He was assigned to various offices around the world, but there is one that I think is particularly interesting. One he spent three years working from.

'Where?'

'Kabul.'

'When?'

'At the same time as Rachael Goldberg was section chief.'

CHAPTER SIXTY-TWO

On 29 June, the funeral service was held at a small church in Abingdon, Virginia, for Luna Elizabeth Rivers. The weather was near perfect – sunny and warm, but not too hot, and with just whisps of feathery clouds in the sky. It was a well-attended event for the popular local girl, who many remembered from their days at the town's kindergarten and elementary schools. Despite moving away at the age of twelve, due to her father's career in the Diplomatic Service, Luna's boisterous, jocular personality meant that she was difficult to forget. Also in attendance, were a number of people from her 'new life' – including MI5 Director Sir Iain MacGregor, the secretary for homeland security and the vice president. Needless to say, the latter in particular, came with a heavy entourage of Secret Service agents.

In true Luna style, and in accordance with her wishes, black dresses and ties were banned and guests were even asked to consider a splash of colour in their attire. She had also carefully selected the music, which she considered to be beautiful but also meaningful. Whether she knew that her choices would have such an impact on her guests was unclear. Perhaps she did.

The front row in the church was reserved for immediate family. Luna's father, Phillip, plus her brother Adrian and his family sat on one side. On the other side of the aisle, sat Tom with their twin daughters, Bronte and Karah.

As Luna's coffin was slowly and respectfully carried into the church, her first chosen song began. Even before the end of the first verse of Birdy's song 'Wings', her father's head had dropped and he began crying uncontrollably. Comforting his father, Adrian put his arms around his shoulders. Phillip managed to whisper, 'My baby girl, my beautiful baby girl,' and then the heads of father and son met. Tom also spent most of the service with his head bowed – gripping the hands of his daughters who sat either side of him.

The service was relatively short, as Luna had intended. *I don't want everyone leaving that church in an even more depressed state than when they arrived*, she had told Tom. As the service ended, her second selected song played. An uplifting, poignant and positive message delivered by Xavier Rudd with 'Follow the Sun.' The longer the song played, however, more and more of the congregation also started bursting into tears.

The wake was held back at Luna's family home. A large sprawling property with an 'in and out' sweeping drive and which was the net result of Phillip dedicating over thirty years of service to the US government at a senior level. Having moved all around the world during his career, Phillip always knew that he would one day return to the town which held so many important memories for him. It was the town where he grew up and went to school. It was also the town where he met Luna's mother, Elizabeth.

He had been on his own for over fifteen years now, since the tragic death of his wife in a car accident. He had tried dating other women, of course. But none of them matched up to Lizzy. She was beautiful; she was strong; she was funny and she was kind. Phillip had resigned himself to being single for the rest of his life, though he knew that he would always have the comfort of his children's love. But now his heart was crushed. His amazing daughter was gone.

Standing in the corner of the sitting room, Phillip stood out not just because of his slight height advantage over the guests but also for his dazzling full head of silver hair. Perfectly groomed, of course, as someone might expect for a career diplomat. Standing and talking to him was his son-in-law, Tom Rivers. One of the few men that he ever felt was good enough for his daughter. And that was before he morphed into some sort of special sleeper agent and saved his country. Phillip noticed a parting of guests and then a very familiar figure walking towards Tom's back.

***

'Phillip. Tom. I just wanted to say how sorry I am for your loss. Though I didn't know her for long, I have to say that I think Luna was an amazing woman. Stepped up when her country needed her and never flinched in the face of danger.'

'Thank you, Mr Vice President. I appreciate it. I think I'll leave you two to have a chat,' said Phillip, sensing there was another reason for Jed Stone's approach.

'That was a beautiful service,' said Vice President Stone, putting his hand on Tom's arm.

'Thank you, sir. It was good of you to spare your time to attend. Especially, now you're running things. I'm sorry that I've been a bit aloof recently. I've been in a pretty dark place.'

'Completely understandable, Tom. We were worried about you for a while. I had reports coming through that you had become a recluse since Luna passed away. No one had seen you or heard from you and you weren't returning anybody's calls.'

'I know, sir. I'm sorry.'

'No need to apologise. Just shows that you're human after all.'

Tom smiled and nodded in reply – aware of his reputation throughout the American establishment of being a relentless and almost unstoppable creation of MI5.

'Can you tell me what the latest is on the president's condition? I've not been keeping up with recent news, I'm afraid.'

'The president is still in a critical condition. Stable but critical is the official assessment. She's obviously not in any condition to make decisions though.'

'Is she going to be alright?'

'Look, hopefully, given enough time, the president will return to full health. But right now, I need your help. Tom, we are facing a threat like this country has never seen before. An enemy hidden within the fabric of our society, whose very existence threatens the principles of our democracy. An organisation of faceless, unelected and powerful people who are focussed on manipulating not only our government but others around the world.'

'I assume you're talking about The Collective?'

'I am. And we need to set about destroying them, if we aren't already too late. This was President Monroe's intention before they shot down Airforce One. We need to pick up the baton and complete the mission. She trusted you implicitly and you showed her total loyalty. I am now asking the same from you.'

'You can always count on me to stand against those who would do us harm, Mr Vice President. That's what I signed up to all those years ago and nothing's changed.'

'Thank you, Tom. Quite frankly though, I'm amazed how calm you are considering the part they played in the murder of your wife.'

Jed Stone's comment had an immediate and noticeable effect on Tom, who straightened his posture and stared intensely into Jed Stone's eyes. Stone was an army veteran and his military experiences had moulded him into a man who was not easily intimidated. Tom's change of physical expression was quite remarkable though. Another side to the man. At last, a glimpse of the same person who pursued terrorists through London and then gunned them down.

'I've been conditioned that way, sir,' replied Tom. 'But I have to admit, controlling myself is proving to be a challenge.'

'Well, I suggest you channel your grief and anger into your new mission.'

'Rooting out members of The Collective?'

'Exactly. And I can use the power of my office to help you. Report to me directly.'

'Are you wanting me to just investigate or … take more direct action?'

'Officially, it should be an FBI investigation. I will speak to the director and tell him to give you whatever you need.'

'And unofficially?'

'Unofficially, if some of members of The Collective should meet an untimely demise, then I won't be crying myself to sleep. As far as I'm concerned this is war.'

'Understood.'

'Do you know where you will start?'

Tom looked over Stone's shoulder. Someone standing on the other side of the room caught his attention. In deep discussion with Sir Iain MacGregor was Director of Homeland Security Rachael Goldberg.

'Yes, sir. I believe I do.'

CHAPTER SIXTY-THREE

June had felt like the longest month ever to Rachael Goldberg. On her watch, there had been a deadly terrorist attack on two American towns; an unsuccessful assassination attempt on the British King; and the downing of Air Force One, resulting in the critical injury and subsequent hospitalisation of the President of the United States. Then to top it all off, Luna River, one of their most important assets, had been killed with a nerve agent along with two FBI teams by the world's craziest terrorist. *Not exactly stuff that you would want included on your resume*, thought Goldberg, as she turned the front door handle to her house.

Goldberg had worked hard to get where she was now. But she had made so many sacrifices along the way. Sometimes she wondered, when she sat alone in her large, detached house in Arlington what life would have been like if she had made different decisions. Sliding doors, they call it. Perhaps, she would have had children and become a stay-at-home mom. She could have met up with friends when the kids were at school and enjoyed a good chat and a giggle over a coffee. Perhaps, if she had been a little less obsessed with her career and fighting her way to the top, she would not now be separated from her husband. Perhaps. But that was not her. She had always been driven and a cosy family life was never going to be her thing.

When her husband-to-be had proposed to her, he had assured her that he could cope with her work life and her ambitions. Foolishly, she believed him. It was clear after just two years of marriage that someone doing a 'normal' job would never really understand. The only person that she had ever had a relationship with, albeit many years ago, and who did get it, was Iain MacGregor. But the large pond called the Atlantic sat between them and both of them quickly realised that it was never going to work.

She looked in the hallway mirror and swept back her bob-style brunette hair. Peering closer into the mirror turned out to be a bad idea, as she noted a few new lines around her eyes. *Pressures of the job, taking their toll*, she surmised. Goldberg turned around, realising that assessing her appearance was not helping her mood. *What would help*, she decided, *would be a big slug of brandy*. Walking into her living room, she switched on the light and took off her grey suit jacket, placing it neatly over the back of a chair. Something caught her eye. Something in the corner of the room. She turned her head to face the figure sat in the shadows.

'Who's there?' she challenged.

'Hello, Rachael.'

'Oh my God! Tom is that you?'

Tom reached over to his side and, with his left hand, flicked on the floor lamp. Goldberg could now clearly see her late-night visitor, dressed all in black and with an emotionless, intense look on his face. Held in his right hand, hanging towards the floor, was his Glock M19 pistol. Attached to the end of the gun was a silencer.

'What's with the gun, Tom? Have you come here to kill me?' said Goldberg, with a brief, nervous laugh.

'Depends.'

'Depends on what?'

'Depends on what you say in the next couple of minutes.'

Goldberg's eyes widened and she visibly swallowed. 'Do you think that I had something to do with Luna's death?'

'Sit down, Rachael,' said Tom, pointing with his gun to the brown leather armchair opposite.

Goldberg complied, perching herself on the edge of the seat cushion. 'Look, I know how it looks. That cop that tried to kill her used to work for me in the CIA.'

'Quite a coincidence, isn't it?'

'Come on, Tom. Really? Give me some credit. If I was going to use an assassin, do you think it would be someone with a direct link back to me?'

'Go on.'

'They used Giorgio because they knew you would find out about his connection to me. They're probably hoping you would kill me.'

'I still might.'

'You think I'm a member of The Collective, don't you?'

'Are you?'

'Of course, I'm not. But I would say that wouldn't I? Look, I'll give you another reason why I'm not Collective.'

'I'm all ears.'

'OK. When I was the CIA station chief out in Kabul, I was directly responsible for the capture of Baqri's brother. I handed him over to the Egyptian authorities in the full knowledge that they would execute him.'

'But Baqri's not Collective. He's a terrorist and he works for himself.'

'Sure. But their objectives cross over. And they need him. Baqri's important for the implementation of their plans. If I was Collective, and I was responsible for the death of his brother, do you think Baqri would still do their bidding?'

'Fair point. Go on.'

'I believe that you've got … we've got … a much bigger problem than you think. I'm talking about Vice President Stone.'

'We've been over this ground before.'

'We have. But then I spoke to his wife who told me that he's never used his cell phone for anything except making calls. She described him as a technological dinosaur who has never even sent a text in his life. When I asked about him playing games on his phone, she told me that he detested them and the people that played them. Tom, I have to tell you that I am convinced we were right about him all along.'

Tom removed the silencer from his Glock and holstered his weapon. After a slow amble over to Goldberg's drink cabinet, he poured a large shot of brandy into each of the two glasses on the side. With a glass in each hand, Tom then stood motionless. It was almost a whole minute before he spoke again.

'I had a nasty feeling you were going to say that.'

CHAPTER SIXTY-FOUR

Mohammed Baqri was sat on the top deck of a 220-foot super-yacht, relaxing on a sun lounger. Back in his shorts and beach shirt, he now sported a Panama style hat, which was tipped down at an angle, so that it covered his eyes.

'Interesting new look,' said Brigid.

'Do you like it?' asked Baqri, not moving himself or his hat.

'Not sure. Your shaved head and tattooed face say gangster … but your clothes say that you really just want to go surfing.'

'I assume you disturbed my relaxion in the sun for a reason?'

'Well, firstly I was wondering how the hell you managed to get yourself a yacht?'

'Oh, it's not mine, my dear! This beauty belongs to Benny.'

'Arms dealer Benny? I thought he had set you up?'

'No, it seems that that was just a ploy by Tom Rivers to get me out into the open.'

'So, I assume we're here for some good reason – rather than you wanting to top up your tan?'

Baqri lifted up the front of his hat, donned his sunglasses and then elevated the angle of his seat.

'Yes, Brigid, we're here for a good reason. And to answer your next question, no we're not in any danger of being boarded by western special forces and arrested. This is because we are just twenty-five miles north of the Russian naval base at Tartus and if you look around, you will note ships from their

Black Sea Fleet in close range. Too much of a risk of conflict for America to come for us.'

'So, why are we here?'

'We're here waiting for Benny to arrive on that helicopter there,' said Baqri pointing at the approaching black Airbus ACH145. 'This is because we have been given another project by The Collective and we needed his assistance in procuring a few things. And transporting a certain person.'

Two men were sat in the back of the helicopter, which was just setting down on to the helipad. Brigid recognised the first one. Heavily lined face with a boxer's nose. Benny Erikson. Renowned global arms dealer and proud recipient of the nickname 'Benny the Bomb' – courtesy of MI5 Director, Ian MacGregor, so the rumour went.

'Whose that with Benny?' asked Brigid.

'That is Alexei Nevsky.'

'Nevsky? The Russian that you used to pilot the HGVs? What the hell have you brought him here for?'

'Some unfinished business. Otherwise known as President Monroe.'

'Hang on! I thought we just killed her by bringing down Air Force One?'

'Stop the press! News alert! Believe it or not, President Monroe is still alive.'

'You're kidding me?'

'I know. Mad. Why don't people just die when I try to kill them? It's very frustrating, you know.'

'There's nothing in the media about it.'

'Nope. The White House decided a news blackout on her condition was a good idea. So, the public don't know what her condition is or even whether she is alive or dead. But The

Collective have reliable sources who have told them that the president actually survived and is currently residing at the University of Kansas Hospital. The really bad news is that they've just brought her out of the induced coma that she had been placed in.'

'OK. Well, that's amazing. How the hell did she survive that? And I'll tell you what's also amazing ... that The Collective have decided to trust you again. I mean your success rate hasn't been the best, has it? Attack on London – failed. Assassination of the King – failed. Assassination of the President of the United States – failed.'

'The London attack was a success, actually. If only to prove that a large mobile EMP could work. And anyway, The Collective admit that they underestimated certain factors. Or should I say, a certain factor.'

'Tom Rivers.'

'Exactly. They never thought that one person could have such an influence on the outcome.'

Baqri turned his attention to Benny Erikson and Alexei Nevsky who were now stood in front of him. 'Benny! How are you? Thank you so much for the use of this lovely vessel of yours. Is everything set-up?'

'It is. The satellite link is now established and we are ready to go,' replied Erikson.

'Excellent. Please escort young Alexei downstairs and introduce him to the control system that he will need.'

'Why am I here?' complained Nevsky. 'I did everything that you wanted. You agreed that I could re-join my family once my job was done.'

'And you will, Alexei. But the job's not finished yet. Please go with Benny here. The sooner you complete your mission, the sooner we can let you go.'

Reluctantly Nevsky did as he was instructed and disappeared below deck. Baqri turned back towards Brigid.

'And how's Tom Rivers taken the death of his beloved wife?' asked Brigid.

'Not well, as you might expect. But do you know she managed to survive for days in the hospital before finally succumbing to the nerve agent?'

'What?'

'Yep, despite everyone else from two FBI tactical teams dying from Novichok poisoning almost immediately, Luna Rivers kept on going. Amazing. I know she has superior genetics, like her husband, but that Dr Patel is something else.'

'Who?'

'You know, the genetics scientist who headed up MI5's Sleeper project. She's supposed to have found a way of enhancing her subjects. And it looks like it works. Personally, I think she's a witch.'

'So, has it worked? Is Tom Rivers now hunting down people?'

'It seems he's about to. That's something that I'm going to really enjoy. The great defender seeks retribution against his former masters.'

'And I guess you're hoping not to be on his hit list?'

'It's fair to say, that would certainly be my preference. I'm relying on the carefully worded letter that I left on Luna's body to convince him that I had nothing to do with her death and that I treated her with the greatest of respect. In any case, he will be getting information on other people through soon. They should become the focus of his attention, instead of me.'

'You better hope so. Does seem like her death hit him hard then?'

'So, it seems. Apparently, he initially just isolated himself from the rest of the world. Everyone has their weakness. For Tom, it's his family. We are never so defenceless against suffering as when we love.'

'Sorry?'

'Sigmund Freud said that you know.'

Brigid rolled her eyes and sat down on the lounger beside Baqri.

'And have The Collective given a name to this new project that they want us to do?'

'They have. Farsight.'

CHAPTER SIXTY-FIVE

The buzz of the apartment's door intercom announced the arrival of an old friend. Tom looked at the screen and the image of MI5 Director Iain Macgregor cowering under his umbrella. It had been pouring down all day.

'Good morning,' said Tom, opening the apartment door and observing Mac's heavy frown and pursed lips.

'Not sure that there's anything good about it,' grumbled Mac, giving his umbrella a shake outside the door. 'If I wanted weather like this, I could just go back to Scotland.'

'Let me take your coat. And perhaps a nice cup of tea would be in order?'

'Tea? Really?' replied Mac, with a hint of excitement.

'Yes, your favourite. Yorkshire tea. Don't tell me, you've moved on to some posh blend, like Earl Grey, since your promotion?'

'Nah. Still drinking good strong tea out of a mug. Get the odd raised eyebrows but I really don't care.'

Tom smiled. 'Take a seat, Mac, and tell me why you so desperately need to see me before you go back to London.'

As requested, Mac sat himself down in one of the two contemporary black chrome and leather sofas positioned opposite the television in the living room. Tom was dressed in dark blue jeans and a t-shirt, but what struck Mac was not his attire but his physique. For someone who had recently lost his wife, it would not be unreasonable for a man to let his appearance slip. But Tom looked as fit as he ever had.

'Tom, I have to say that your recovery from your injuries has been remarkable. You seem to be walking around normally. And I suspect that you may even be working out at the gym again.'

'You're right, I am. Nearly back to normal. Just got a few scars as reminders. But I doubt you delayed your flight back to the UK just to see if I'm walking alright.'

'OK. To be honest, we're concerned about your mental health.'

'We? You mean you and Prisha Patel?' said Tom, placing two mugs of tea on the coffee table and sitting down on the other sofa.

'Yes. Look, Tom. You know Prisha. And you know we take her opinion very seriously. She's a world leading psychological expert. And she knows your mind better than most. It's her processes that condition and enhanced you. But even she thinks that the level of control that you are exercising is extraordinary.'

'I'm fine, Mac. Really.'

'We're concerned that you've bottled up your grief.'

'And I'll just suddenly flip and start killing people?'

Mac took a sip of tea before replacing it back down on the table. 'You do have the ability to become a killing machine, yes.'

'Mac, I'm just staying focussed.'

'This wouldn't happen to have anything to do with your assignment from Vice President Stone, would it?'

'Might have. Apparently, he requested an extension from the prime minister for my secondment to the US.'

'A request that the prime minister couldn't exactly refuse, after all the efforts that President Monroe made to save the King.'

'He did end up looking a bit stupid, didn't he? Accusing America of collaborating with terrorists.'

'More than a bit, I would say. President Monroe bought herself a lot of political capital with what she did – not just with Britain either. I don't believe that there are many world leaders who would have done what she did.'

Tom raised his mug of tea to have a sip but stopped short. 'Mac, I'm really concerned about the president's safety. The Collective clearly regard her as an obstacle to their plans. They tried killing her once and I'm sure they're going to have another go.'

'I agree. And I also think that they are likely to target other high-profile people whom they regard as a potential problem.'

'And then replace them with their own members?'

'Exactly. So, I imagine that Stone wants you to counter that. Identify and take out members of The Collective instead?'

'That's what he says.'

'You're probably thinking of visiting Rachael Goldberg first? I've known her for years, Tom. Doesn't it seem a bit convenient that the cop who tried to kill Luna, used to work for Rachael at the CIA? I can't honestly believe that she's Collective.'

'She's not.'

'How do you know?'

'Because I've already paid her a visit. She's not the member of The Collective. Vice President Stone is.'

'What?' asked Mac, sitting forward on the sofa. Are you sure?'

'Pretty sure.'

'Stone's acting president. And there's going to be others, you know. Are you planning to deal with all of them on your own?'

Footsteps from behind caused Mac to quickly look over his shoulder towards the bedroom door.

'Oh, shit!' he gasped, nearly falling off the edge of his seat.

'But he's not on his own,' said the voice from the doorway.

CHAPTER SIXTY-SIX

Very slowly, Mac rose to his feet and turned to face the apparition that had appeared to his side. He stood in silence with his mouth slightly open and simply stared.

'You look like you've seen a ghost,' said Luna.

'How … what?' murmured Mac, for once unable to put a coherent sentence together. It took a little while before he spoke again. 'What the hell is going on? You were dead. I went to your funeral. Did you just stage your own death? You clearly did. And you didn't think that you could trust me enough to let me in on it?'

'Mac, why don't you take a seat again and we'll explain?' said Tom, placing his hand reassuringly on Mac's arm.

Mac complied with the request. A heavily furrowed facial expression clearly displayed his current mood. Luna then sat down on the other end of the same sofa and turned to face him.

'Go on then,' said Mac abruptly.

'You're aware that someone tried to murder me when I was lying unconscious in a hospital bed?'

'Officer Giorgio?'

'That's right. He was a grunt working for The Collective. Though Tom killed him, they would have just sent more people after me.'

'Why?'

'When I was captured by Baqri, he told me that they wanted me dead. He assumed that I was going to die from the nerve agent poisoning, so while my condition got steadily worse, he just prattled on about Tom.'

'You've lost me.'

'I overheard him telling Brigid Doyle that The Collective had decided that instead of repeatedly trying to kill Tom, they could actually use him to help them complete their objectives.'

'By killing you?'

'Exactly.'

'Nope. Still don't get it. Surely, Tom would go after them if they murdered you.'

'That's right, he would.'

Mac shook his head, clearly still baffled by Luna's explanation. 'Am I missing something here?'

Tom said, 'The bit you're missing is that we don't actually know who the members of The Collective are, do we? We have some suspicions, of course, but what if we suddenly started receiving convincing intel as to their identities.'

'Which was false and contrived and provided by The Collective?'

'Yes, but I wouldn't know that.'

'And you went after them?' said Mac, nodding. 'But in reality, those people weren't actually the bad guys. They were the good guys.'

'Completely consumed by the need for revenge, I would hunt them down one by one.'

'And what you unwittingly then become is a super-assassin for The Collective. You would be removing all their enemies for them.'

'Correct. I could clear a path for them by removing various important people and allowing them to replace them with their own.'

'But you're conditioned to control your emotions.'

'It's their belief that my brutal murder would breach that conditioning,' said Luna. 'Push Tom over the edge.'

Mac sat back into the sofa. 'So, when did you decide to fake Luna's death?'

'When she woke up at the hospital. She told me what Baqri had said and we decided that we had to make it look like the Novichok poisoning had been successful. The doctor was sworn to secrecy.'

'Wow. And then we had a funeral. I have to say that you are a family of amazing actors. I was certainly convinced that you were dead.'

'It *had* to look convincing.'

'And you were all in on it?'

'Not all. We had to tell the girls. But we thought that as they are under your protection in the UK, then it will be easier for them. They know the importance of never speaking about it.'

'And Phillip?'

'Luna's Dad didn't know. His grief was genuine.'

'Oh my God!' said Mac, looking at Luna. 'Your Dad thinks that you're dead!'

'I know,' replied Luna. 'I feel terrible about it. But if he understood what was happening and that playing dead would actually save my life, he would understand.'

'Him showing raw grief and emotion, would have convinced anyone,' added Tom.

'Sounds a bit like you used him to me,' said Mac.

'That's not fair, Mac!' exclaimed Luna. 'We are facing a threat like nothing we have ever seen before. If The Collective end up dominating the halls of power of every major country, then the democracy that our countries were built on will be gone, and the people won't even know it. Anyway, I may not even survive our forthcoming fight with The Collective. In which case, my dad doesn't need to know anything different.

But if I survive … well … I'll have to deal with that when the time is right.'

'Mac, what you need to realise is that the apparent death of Luna gives us a couple of big opportunities,' said Tom.

'Go on,' said Mac.

'Firstly, it means that we have Luna off the radar. She will be a critical asset that they just won't be expecting.'

'OK. And the other?'

The sound of the door intercom buzzer interrupted Tom before he could reply. He walked over to the apartment's door, looked at the display and pressed the door release for the main front door of the building.

'Well, the other one is that it helps us solve what seemed like an impossible question,' said Tom. 'The question of who is in The Collective and who isn't.'

'How's that?'

'OK, not so much who is in it, but more who isn't.'

'Like with Rachael Goldberg you mean.'

'Correct. Clearly, they want Rachael eliminated. They used someone who was directly linked to her for the attempt on Luna's life at the hospital. A link that was easy for you to discover, Mac.'

'Bit too easy.'

'Sure, but I would expect further supporting evidence to start appearing soon,' said Tom, peering through the apartment door's spy hole.

'Then we will see who else is highlighted through intel as being Collective. They almost certainly won't be and we can regard them as friendly,' said Luna.

'I'm really not sure how you and Tom can possibly take on the might of The Collective without proper support,' said Mac. 'At the end of the day, I'm the director general of MI5 – not the CIA or the FBI. I work for the British government. You're going to need help over here too.'

'I couldn't agree with you more,' Tom replied, opening the door.

'Rachael!' said Mac, jumping to his feet.

'Hi, Mac. Good to see you,' replied Goldberg, walking straight up to Iain MacGregor and kissing him on the cheek.

'Let me take your coat, Rachael. Please, sit yourself down,' said Tom indicating with his hand to the empty seat on his sofa.

'So, at the moment there is just the four of us to take them on,' said Luna.

'But we'll get more on the way,' added Tom.

'What about President Monroe?' asked Mac.

'I think the president is absolutely critical for our success. To be honest, I can't see how we can win without her. But she'll be their first target. Having her in power will really hamper their ambitions. They can't take the risk that she will fully recover and take back power from Jed Stone.'

'I agree. I really believe that with President Monroe back in the Oval Office, then we'll be in with a fighting chance,' said Goldberg.

'We need to make sure she's protected,' added Luna. 'There's only a certain amount that the Secret Service can do though.'

'With that in mind, I'm off to see the president,' said Tom. 'She needs to know what we know.'

Tom looked at Luna, Rachael Goldberg and Iain Macgregor in turn.

'I think that it is no exaggeration to say that the fate of the free world is now in our hands. Be under no illusion, if we fail then the world will be ruled by unelected shadows. We must prevail or democracy will fall. Today the fight begins.'

CHAPTER SIXTY-SEVEN

Not surprisingly, The University of Kansas hospital had become more of a fortress than a medical centre since the arrival of President Monroe. Local cops and marines stood guard outside the front and a broad mix of FBI, Secret Service and even more Marines occupied the reception area. The flow in and out of the hospital had become painfully slow, as visitors were corralled into queues, separated by barriers, allowing agents to perform their necessary checks.

Having shown his ID on arrival, Tom was escorted by the senior Secret Service agent to the elevator. He was delighted to hear that the agent's instruction had come from the president herself – a good indication that her health was continuing to improve. Tom pressed the button for the top floor and, as the doors closed, considered the fact that he was once more in a hospital. He seemed to have spent an inordinate amount of time in medical centres recently. It also occurred to him that during both his stay and that of his wife, they had both been subjected to assassination attempts. *But why a hospital?* he pondered. *Well, the victim would most likely be in a fixed location and immobile, to start with. And it would be somewhere open to the public, making complete security almost impossible*, he reasoned. But the difference on this occasion, was that the president had the benefit of a small army protecting her. Even Baqri and his Collective friends would find getting near her to be impossible.

The doors opened and Tom stepped out to be greeted by another Secret Service agent.

'Mr Rivers,' said the agent, as a statement of fact. 'I'm agent Barratt. If you would follow me, please sir.'

'Barratt? You're not related to John Barratt by any chance?'

'He was my father, sir. I'm Rob Barratt.'

'I'm so sorry for your loss, Rob. I met your Dad a number of times. He was a fine man. You look a bit like him you know.'

'So I've been told. Same square jaw line apparently.'

'And immaculate appearance. I imagine that when he was younger, there would have been a striking similarity. And you decided to follow the same career choice?'

'I'm actually the third generation of Barratts tasked with protecting the President of the United States. Runs in the family, I guess.'

'Guess so. Shouldn't you still be on compassionate leave?'

'I had to return to work. Sitting at home really wasn't helping. I needed something to keep my mind focussed. I have been approved to re-commence field duty by the way.'

'Of course. I get it, Rob.'

'I'm sorry, sir. The president is waiting,' said Barratt, indicating with an open hand.

Tom passed several more Secret Service agents standing in the corridor before he arrived at a room which he guessed was that of the president by the level of security outside. Tom spotted a familiar figure walking away, as Barratt gave him a polite nod of the head and opened the door. *A suite of some sort*, Tom surmised as he walked into the room. Much bigger than a standard hospital room with a little more furniture. Still no getting away from the fact that it was just a white clinical room, at the end of the day.

As he approached the bed, President Monroe turned her head to face him. It was certainly a strange sight for Tom – seeing the president sat up in bed with numerous pillows propping her up.

'Madam President,' said Tom, approaching the bed. 'How are you feeling?'

'I'm making slow progress, apparently. And trying really hard not to be the worst patient ever. I'm really not cut out for just lying in bed all day,' said the president in an uncharacteristically quiet voice.

'Was that the First Gentleman I saw walking down the corridor?'

'Yeah, he's gone for a coffee while we have our chat. He's been an absolute rock, Tom.'

'He's a good man, ma'am.'

'But enough about me – how are you doing? I see your walking has improved dramatically. Amazing recovery.'

'Yeah, still not able to sprint around though.'

'Not really surprising, is it? Look, I just wanted to say how sorry I am to hear about Luna.'

Tom looked around to check that agent Barratt had definitely fully closed the door behind him. 'She's alive, Madam President.'

'What?'

'Luna's alive. She managed to survive The Collective's attempts to kill her but we were sure that they would keep trying.'

'So, you faked her death?'

'We did.'

'Does Jed know? I saw him earlier and he was telling me the good news that you had agreed to spearhead the search for members of The Collective.'

'Madam President, we believe that Vice President Stone is one of them.'

President Monroe paused for a few seconds before responding. 'Oh, Tom. Come on. We've been over this ground before.'

'And we were right the first time. Even Rachael Goldberg is convinced.'

'That doesn't make any sense. Why would he want you tracking down his fellow members?'

'He wouldn't. He's hoping that I will hunt down and eliminate those *that I believe* are Collective members.'

'Acting on false information?'

'Exactly. The idea being that as I am so consumed by the need for revenge, I would simply act on any evidence given to me. But the targets would be people in powerful positions whom The Collective believe are unlikely to turn to them if asked. Or perhaps they have already been approached and refused. And then…'

'They are replaced by the converted,' interjected Monroe, looking up at the ceiling. 'Giving them full control of the government.'

'Yes, Ma'am.'

'Dear God. I've made a complete mess of this, haven't I?'

'I'm sorry, Madam President, but you really haven't. We were both unsure about Stone. And look at what you've achieved. You've saved the King's life. Twice. As a result, the coup in Congo has failed and instead of international isolation, America now has stronger ties with its allies than ever before. Plus, it has now gained a number of new allies. Baqri has no more polonium or Avangards to launch at the United States and the whole thing will have cost The Collective big time.'

'But all those American lives lost. That was on my watch.'

'It would have been on anyone's watch. Those polonium attacks happened before you even knew what you were really dealing with. Many more people could have died if you hadn't made the decisions that you did. I'm pretty sure that history will judge you as an exceptional leader.'

'Thank you, Tom. I appreciate that. So, where do we go from here? Are they going to try and kill me again?'

'I believe that they will have to. And sooner rather than later with your condition improving. You're their biggest barrier to controlling the government of the United States. So, we need to get you back to full health and sitting again in the Oval Office, if we are to have any chance against them.'

'At the moment, the doctors are saying that I'm in no condition to resume my duties. To be fair, after a while, I did start to lose concentration when I met with Jed Stone earlier.'

'Did the Vice President know that I was coming, by the way?'

'You only called me fifteen minutes before you arrived. I didn't have a chance to let anyone know apart from the Secret Service.'

'Well, it won't take long now till he finds out.'

'So, what do I say to him? When he asks about your visit?'

'Just tell him that I came to check on how you were and that you put your full support behind his initiative to track down Collective members.'

***

Tom glanced at his phone's screen – the ringing rudely interrupting the conversation. He stood up and, having answered the call, walked slowly towards the window. The call was brief but, even after it ended, Tom continued to remain perfectly still and just gazed out of the window and across the skyline. He turned around once again to face the president.

'When you saw VP Stone, what exactly did you discuss?'

'Mainly an update on the casualties of the attacks and then we discussed the usual matters of state. I started feeling tired and he left.'

'And nothing else?'

'Such as?'

'Anything unusual?'

'I don't think so. Why do you ask?'

'Well, that was Sir Iain MacGregor on the phone. Baqri's been located on a yacht anchored just north of the Russian base at Tartus.'

'Damn! That's going to be too risky to take him out there.'

'I agree. But there's a second part to the intel which worries me.'

'Go on.'

'An unmanned reconnaissance drone has identified Alexei Nevsky arriving on the yacht via helicopter. We don't know who to trust at the CIA, of course, so Rachael had this verified by one of her old team who is now quite senior.'

'Nevsky is the Russian who piloted the Avangard HGVs for Baqri, right?'

'Right. So, my question is why has Baqri flown in Nevsky to join him? All the Avangards have been used. So, what's the point? And it's not like they're best of friends – he will be there under duress. My understanding is that Baqri has kidnapped his wife.'

Tom walked back to the president's bed and sat down in the chair beside it. He leaned forward. 'Madam President, please have another think. Was there anything that the vice president said which was slightly odd? Anything at all?'

Monroe thought. 'Well, the only thing was when we were discussing my health. He asked me about whether I was due for any appointments today – you know like having a scan or something. I told him that I wasn't. But then I overheard him asking a doctor standing outside my door exactly the same question. I remember him saying *so the president isn't going to be moving from this room for the whole day?* I was a little irritated because I thought that Jed was questioning my memory.'

Tom sprung to his feet and marched over to the door. As he opened it, he looked back at Monroe. 'Madam President, we've got to move you. And I mean right now.'

CHAPTER SIXTY-EIGHT

'Rob,' Tom beckoned, poking his head around the door. 'We need to move the president to the back of the hospital.'

'Sir?'

'I think there's another attempt on her life coming. Likely to be an aerial attack. Tell the First Gentleman's security detail to move him as well. And get the FBI to start clearing the other rooms around here.'

'But we haven't got anywhere to take the president yet.'

'I don't care. Just get her out and away. We have no idea how long we've got – it could be minutes or even seconds for all we know. Ask the senior Secret Service agent to secure a new room for the president. Now.'

Within minutes, the area around the president's room was teeming with Secret Service. The president's bed was swiftly pushed out into the corridor and, with half a dozen agents in front and the same number to the rear, it was moved at jogging speed down to the first junction. Tom watched from the doorway as the agents turned it right around the corner and away towards the back of the hospital.

Outside the president's former room, chaos had ensued. Doctors and other medical staff plus the FBI, cops and marines were all trying to evacuate the other rooms.

'C'mon, c'mon,' shouted Tom, over the now deafening noise. 'Let's get a move on people.'

'We've got some patients who we're struggling to move,' one doctor shouted back.

'I get that. As quick as you can doctor. Your patients are in significant immediate danger.'

Something caught Tom's eye and he looked back at the window behind him. In the distance he could make out something flying towards them at high speed. He didn't need to look any further – he knew what it was.

'Everyone get down! Take cover! Get down!' he shouted, whilst launching himself through the open doorway opposite and rolling himself under the bed.

***

Tom's ears were still ringing from the huge blast which rocked the building when he opened his eyes. He blinked several times but the dust was so thick that he was struggling to see through it. He felt something run down his nose and drop to the ground. Blood. He looked out from under the bed and what he saw was no longer a working medical facility but something more akin to a war zone – just complete and utter devastation. Beyond the rubble and debris immediately in front of him, he could see that the door had been blown off its hinges and a ceiling strip light fitting was leaning against the door frame – propped up on one end. He crawled out, stood up and pushed the light fitting that was blocking the door to one side. Holding on to the door frame, the inevitable coughing started – an unavoidable effect of that much concrete dust.

Tom looked up at the room that had been, until a short time before, occupied by the President of the United States. It was gone. Not just slightly damaged – but completely absent. Only part of the corridor remained directly in front of him with just an open space beyond. He glanced back at the bed that he had taken cover under – now completely covered in various parts of the ceiling as well as debris that had been blown in.

Tom looked along the corridor. Two motionless bodies were lying strewn across the floor just fifteen yards from him. He could now clearly hear cries of help from further along. He made his way across to the first body. Barely recognisable through the layers of dust covering him. Tom realised that it was the doctor he had spoken to just before the explosion. A young guy who must have been in his mid-twenties. And beyond him, his elderly female patient. Both lying perfectly still and completely silent.

Tom rolled a large lump of debris off the doctor's chest and placed his fingers on the side of his neck to test for a pulse. He felt a hand on his shoulder. He looked up to see another young doctor dressed in her scrubs with other medics behind. Clean green scrubs. It was clear that an influx of medical staff had arrived from other parts of the hospital.

'I'll take it from here,' said the doctor reassuringly.

Tom nodded and stood. He looked down at the two casualties and clenched his fists. 'Baqri,' he raged through gritted teeth. 'This needs to stop.'

He felt a presence behind him. It was Rob Barrett.

'Mr Rivers, the president has instructed me to come and check on you,' said Barrett, wide eyed at Tom's appearance.

'Tom. Please call me Tom. My bank and those that want to send me bills call me Mr Rivers.'

'Yes, sir … Tom,' said Barrett, glancing down at Tom's arm.

'What?'

'It's your arm. You've got some small bits of shrapnel lodged in it. Do you want me to get that looked at?' said Barrett looking at a slow trickle of blood dripping off the end of Tom's fingers.

Tom looked down. 'Oh yeah. So I have. I tried using my arms to protect my head from the blast. I'm sure I'll live for a little longer, Rob. And the staff here have definitely got higher priorities to deal with than me. How's the president?'

'She appears to be fine. No worse for her race across the hospital.'

'Excellent. I need to see her. We need to be on the attack for a change.'

CHAPTER SIXTY-NINE

'Jeepers, Tom!' exclaimed President Monroe, staring at the dust and blood covered person standing in front of her.

'Madam President. Good to see you alive and well,' replied Tom Rivers.

'Thanks to you, Tom. Many others also owe their lives to you, I'm sure. I've asked for an assessment of the casualties but if you hadn't had that area evacuated when you did … well, I dread to think.'

'I'm afraid there were some who just couldn't escape quickly enough. They didn't make it.'

'I know. I'm glad you managed to though.'

'Well, it seems that I just needed the right motivation. Seeing an unmanned drone flying straight at me sort of worked.' Tom glanced down at the ground. 'I'm afraid that I'm bleeding on your floor. My apologies.'

'Tom, you look terrible. I can barely recognise you. Rob, find him a medic, will you?'

'I'm fine really. We need to talk, Madam President,' said Tom, as Rob Barrett exited the room. 'Baqri's going to try and kill you again. I'm sure of that. The reason is that The Collective will now know that your health is improving. They will also realise that the moment you are well enough to take your powers back, then they've got a problem. So, they will need to act soon. Or, should I say, they will need Baqri to act soon. But I think the best form of defence is attack. We have to turn the tables on him.'

'How do you mean?'

Tom walked over to the side of the president's bed, sat on the edge of the chair beside it and cradled his arm in a slightly elevated position in an attempt to reduce the bleeding. 'I want your permission to hunt down Baqri. Capture him preferably – his intel on The Collective could be invaluable. Kill him if necessary. But he's got to be stopped.'

'I agree. But as far as Jed Stone's concerned, you're supposed to be on the hunt for those that he would like you to believe are Collective members – not Baqri.'

'And he needs to keep believing that. I'm sure Jed and the rest of his Collective friends won't be overly happy if they think that I'm actually trying to get Baqri.'

'Do you even have enough resources to do this?'

'We will have to. Don't forget Luna is completely off the grid and we should soon be able to start working out who else we can trust apart from Rachael and Mac.'

A short knock on the door interrupted them and Rob Barrett re-entered the room. The nurse that accompanied him had clearly been well briefed as she started immediately tending to Tom's wounds.

'I've got a casualty update, Madam President. So far, there have been six fatalities from the blast and fourteen injured,' said Barratt.

'That's terrible, of course. But it could have been so much worse,' replied Monroe.

A buzzing noise from Barrett's inside suit pocket alerted him to a call on his phone. Having answered it, no actual conversation followed. Barrett held his phone out to Tom.

'It's Baqri. He wants to speak to you and the president.'

'How the hell did he get your number?' asked Monroe.

Barratt shrugged his shoulders and shook his head.

'Probably best if you could leave us for a few minutes please,' said Tom to the nurse, who immediately complied. He put the phone on the table that sat over the president's bed and pressed the speaker button.

'This is Tom Rivers.'

'Oh Tom, Tom, Tom. What are you doing there Tom?'

'Trying to stop you from murdering innocent people.'

'I hope you're not trying to include President Monroe in that group? You're just *so* desperately naive – aren't you? Tom Rivers – the champion of good. But it's not that simple though, is it? There's nothing innocent about this president that you are so dedicated to protect. She's a warmonger and a mass murderer of the weak, as has been every president before her. She should die and her country should burn – I'll actually be doing the world a favour. So, stop getting in my way.'

'You're a murdering psychopath, Baqri,' said Monroe.

'Oh, you're sounding better, Calamity. What a shame. Don't worry, I can change that.'

'I don't think so,' said Tom.

'Oh, I do. There's no place that you can hide that I won't find you, Madam President. And there's no one – not even Tom Rivers – who will be able to protect you. You will die. Make no mistake, I'm coming for you, President Monroe. I'm coming for you.'

Tom looked over at the president with an intense, piercing stare. His eyes narrowed. 'And *you* make no mistake, Baqri. I'll be right there to stop you.'

AUTHOR BIO

T.J. Hawkins is a British author, born in Devon, brought up around Canterbury and now lives in the beautiful English Lake District. A firm believer that variety is the spice of life, he joined the police straight after school and then worked much of his life in the licenced trade before becoming a professional in the property industry. Married to the lovely Sarah and a proud Dad. A keen cook and loving everything Italian.

Always grateful to have inherited his father's genetics, he has yet to have a single filling in his mouth despite being in his late fifties and having a very sweet tooth! At six foot three inches and weighing in at over two hundred and twenty pounds, his paternal genes became the inspiration for the creation of his first novel *Sleeper* and the book's protagonist, Tom Rivers.

GET THE NOVELLA 'DARK AS NIGHT' COMPLETELY FREE!

Discover where it all began for the psychopathic villain of the Tom Rivers thriller series!

Simply go to:

https://tjhawkinsbooks.com/subscribe

Plus advance notice of new books in this series with special pre-order discount days before the official release.

PERSONAL NOTE

I really hope you enjoyed reading The Alpha Particle. As an indie author, I rely heavily on recommendations for my book(s) to be seen. I would, therefore, really appreciate it if you were able to leave a review on **www.amazon.com**

Thank you!

Find me on:

www.tjhawkinsbooks.com
Instagram @tjhawkinsbooks
Facebook Facebook.com/tjhawkinsbooks
Twitter @tjhawkins

Printed in Great Britain
by Amazon

60144454R00221